The Murder Place

PAUL J. TEAGUE

THE MURDER PLACE / PAUL J TEAGUE
1st paperback edition 2017.

ISBN: 978-0-9933255-8-8

Also by Paul J Teague

Don't Tell Meg

The Murder Place

The Forgotten Children

Dead of Night

Writing sci-fi as Paul Teague

The Secret Bunker Trilogy

The Grid Trilogy

Chapter One

There would be more deaths to come because of what happened in that house. Something had been set in motion which hadn't yet found its end. As the couple walked past the three battered For Sale boards, their interest was not in finding a new place to live but in getting a look inside.

The hedge was overgrown, brambles had begun to work their way through the thickening undergrowth, ready to strangle anything that dared to resist. The gravel driveway was overrun with weeds, the paintwork was starting to flake, and the windows were covered with a film of dirt where they hadn't been cleaned in months.

To the casual passer-by, this might have been a place where an elderly couple had once lived; it had the feel of a home once dearly loved but now sadly neglected. Perhaps they had died and the house had been put on the market by children who lived miles away and wanted to get it off their hands.

The estate agent's car was in the drive. At least they wouldn't have to wait around. It was August, but you wouldn't have known it other than from the unbridled growth of anything that had roots. It was wet, chilly and grey. They were wearing light jackets and carrying an umbrella. This was British summertime after all.

They could see that the front door was slightly ajar. Six months previously that would have been a clue as to what was happening inside, but now it was nonthreatening, a simple sign that they were expected and that they'd arrived on time.

The couple took a moment to survey the front garden. A normal couple, it would seem. He had dark hair and a well-groomed beard. Although he was dressed for the weather, it was obvious that he was very well built under those layers of clothing. The edges of tattoos could be seen peeking from beyond his collar and sleeves, his hands were patterned too. This man was no office worker, he was strong and oozed physicality. She had stunning red hair and a small tattoo on her neck. She was confident and attractive, a good match for her companion. They looked like regular house hunters, a young couple doing the rounds of the homes that were for sale.

They scanned the house from the end of the gravel drive. The grass had been overpowered by weeds, which were now almost waist high. The blooms of roses and shrubs made stifled cries from the sea of greenery, but they'd soon be swallowed up, and what was left of a garden would disappear.

It was as they'd heard it described: abandoned, unloved, rejected. The previous occupants had left the house and their former lives and moved away. He was still local, living on a caravan site, they'd heard. She was gone. She'd not been seen since the funeral. Everybody assumed that it had been too much for the marriage. How could you live through something like that and everything stay the same? People had heard that she was pregnant, but there was no proof of that. Only a rumour.

'Hello! Mr Elliot?'

The man took the lead, pushing the door open and calling up the hallway. To the side of the door was a pile of post, free newspapers, leaflets and charity bags. The estate agent must have retrieved them from below the letterbox.

Mr & Mrs P Bailey, Mr P Bailey, Ms M Bailey, Mrs Meg Bailey ... there was every combination of name on the envelopes. All untouched, all unopened. For a moment he considered taking one of the envelopes as a souvenir. Was that illegal? It would be easy to take one which was obviously junk mail, nobody would notice that. It would be doing everybody a favour.

He could hear a voice from the kitchen. It wasn't Glenn Elliot the estate agent. It was a woman, making a viewing arrangement with another person on her mobile phone.

'One moment!' she shouted, and then returned to her call.

The man sifted through the envelopes and found one which wouldn't be missed: *You have won £50,000 in our UK-wide, instant win contest! Open now!*

It was unlikely that there was a cheque for fifty grand sitting in the envelope. He smiled at his female companion. She knew what he was doing and it excited her. She wanted to take him, then and there in the house. Even better, in the bedroom where it had happened. But the estate agent was still kicking around; she'd have to make do with fantasising as they took their tour.

They waited by the door, keen to give the impression that they were genuine buyers. They surveyed the ceilings and skirting boards, looking for who knows what, eager to convince their guide of their sincerity.

They'd had to undergo a probing line of enquiry. There had been a lot of trouble at the house, what with sightseers and voyeurs. It had got much worse since the website listing went live. It was there for all to see on Great House Move. The hits on the page had gone through the roof, yet no offers had been made.

They heard the woman winding up her call. He knelt down and ran his hand along the skirting board, and she inspected the joins of the wallpaper, which was beginning to come away from the plaster.

'I'm so sorry to keep you. I'm Melissa Drake. Mr Elliot sends his apologies.'

She reached out her hand towards them. The man stood up and grabbed it confidently, after wiping whatever he'd found on the skirting boards onto his trousers.

'Alan and Ruth Simpson,' he said, looking at his female companion. 'Pleased to meet you!'

The woman stepped forward, grasping Melissa's hand.

'Yes, Ruth Simpson,' she said, as if fixing the name in her own mind. 'Thank you for meeting us today. We appreciate that you've had some problems with the house.'

'You could say that,' Melissa replied, keen to get the viewing over and done with. As far as she was concerned, the sooner that house sold, the better. It was the second time Glenn Elliot had dumped it on her at the last minute. It had been agreed that, due to the nature of what had gone on there, he would accompany all viewings as he was the owner of the business. But something was going on at home – he'd come in unshaven earlier that week. He'd rung her at short notice and asked her to cover for him.

'I'm so sorry to do this to you, Mel, but something has come up. Urgently. We need to get this property off the books, so we can't be cancelling any appointments. They seem genuine enough, not the usual weirdos and souvenir hunters. I'll make it up to you, honestly. How about I assign you the property that came in this morning on Stallion Road? There's a great commission on that one and it's sure to move quickly.'

Melissa was desperate for the money; the promise of an expensive property and a fast commission was too much to resist. She was broke. That car on the drive didn't buy itself. The interest rate was phenomenal, but it allowed her to create the illusion that everything was fine. It wasn't. Everything in her life was turning to shit. She said yes to Glenn, even though it gave her the creeps going to that house.

The first time Glenn had dropped her in it, it was a no-show. Some guy wanted to take a look around, a property investor so it seemed. She didn't even go into the house that time. She'd put the keys in the door, hesitated, and then decided to wait in her car out on the drive.

Emboldened by the thought of the commission on Stallion Road, she'd gone straight in this time. She'd got no further than the kitchen when her phone had rung. She was grateful that they'd been punctual, she didn't want to be in there alone.

'Shall I show you around then?' Melissa asked. 'I'm afraid that I'll need to accompany you all the time, because ... you know ... because of the problems that we've had.'

'Of course, that's fine, we know the deal. Mr Elliot

explained it to us when I called. Has the price changed at all, or are they still asking for the list price? It is *they* isn't it?'

He'd risked a probe, he hoped it wouldn't show their hand. As it was, Melissa ignored it.

'I think they'd take any reasonable offer to be honest with you. Winter will be here soon, although you wouldn't know this is summer. The house is already showing signs of not being lived in. I think if it goes before autumn, they'll be very happy.'

They entered the lounge. That was where one of the bodies had been hidden. There was no carpet anymore, no underlay even. Initials were carved on the windowsill.

'Is this what they do?' she asked, running her fingers along the uneven wood.

'Yes, it's why I have to accompany you all the time. There are more in the main bedroom upstairs, people carving out their names. I'm not sure what they get out of it. Some macabre thrill I think. It's very sad. Two people died here. Five people died in all. It was terrible. I don't know how people can be so horrible about it.'

But the woman knew. She wanted to lead him upstairs and take him in the bedroom. The thrill of the thought made her face redden. She pretended to look out of the window, exhilarated by the idea of what they were planning.

So this is what it had come to. The beer trickled into the pint glass as I made small talk with the fat guy at the bar. Some generic holiday-maker. Middle-aged. Manual worker. Overweight. Opinionated. Bigoted. I didn't pick up on any of his comments about the number of migrant workers on the site or the noise being made by over-excited kids. I needed the money, and the bar work was helping me to keep my head above water. It was also helping me to forget.

Six months had passed since I lost Meg. Not a word from her in that time. I might have been a father for all I knew, but nothing. Just silence. And an unpaid mortgage.

I'd moved out of the house after the deaths. How could I have gone back there? There were too many memories. It's hard to make a happy home when all you can picture is the beaten corpse behind the sofa in the lounge and the guy with multiple stab wounds in your double bed.

I'd had to move out. I'd grabbed my clothes, and then got a house clearance company to do the rest. Most of our junk was in storage, like our marriage, waiting for some bugger to come along with the key and let some natural light in.

After the police had had their fill, I arranged for the bloodied furniture to be disposed of. The carpets were torn out and dumped. I don't know what happens to stuff like that. I assumed it hadn't been thrown onto the local tip, but who knows in these days of local authority spending cuts? No, it must have been properly disposed of, they'd need to deter the trophy hunters.

Every now and then I drove by. I'd asked Glenn Elliot to collect the post. I used a postal redirection service at first, but it had been too painful seeing Meg's name everyday, so I cancelled it. Glenn Elliot said he'd pick up my mail whenever they had a viewing, and I could collect it from the office. He'd screen Meg's post and keep it in a box. If I heard from her, he'd be happy to send it on.

How can you disappear like that? She'd stopped paying into the joint account straight away. I was pissed off by that. I was her husband still. I was the only one who knew what she'd done. Surely she didn't have to shaft me over the bills?

Her work wouldn't tell me where she'd gone, at her request apparently. Confidentiality and all that bollocks. She'd probably put in for a transfer, until the baby arrived. I was completely in the dark about what was going on. She'd disappeared from my life and left me with the bills and the house.

It wasn't that I couldn't cover the costs, but it was a struggle on my own. The mortgage was hefty. I suppose we'd always assumed that if we did have a family, we had the big house already. We'd never discussed it, but I guess it's a subconscious thing for all couples. Room for us and a couple more if ever we needed it.

I'd moved over to the Golden Beaches Holiday Park and rented myself a static caravan while the holiday-makers were away for the winter. I hadn't expected to stay there long. It was what was available at the time.

Turns out I really liked it. Static caravans are amazing things. I'd never even been in one until I rented at the Golden Beaches. It was luxurious. I had a bath, a shower, a kitchen, three bedrooms, a massive lounge. And it even had mains gas and electricity. It was brilliant. For an extra twenty quid every month, they sent in the cleaners for me. They were mucking out the caravans anyway. It was much quieter at first over winter, so they were happy to take my money.

When things started to get tighter for me, and the house didn't sell, it turned out that it was easy to get extra work. Vicky, the owner of the park, had taken quite a shine to me, so she was happy to help. I started pulling pints in the bar whenever my shifts at the radio station allowed. I was grateful for the work, in spite of the occasional arsehole among the clientele.

My life had taken a complete U-turn. My wife was gone, my best mate dead and my home a house of horrors. Until I got rid of the property, there was no moving on. Strictly speaking, half of the house was Meg's. It was difficult to know what to do until I could talk things through with her.

I was lonely. It's hard to say that, it would have embarrassed me to admit it at the time. I was missing companionship, and on the holiday park female company was easy to find, especially when the season began to pick up and the holiday-makers arrived. You won't believe how many single mothers take their kids to these places. And they're all gasping for a bit of male attention. I wash everyday, keep myself tidy, and can sustain a conversation for more than five minutes. At the Golden Beaches Holiday Park, I was hot stuff and I made the most of it.

I felt so sorry for the poor fools who poured their hard-earned money into spending a week on the site. The place itself was great: plenty of bars, music and entertainment to suit all tastes, a half-decent restaurant and a babysitting service for the kids. Perfect for single mums wanting a night out – with a guy who worked on the radio and was chatting them up in the bar.

But Golden Beaches? More like sand covered in crap! I'd reported many times on the sewage problem in the resort. On a bad day even the seagulls would abandon the place. How they got away with calling it Golden Beaches I'll never know. But they came there in their hundreds when the summer season started, and the place stayed busy and active until mid-September. It was what I needed to take my mind off everything that had gone on.

Vicky walked into the bar. It gave me the perfect excuse to brush off the fat guy. To be honest, it was people like him who were making life so easy for me with the women. I was like Colin Firth to most of them: posh voice, no beer belly and good oral hygiene. That was as good as it got at the Golden Beaches Holiday Park.

'Hello, luv,' she began, leaning over the bar and exposing her extensive cleavage.

She was sixteen years my senior and had lost her husband to a heart attack five years before. They'd built the holiday park together, but he'd been abusive towards her and she was pleased to see the back of him. She made no attempt to hide the fact.

'I'd have put my foot on his throat to finish him off!' she'd laughed at an after-hours' lock-in one night. 'It was the happiest day of my life when he finally croaked and I never had to have the fat sweaty bastard wriggling around on top of me ever again ... but at least it only ever lasted a few seconds!'

She filled the bar with her raucous laughter, but I'd seen enough of human sadness in my life as a journalist to know that it hid despair and loneliness. At least we had that in common. But I didn't fancy Vicky, she was like another species in terms of the kind of woman I went for.

Unfortunately, she was highly excited by my presence on the holiday site. She'd listened to the radio station for years, she woke up with us in the morning, went to bed with us at night. She knew all the presenters by name, had memorised lots of details about their lives and hung onto our every word.

When I turned up, answering an ad in the paper for winter lets, she couldn't believe her luck.

'Do I know your voice, luv? You sound familiar.'

She looked me up and down, and then the penny dropped.

'You're that Peter Bailey from the radio. I've got your picture on my fridge. You're one of my favourites, I love your voice … '

Then she treated me to an impression: '"The ten o'clock news, I'm Peter Bailey, with the latest headlines from around the county … " Ooh, I love the way you say that!'

I smiled, thinking that I'd probably pass on the static caravan. But I'm pleased that I hung on in there, because once she showed me the executive range and revealed the price, I was happy to tolerate a bit of fandom. In fact, she dropped the price to make sure that I couldn't refuse. She probably thought there would be some free publicity in it for her or perhaps some reflection of my very limited fame.

When I first came to her for a place to stay, she didn't know what had happened. It was a few days afterwards that the shit really hit the fan.

Once it was revealed to the press that a local radio personality had been caught up in a gruesome murder, it was everywhere. For a while I thought Vicky was going to throw me out, but once she saw my celebrity connections with people like Alex Kennedy from one of her favourite TV shows, she changed her tune.

'Do you actually know Alex Kennedy?' she'd ask. 'What's she really like? Is she as nice as she seems?'

I didn't mention that Alex and I had lived together for several years, but I did feed the goldfish by dropping the occasional celebrity morsel into our conversations.

I liked Vicky, although there was no way I was going to give her what she really wanted: a night – or more – in the sack with a local minor celebrity. For her, it would never get better than that. She'd probably want me to read news stories to her while I was giving her one in bed.

No thanks, Vicky, but I was happy to be her friend. Which is why I despised myself so much afterwards, once I'd screwed everything up. Vicky deserved so much better.

———

I've never been a fan of counselling. It's all too introspective for my tastes. I'd rather work through my issues the good old-fashioned way, a subtle combination of suppression and melancholy. It worked well for me for years. However, I changed my tune after my experiences with Martin Travis.

I had despised and resented Martin from the outset. Meg had opted for marriage counselling. I'd agreed for the sake of the relationship, and I'd begrudged every wasted minute. At first.

Imagine my surprise when the man I thought harboured a secret desire to shag my wife, *his* client, turned out to be gay. I never saw that one coming. In fact, as I reflected over the events that had occurred six months previously, Martin was the only person who came out with any shred of integrity. Everyone had lied to cover their arses, everyone except Martin and Sally. Sally had died taking the truth with her and that had allowed Meg to cover up what had really happened.

I was still finding it difficult to forgive Martin for

owning a Brompton bicycle, but at least he had shaved off the ridiculous facial hair that had bothered me so much. He'd moved up the ranks, but only from 'that tosser with the dodgy beard' to 'the wanker with the Brompton'.

I respected his integrity, I was grateful for the support and friendship that he'd offered to Meg, and I'd be forever appreciative of him taking more pellets from Sally's gun than I had. However, he still wouldn't tell me where my wife was.

I'd decided to continue the counselling. With Meg gone and nobody close to speak to, I'd felt the need to get it all out of my system. Even better, I discovered that I had health insurance for it from the radio station. I could continue to skip off work for two hours a week, talk about what was on my mind, and get the bill picked up at the end of it.

I was ready for a move from work. My heart wasn't in it anymore. Not the job, the place. It's where Jem and I had met and been friends. Turned out he was a cheating, scheming piece of shit. My judgment in friendship turned out to be completely skewed. Another Pete Bailey classic. I can't spot a man who's gay. I can't spot a rapist. My social skills appear to be impaired.

I was ready for a move to a new radio station. It would be easy enough to do, but I needed to sort out the house first and see where I was with Meg. My life was in limbo, but I'd move on as soon as I could see a way forward. I needed some time, I had a lot of issues to work through.

I'd turned to Martin for advice and support, and he'd rejected me outright. It was nothing personal, he was at great pains to emphasise that. Mind you, I was sure he'd never forgive me for the scratches that I'd left on his beloved Brompton. He felt that there was a conflict of interest; besides, he specialised in relationship counselling, I needed something broader than that. It was part relationship counselling, part bereavement support and part psychoanalysis. At last I could be like those Americans on TV, whining about my emotions while running up a huge bill for my trouble.

Martin was in contact with Meg, I knew it. He wouldn't admit it, and I had pushed him on it, but his integrity remained intact and he wouldn't budge. He reminded me of client confidentiality and wouldn't be drawn on where she was. Why couldn't he have been a scheming turd like the rest of us?

Part of me continued the counselling because I wanted to have a good reason to keep visiting the clinic. Seeing Martin regularly was the only way I had to stay in touch with Meg. Even when I was assigned to Blake Crawford, I'd see Martin in the corridors from time to time. It did bring back horrible memories, though. Every time I went for a pee there, I'd be reminded how I'd had to climb through the window of the toilets to try to save my wife.

Blake's support was really beneficial. He was very different to Martin, older for starters. I prefer to take my advice from people I feel are old enough to have been through the mill themselves. Martin was a youngster, a gay one at that, and part of me couldn't stop questioning his suitability to advise me on my heterosexual marriage.

I knew the drill, of course. Counsellors don't advise, they guide. It's immaterial what life experience they've had, they're trained in counselling, those are the skills that they need to help. Fair enough. I still preferred Blake.

I was sitting out in the corridor, waiting for my session to begin. I'd told a white lie at work, left early to avoid reading the midday bulletin. I was going through the motions. I'd give it another month, then start looking at the jobs pages seriously. I didn't know then that I would have left the city within the next five months, and would never want to go back ever again.

Martin Travis opened his door and saw his previous client out of the office.

'Martin!' I said, pleased that I'd caught him.

'Hi Pete, can't chat, it's a bit of a busy day ... '

He knew what was coming.

'Heard from Meg recently?' I asked. 'Any mention of a baby?'

His face coloured. It wasn't fair of me, I knew, but he was the only connection I had with her. With no family of her own, when Meg disappeared so did all my connections with her. Martin was my lifeline.

'Now, Pete, come on, you know that I can't discuss anything to do with Meg. I'm sure she'll reach out to you if and when she's ready. But I really can't talk about this.'

Blake came out of his office.

'Ah, Pete, I thought it had to be you. Hassling poor old Martin again. Come on in. He's not going to say anything to you, you should know that by now.'

I did, of course, but it was worth a try. Journalist Pete Bailey asks the questions that need to be asked. And is told to get lost.

I took a seat in Blake's office. It was posher than Martin's – it was Blake's clinic after all. I settled in on the large leather sofa. Very comfortable too. Martin's was covered in some cheap fabric. I'd caught a glimpse of it through the door. It had been changed since he'd bled all over it six months previously.

'So, Pete, how are things? I see that you're still worrying the same knots that you were when you first came to see me. Good job the insurance is paying for this, isn't it?'

That's why I liked Blake. He was a man of the world. He told it to me as it was. He knew my weaknesses.

I laughed. I think that Blake had begun to fill the void that Jem had left. My best friend had turned out to be a sexual predator. I still found it hard to believe.

Blake was probably ten years or so older than I was. Either that or he'd been working a lot harder than me. His hair was almost totally grey. He had the firm hand of a man who knew exactly what he was doing. And he didn't beat about the bush like Martin. If he thought I was being a prat, he told me so.

'Still shagging the single mums at the caravan park, Pete? You need to stop that, you know. You're using one-night stands to avoid dealing with your issues.'

I knew that. And Blake had told me many times. It had begun with Ellie. We'd slept together to help me hide away from my problems with Meg. Now I was doing it all over again: shagging single mums who were on the campsite for a week, grateful for the relief from caring for their kids, and happy never to see me again. They'd had their fill of feckless blokes. They wanted physical contact and closeness, and they were ready to have it with me, but they weren't rushing back into relationships any time soon. That suited all of us.

'You're right, Blake. I can't defend it. I'll stop it eventually – I can't stay at Golden Beaches forever. But, for now, it numbs me. It stops me thinking about everything. And it's harming nobody.'

'Why don't you think about picking things up with

Alex Kennedy? You said that you lived together for several years. You've worked out for yourself that your resentment with IVF was likely based on you losing the baby with Alex. Are there some unresolved issues there, do you think?'

There were lots of unresolved issues in my life. It's why the single mums were proving so attractive. It was oblivion. When making love to Janine from Paisley or Terri from Manchester, I didn't have to confront my demons. Janine or Terri or whoever it was got to forget their depressing life on benefits and I got to forget the mistakes I'd made in my own.

'How are your money issues, Pete? You were worried about that last time we spoke. Have you considered approaching Meg through legal channels?'

Damn, this again. Legal channels. There was no way I was doing anything involving the law unless I had to. We'd all escaped with our reputations intact. All of us: me, Meg, Ellie, Alex, Jenny – each one a liar, none of us called to account for our actions. No way was I voluntarily inviting anything that involved the legal profession back into my life.

'It's complicated, Blake. I want Meg to come to me first. We'll need to talk, we have to sort this out. I want to know about the baby. But yes, money is a bit tight at the moment.'

I decided to deflect. It's another coping technique that I use, according to Blake.

'I'm so desperate I'm considering pinching Martin's Brompton when I leave today and trading in my car.'

Blake looked at me as if to say 'Really?'

'The truth is, Blake, I'm lonely and miserable. I want my wife back. I hate my life. I've had enough of my job. I want to see Meg again.'

Chapter Two

'Where are you moving from?' asked Melissa, rapidly resorting to the estate agent's standard set of questions. She preferred to steer things away from the house's gruesome history.

'We're not from round here,' he replied, a little too quickly. 'We've moved around a lot, and we'd like to settle in this area.'

'Do you have somewhere to sell? I'm afraid I didn't get to look over your notes before our appointment.'

'No, we're cash buyers,' he replied, knowing that this was like foreplay to an estate agent. A cash buyer, no chain, no mortgage applications. All they had to do was to say yes and a commission cheque would soon be on its way. If it came quick enough, she might even be able to make her own mortgage payment. Ironic that she sold houses for a living but could barely afford to stay in her own.

They moved through to the kitchen. Every sign of domesticity had been removed. It was soulless now.

The woman lingered in the lounge, imagining the body lying there, bleeding out onto the carpet. She could still see the signs of cleaning. It was a professional job, this wasn't a task for Mrs Mop. But however much industrial strength bleach had been used, you could still see the discolouration on the floorboards. She knew exactly where he'd died. She knew what she was looking for. It wasn't the first time they'd been to a house like this.

The man kept Melissa talking, letting his partner linger and savour what had gone on there. It was his gift to her, and she'd reward him later; she always left these places desperate to screw. It was an aphrodisiac for her, a delicious experience, a chance to relive violent events.

'The garden is going to need some landscaping work. And can you see how the wall seems to be leaning out there?'

He was distracting her. They'd learnt long ago that estate agents get excited when you start to talk about changes that need to be made and jobs that have to be done. It shows them that you're thinking about what it would be like to live there. You're picturing your new life. They smell your blood. Or, at least, your cash.

Melissa was already spending the commission cheque. If she landed both Stallion Road and this dump, which she'd assumed they'd never sell, she'd not only be able to pay off the mortgage arrears but could also grab a weekend away. With her new man. Well, one of them at least, she'd decide when the money got paid into her account.

As Melissa leant over the kitchen units to check out the garden wall, the woman was taking photos on her smart phone: the lounge, the carvings on the windowsill, the entrance hall and – while her back was still turned – the kitchen, cataloguing every inch of the place for reference later. They'd read the reports and newspaper cuttings, placing each body and reliving every blow. They didn't need Netflix. This was as close to the real thing as they could get. For now.

The lounge, dining area and kitchen were part of an open loop, so they walked back into the hallway and towards the stairs.

'You go ahead,' he said. 'I'll be upstairs in one moment.'

Sensing Melissa's hesitation, he added something extra to boost her confidence.

'I love this front garden. I can picture us now, sitting out there in the sunshine. If we ever see the sun again!'

Melissa laughed and, smelling a sale, she walked up the stairs. The woman followed behind her and they headed towards the bedrooms. She knew what he was about to do.

As the women disappeared onto the landing area, the man took a small knife out of his pocket. He moved over to the front door where he made a carving in the woodwork: R&L, right in the bottom right-hand corner of the door. It was like a wolf's scent, marking territory, warning other sickos to keep well away. It would stay there unnoticed, even after the house had sold. But they would always know it was there. It would be something that only they knew about.

He finished his handiwork, then ran up the stairs two at a time, anxious not to pique Melissa's suspicions. They were in the spare room. There had been a struggle in that room. The one who was decapitated, Jem, had a fight with Bailey in there. They were nearing the bedroom. That would be the crescendo of their house tour. They needed to work Melissa up into a frenzy, make her hungry for the sale, distract her for the main event.

'I don't know about you, but I love the place, don't you ... Alan?' she said. There was a hesitation over his name. Melissa sensed it momentarily, but her attention was diverted by the woman's enthusiasm for the property.

'I love it, Ruth. I think it's exactly what we've been looking for. It won't take too much to get it the way we want it.'

'I'm a bit concerned about the damp that's beginning to come through the walls, it looks like quite a redecorating job.'

Melissa jumped straight in.

'If you're thinking about making an offer, I'm sure that we could get the price down lower, especially for a cash buyer … if you wanted to move fast?'

She was already on the hook, they had to reel her in now.

'We're only in the area today, we have to travel home tonight. We've looked at several properties already today, but we're most excited about this one. You wouldn't check that out for us, would you? I think that if we knew that the repair costs would be covered, we'd be happy to move quite quickly.'

Melissa's eyes lit up. She was already in that hotel spa bath with Logan, or Olaf, or whichever of her men she decided to take with her for her weekend away.

'I'll go and call the office now,' she said. 'I'll leave you to chat about it. Give me a shout if you need me, I won't be far. I'll be in the kitchen.'

Melissa walked off down the stairs, leaving them alone on the landing.

They smiled at each other and walked into the main bedroom, excited and expectant.

It had been stripped bare, like the rest of the house. The carpets removed, the underlay gone, only the carpet grippers remaining along the edges of the floorboards.

21

This is where it had happened. This is where Tony Miller had met his brutal end, stabbed to death, abandoned in the marital bed. This was the place they'd slept together. Their sanctuary, their most private place.

She walked over to the bedroom window and examined the deep windowsill. Older houses were always great for big windowsills. There were more carvings in the woodwork: initials, hearts, names. People like them who'd come to this house to see where it had all happened.

She sat on the low windowsill, pulling up her short skirt. She wasn't wearing anything underneath. They'd come prepared for this, they'd have to be quick.

Downstairs, they could hear Melissa talking to somebody in the office. She'd be stuck to her mobile phone for a few minutes, probably check her emails and Facebook while she was there.

The woman parted her legs slowly and moved her skirt up higher. His hands moved to his belt, he undid the buckle, hurrying now, frantic to take her. He dropped his trousers, letting them remain at his feet, his excitement revealed by the bulge in his boxers. He pulled them down to his ankles, knelt on the floor and slipped inside her. She was ready for him, desperate to take him in this special place. As he came inside her, she pictured the bloody body staring at her from the bed, watching her as they had sex in that room. For a moment she pretended that she *was* her – Meg – and that *she* was the one who'd killed him. It felt delicious. She wanted more.

I was enduring another evening alone on the campsite.

I'd been at work most of the day, popped out for my session with Blake, then had to return to the office to finish off some news story about a man who'd been taking pot shots at ramblers as they walked through the footpath on his property.

It was quite a funny story, although I came over all disapproving when I recoded the voice links for the radio report. He'd shot and wounded twelve ramblers, cursing at them as he did so. He'd had one of those rapid-fire air pistols, no need for a licence. He claimed that he'd been shooting at cardboard targets in his garden and that the ramblers had got in the way.

Turned out he was pissed off with them dropping their sweet wrappers in his garden and letting their dogs shit all over the place. I had every sympathy with him, but as a respectable member of the broadcasting community, I couldn't let on. I had to disapprove of his actions and make sure that I didn't glamourise violence in any way.

He'd used the same sort of pistol that Sally had got hold of. I still had a small scar above my eye as a souvenir. Those things hurt. There was very little chance of them killing anybody, but they were scary when one was pointed right at you. They look like real guns too – I was surprised that the manufacturers were allowed to do that. I'd suggest it as a follow-up radio investigation: 'Lookalike pistols put public at risk!' I'd drum up some sensational headline, see if I could get the newsroom interested in the story.

I'd got back too late to take a shift in the bar, even though Vicky had texted me earlier to see if I was available.

Fancy doing some pulling in the bar tonight? You can pull me if you want to :-) LOL V xxx

I was pretty sure that constituted sexual harassment at work, but I let it slide. Vicky was no threat to me. She knew it was a bit of a joke, she understood that it would never happen.

No can do I'm afraid, working late tonight, breakfast shift on Wednesday, early to bed for me! Pete

Never mind, maybe I'll come over and join you later V xxx

Now that *was* sexual harassment, but I'd continue to encourage it because Vicky should have thrown me out of my caravan a long time ago. The original deal had been for winter, until the new season started.

When the first holiday-makers arrived at Easter, there were still plenty of unoccupied units, so she gave me a stay of execution. As things got busier, she got me involved in the bar work and it suited her to have me around. I paid the rent on time, I made myself useful, and she liked being in the orbit of a local celebrity. It gave her a thrill to hear me reading the news on the radio in the morning and then see me returning to my caravan on *her* campsite in the afternoon.

It suited me to be there, but Christ it was boring on an evening when I had nothing to do. The TV was poor, they only had free-to-air in the caravans. The internet was even worse. I'd had to upgrade my data package on my phone so I could tether my laptop and get a decent signal. That's the joy of being beside the seaside, I guess: grey British seas and crap services. It's a holiday destination made in heaven.

I decided to catch up with Alex. She'd been nagging me to come over, she was desperate to pay me a visit and see how I was doing after the events of six months earlier.

The official version was that Sally had killed the two men in the house, and then gone on to put Jem's life in mortal danger. I was the only one who knew that it was Meg who had killed Tony. But the way I saw it, Meg wasn't guilty of first-degree murder. She'd killed him in self-defence. As for Jem, he'd been decapitated because of Sally's actions. Sally's death was suicide, she'd jumped of her own accord. The case was done and dusted as far as we were all concerned; none of us came out of it with very much credit and it was best laid to rest in the city's cemetery.

Alex was on Skype. I sent her a text message.

You alright to chat? Video okay?

Pete, you're alive. Dial in, I'm here. Just out the shower :-)

I dialled in and there she was on the screen. Not quite as glamorous as her TV persona. She had a towel wrapped around her head and another wrapped around her body. How do women do that? *Why* do they do it? I've never understood the towel-around-the-head trick, it's like they're born knowing what to do. It's the same as taking off a bra under clothing. I've never figured that one out. How does it work? Surely you have to pass your arm through a strap at some stage?

'How are you, Pete? You're terrible, I know you've been avoiding me!'

'I know, I know! I've been … preoccupied, Alex. You know how it is. You're busy too.'

'The series ends tomorrow night, I've got a few weeks clear. How about I come up and pay you a visit? Where is it you're staying? The Golden Showers resort?'

She laughed at her own joke, and I caught a brief glimpse of cleavage as her towel dropped slightly. We'd been in love once, before Meg, but we'd gone our separate ways. That was a long time ago, we were just good friends. We'd become closer again because of what had happened. If it hadn't been for Alex, I'm not sure how things might have turned out.

I tried some evasion tactics. I'm not even sure why I was putting her off. Perhaps I was scared that she'd get me to talk about Meg's confession, her final words before she disappeared. That was a secret I had to keep. It was between me and Meg, it would bind us for life. If that information ever came out, things could go very bad, very fast. That was it. I was worried about being close to anybody because there were things that I couldn't share. How could I ever be completely truthful with anyone ever again?

'You're going to try and wriggle out of it, you bastard! Come on, it's me. I'm dying to see you again, Pete. What have you got to hide?'

The truth was, I had a lot to hide. However, I was ready for some easy company. Alex knew me of old, it would be great to see her again. There's only so much time you can spend in the company of work colleagues, fat blokes in bars and single mums. Eventually you need real company, a friend, and that's what Alex was offering. I'd missed that easy companionship since Meg went.

'Oh bollocks, okay then, but you know that I'm living in a static caravan don't you? You'll get none of your celebrity lifestyle up here. It's all beer, litter on beaches and bad internet connections where I live. Although I do hear a rumour that Stephen Fry is thinking of moving in.'

Alex burst out laughing and that darn towel dropped down a few more tantalising centimetres. If I didn't know otherwise, I'd say that she was doing that on purpose. Intentional or not, it was making me think back to our life together. It was so long ago. We were much younger then. She probably wouldn't even fancy me, I'd got a bit wider around the waist and I'd abandoned the gym some years ago. I was still in good nick compared to other blokes my age, but I wasn't the young buck that she'd once known.

She looked hotter than ever, mind you. Alex had improved with age. I guess it was the expectations of a life spent on TV. No saggy bits or dark circles under the eyes allowed. She had to keep in shape and look her best. A few days on a static caravan site would probably be a nice change for her.

'Okay, okay, you've ground me down. When are you coming?'

'Last show wraps Thursday night at ten o'clock, and there's a debrief meeting on Friday. How about I hop on the train at Euston and join you on Saturday morning before lunch? Do I need to bring anything?'

'Those times work fine for me, and no, don't bring anything. I'll pay for guest service over the weekend; they'll deliver towels and extra bedding. I've got two spare rooms here. I'll move all my crap out of one of them. It'll be good to see you.'

'Don't put yourself to any trouble, Pete. We've shared a bed before, and I'm quite happy to go top-to-tail if we need to. You don't still fart like you used to, do you? Actually, maybe I will have that separate room!'

We both burst out laughing, remembering some of the fun we used to have together, and I caught a momentary glimpse of nipple as Alex moved backwards and forwards.

As it turned out, she would share my bed again. But not before I met Rebecca.

I had a couple of days before Alex's visit, and the more I thought about it, the more appealing it became. I started planning some of the things that we could do while she was staying with me, it would be good to catch up. After Meg, Alex knew more about me than any other person. We'd spent five years of our younger lives together. Even if it hadn't worked out for us, that counts for something.

My static caravan needed a makeover before she arrived. She was always the tidier half of our relationship. The spare rooms were packed with boxes, I'd need to move them over to the self-storage warehouse where all my other belongings were kept.

I'd been surprised by how little of life's crap I actually needed after Meg left. The caravan came equipped with all the basics: beds, cooker, microwave, TV, kettle. Once I'd got my clothes, toiletries and tech, that was all I needed.

I'd brought much more than was necessary for such a small space, so Alex's visit would give me the boot up the butt that I needed to clear it all out. The advantage of working the early shift is that you get an afternoon that you can use productively. I did exactly that, leaving the office promptly and heading straight back home. Home was now the caravan park. I'd long ceased to make my way back to Ashbourne Drive on autopilot.

It had taken a few months to lose that habit. I'd finish my shift and jump into my car, with thoughts of Meg and home on my mind. A couple of times I even got as far as the drive before I realised my mistake. I never wanted to enter that house again. I'd got my stuff and then let the clearance guys move everything out to the storage units. I didn't want to know, it was too painful. I gave them instructions for gathering together the junk that was now sitting in the boxes in my two spare rooms, but didn't go back again. I'd paid people to take care of it all, it's why I was so short of cash, but I knew I'd be okay again, once the house was sold and I was back on my feet.

I'd barely even opened the boxes that I'd loaded into the back of my car. They were full of books, paperwork and the stuff of life, but everything was online nowadays and I didn't need most of it anymore. I read books on my smart phone, kept my bank accounts in the cloud, and watched TV on demand from Netflix. There was nothing holding me to that city, I could walk away whenever I wanted, start afresh and forget the past.

I loaded up the last box into the back of the car, slammed the boot shut and set off for Boxed In, the warehouse where my old life had been locked away for the past six months. As I got closer to the industrial estate, I found myself getting nervous. I'd never even been to the storage unit, all I had was a key and a unit number.

It wasn't what I'd expected at all. It was a vast space, lined with storage rooms in all sizes. Each had a solid green metal door and a locking mechanism which looked pretty secure. I hadn't got a clue where my unit was, so I signed in and asked the chap at reception to guide me through the maze.

'Hello, Mr Bailey!' he said cheerily. I knew what was coming. He'd heard me on the radio. There would be no anonymity here.

'I was only listening to you on the radio this morning. Thanks for using our service. Anytime you want to give us a mention … '

How many times had I heard that one? I don't know what he thought it would do for his business. A mediocre local mini-celebrity, one step up from the High Street butcher, mentioning a storage warehouse. Did he think that all of a sudden the entire population of the city would hear my words, realise that they'd got a load of junk that needed to be stored more effectively, and beat a path to his door? People have funny ideas about the power of TV and radio. Sure, some things take off, but Boxed In Ltd was unlikely to be one of them.

I exchanged pleasantries and tried to steer him off the scent. He didn't take the hint.

'Terrible business with you and your missus,' he persisted. 'So many people dying, it was a tragedy. Shocked the whole city it did. It must be hard to keep your life going after all that?'

I didn't take the bait, instead I made non-committal responses and tried to remember where in the maze of storage rooms my own unit was located.

'There you are, Unit 205!' he announced.

I was damned if I could work out where we were, the place was huge. I could make no sense of the numbering system. You could get lost in there for days. My guide through the labyrinth hovered for a while, no doubt hoping that he'd get a look inside. I made it clear that it was time for him to get lost, in a nice way of course, and he finally took the hint.

I felt in my pocket for the key. There were several different sizes of storage room, and I'd got one of the bigger ones. No wonder it was costing me an arm and a leg. If Meg would only make up her mind what was happening with us, we could move on, divide it all up, throw it on the fire, whatever.

I inserted the key into the heavy padlock and opened the clasp. The door slid upwards, like a garage door. It was dark, and I could just make out the silhouettes of my former life. I looked around for a light switch. It was right next to me. The storage unit lit up.

My life with Meg came rushing at me at great speed. A lot of furniture had been thrown out and destroyed. Our bed, for instance. It was soaked with the blood of Tony Miller, nobody would ever be sleeping on that again. One of the settees had gone too, the one covered in the blood of Jason Davies. I got a flashback to the moment when I'd found his body, his throat slit, his head pounded by a baseball bat. I wanted to be sick. I'd begun to put those images behind me, now they were back with me once again.

The second sofa was to my left, piled with boxes. It had borne witness to everything that went on in the house that night ... the stories it could tell.

I needed a break, it had been overwhelming to see all my stuff again. I headed back to the office at the entrance of the warehouse, taking a long detour along the way as I made wrong turns and kept hitting dead ends. You needed a sat nav to get around that place.

The guys in the office found a trolley for me and I loaded my boxes from the car onto it. After two trips, all my stuff had been moved into the storage area.

I'd settled down a bit since first seeing all of our belongings stuffed into that one place. It had been a shock, much more than I'd expected, but it was over, the nightmare had ended six months previously. I offloaded the boxes and played the inevitable game of cardboard-box Tetris that was required to squeeze it all in. There was no way I was going to move up to a bigger storage area, it was costing me enough already.

After a while, it became evident that there was no way I was going to get everything inside, not without a reshuffle. The removal guys had thrown it in, they didn't give a toss whether it had been done in the most sensible way. This job was going to take longer than I'd thought.

I moved the boxes out into the corridor to give me the space to organise things a bit more strategically. There was nobody in the warehouse, it was all quiet. Like me, most people dumped their junk, locked the doors and seldom came back. I wondered if anybody would even notice if everything got sent to the tip.

I began to come to boxes which I hadn't seen before. They'd been packed by the removal guys, and I hadn't got a clue what was inside them. My curiosity was aroused, and I started to open up the flaps to get a sense of what was inside. There would be stuff in there which had been in the loft for ages, things that had been long forgotten by Meg and me.

I started to open up boxes and rummage around inside them. I hadn't got a clue what I would find. It was the proverbial Aladdin's cave, only there was no gold or precious jewels, only endless heaps of junk that should have been thrown out years ago. Then I came across a box packed with things I'd never seen before. Most of it was rubbish: childhood toys, musty old Enid Blyton books, birthday cards which seemed to increase from age six to seventeen years old. But tucked at the bottom was an old shoebox with two elastic bands around it to keep the contents safe inside. I opened it up and found a bundle of photographs. I'd never seen any of this stuff. It all belonged to Meg. She'd never shared any of it with me before.

Chapter Three

She looked directly towards his smart phone, which he'd propped up along the skirting board, directly opposite.

'You filmed it. Good,' she said, as he got up from his kneeling position and hoisted up his trousers, then buckled his belt once again. She took a moment to tidy herself up, pulling her short skirt down from around her waist. Downstairs they could hear Melissa Drake finishing her call to the office.

'Am I too flushed?' she asked, as he switched off the video recorder on his smart phone. They'd watch that later, on the HD TV. It would become a part of their personal porn collection. It might even make it to one of the porn websites, depending on how visible her face was. For regular videos they used masks, the Venetian kind, the type people wore at masquerade balls. She always kept a couple by the bed, it was a thing of hers. He didn't mind. The hotter she was, the better, as far as he was concerned. Sometimes she'd tell him to put on a mask. He'd know then that the camera was coming out. It was getting uploaded to a website. It would be another of their secrets; it gave him a thrill to think of strangers getting off on watching them together.

'Have you got a tissue?' she asked, hearing the sound

of Melissa's footsteps as she made her way up the stairs. He handed her one and she swiftly wiped herself down. She finished straightening her skirt as Melissa re-entered the main bedroom. He distracted her, seeing that his companion needed a moment to cool off. She looked out the window, pretending to survey the garden.

'I've not been able to raise Mr Elliott – Glenn – I'm afraid, but if you can leave me a mobile phone number, I'm sure that he'll get back to me as soon as possible. I really don't see a problem with dropping the price slightly. It's been on the market for a long time, and I think the owner is keen to get rid of it.'

'It was a terrible business. We saw the news reports at the time. What a shock for the poor bloke. Does he still live locally?'

He had the answer already. They knew exactly where Pete Bailey was living. He didn't expect Melissa to tell him, she was too professional and old school to make such a rookie error, but he wanted her to think that they were deadly serious about buying the property.

Nowadays you could find most people from the information that was freely available online. Pete was easy. They knew where he worked. It had been all over the papers at the time, the journalists had loved that one. He was one of their own. He was on the radio most days, and they could be sure of his whereabouts when he was broadcasting live. They'd followed him home from work one day, and he'd led them directly to the Golden Beaches Holiday Park. That's all they needed: mobile home pitch, car number plate and work location. All they had to do was to wait and watch.

'Yes, he's still local,' Melissa answered, 'but I think he'll be moving on after all this. Poor chap, it's a lot to happen to one man.'

The woman turned around, she could feel the flushing in her face had subsided. She'd been standing there at the window, thinking about what they'd done. In that house, the murder place, where it had all happened. Pete would come next. They knew where he lived, and now they'd seen the house itself, she was desperate to move on with her plan.

'Is anybody else interested at the moment?' the woman asked. 'What's the competition like?'

Melissa thought that she was looking a bit hot and bothered. She'd put the boiler on when she'd arrived to take the chill off the place, maybe it was running a bit high.

'In actual fact, somebody else will be coming around later today. The office mentioned it to me a few minutes ago. I won't be doing the viewing, it'll be Glenn, but I'll make sure I speak to him before he sees them. If you want to put an offer in, yours would take priority, of course. What sort of price are you thinking of?'

They'd both done this before. Estate agents were easy. It was simply a matter of dropping the offer below the asking price: not so low that it would be rejected out of hand, high enough to show that they were serious. They didn't want to be seen as time-wasters or carpet-treaders. The woman looked at her companion.

'I was thinking maybe £3,000 below the asking price?' she suggested.

'Yes, something like that. I reckon we'd have to paint through, and the garden needs sorting out. How about £4,000 below asking price, but we'd go to £3,000 if he knocked us back? Do you think that will work?'

Melissa tried to contain her excitement. As an estate agent, she was playing her own games. Glenn Elliott *had* been back in the office when she rang, but she wasn't going to tell them that. She needed to leave them hungry. She had to sow the seed of doubt that they might not get the house. It was true that somebody else was coming to look around later, but she sensed that these two were hot to trot. All of her antennae as an estate agent were vibrating, she could feel that an offer was imminent.

'I think you're in the right ballpark, I'm very confident that the vendor will be interested in that offer.'

'May we take a look out the back?' he asked, glancing briefly at his female companion before he spoke. Melissa didn't spot the signal, but then she wasn't ready for it in the way the woman was.

'Of course, of course,' Melissa replied, feeling in her pockets for the keys. 'Let's head downstairs and I'll open up the back door. It's a bit stiff, I think. The handover notes for the house say it needs a good shove to get it open. The sooner somebody's living in this place again, the better, if you ask me.'

They walked downstairs and Melissa struggled to open the door.

'Here, let me help,' he said, moving in to assist.

'I can't budge it,' she said. 'Thanks, see if you can get it open.'

'I see you put the boiler on,' the woman said, distracting Melissa. 'Is it playing up or does it seem to be working okay?'

This was his cue. While Melissa gave the usual reassurances about the boiler, he slipped one of the keys off the metal ring on which they were stored. There were plenty of keys on there, along with duplicates – they'd be in and out of the key cabinet in the office all day. He gave the door a pull and it came open.

'Ah, well done!' said Melissa. She led the way outside. The woman followed, the man held back. He was making sure that he'd left them a spare back door key, when Melissa popped her head around the door. She almost caught him moving the coloured key covers around so that they'd think it was a key from another property that had been lost. He smirked as he thought of the confusion that he was about to subject them to. Somebody in the office would be in real trouble when they realised that one of their keys had been misplaced.

'Everything alright, Mr Simpson?'

He covered up his tracks.

'Yes, no problem. I was taking a closer look at this door to see if I could make it easier for you next time you're doing a viewing. It's actually a hinge problem rather than a damp problem. I've tightened the screw using the edge of one of these keys. That should do the job until we can get workmen into the place.'

He'd said exactly the right thing. It's what all estate agents look for. The minute viewers start talking about a house as if they're already in there, it's as good as sold.

Melissa did a happy dance in her head. She was calculating the commission as he spoke. The man moved his hand to conceal the stolen key in his back pocket. He gave back the key ring. It was so laden with colour-coded keys that they might go for days without realising what had been done.

They'd got what they'd come for. They had no intention of buying the house. But they would be coming back there again, this time without the complication of an estate agent in tow.

For some ridiculous reason, I hesitated before tearing open the shoebox and working my way through the photographs. I felt as if I was invading Meg's privacy, yet she was my wife. I'd still not had any formal approaches from her legal representatives, if she even had any; she'd disappeared without a trace, not making any moves to end things between us.

I decided to look. She'd never shared these photos with me. How bad could it be? I knew that she'd lost her mum and dad in her twenties and that she'd had a sister. They'd been killed in a car crash apparently. It's pretty horrible that — almost an entire family wiped out in a single accident, and no relatives. It's amazing how a family tree can so suddenly hit a dead end.

I'd never questioned Meg's family history. Why would I? It had come up early in our relationship, the parent conversation. It turns up as sure as night follows day. Only, when I asked the question, it became an immediate no-go area for us.

At the time we met, both my parents were alive. I had two brothers and a sister. We all got on, but like most modern families we lived miles apart and seldom saw each other. My dad died of a heart attack within three months of retiring, when I was in my mid-thirties. He'd worked all of his life in a job he hated, craving retirement at the age of sixty, and then he'd dropped dead within weeks of reaching his Holy Grail.

Mum was showing signs of going on forever. It had shaken her when Dad died, but she was amazing. She'd taken the punch then got up in the ring and carried on fighting. I was proud of her. People say women of that generation were dominated by men, but it's the men who keel over with heart attacks and strokes, and the women get on perfectly well without them.

'How about you? Where do your mum and dad live?' I'd asked Meg.

Silence. Oh shit, were they dead? We were getting to that age when you couldn't assume both sets of parents were alive – you had to leave wriggle room in case they weren't.

'Mum and Dad are both dead,' she'd replied. Her answer was curt and tense. She was shutting me down. 'They died in an accident when I was young. Along with my sister. It was horrible.'

'I'm sorry,' I said, moving in close to offer some comfort. Her body was stiff and unwelcoming, I'd touched a sensitive spot.

And that was it. Meg was happy to talk about my family – she got on really well with my brothers and my sister, but her family became a complete no-no as far as polite chitchat was concerned. I'd warned my family off the topic before they met Meg, and it never came up again.

She'd make the very occasional slip, mention her mum and dad or begin to share a memory of her sister, but other than that, nothing. We never went to family gatherings, there were no Christmas or birthday cards for her from long-lost aunties and uncles. That part of her life was non-existent, it was something that we never talked about.

Being the in-tune kind of guy that I am, it had taken me far too long to understand why Meg had become so keen to have a child of her own. She was making a family, creating roots where there were none. I'd missed that completely, oblivious within the cushion of my extended family. All of my siblings had kids, the Bailey family tree would continue to sprout and flourish. But for Meg, family had meant something completely different.

As I began to sort through the photographs, I became aware of how much I wanted to see those pictures. I had thought that none existed. People do funny things when parents die. Some go off and have affairs, suddenly threatened by the meaninglessness of their lives. Others take trips of a lifetime and blow their savings, finally aware of their mortality. After a while I'd taken it as a private matter for Meg. She had kept no photos, no memorabilia, I had to respect that's how she wanted to play it. Yet, here they were. They had been hidden from me. They did exist after all.

The first photos were black and white. Future generations will never have that experience of looking at images that were taken decades beforehand, curled and folded from years of handling. There were names on the back, written in handwriting belonging to a generation that would soon no longer exist. It was neat, even, and beautifully penned in brown ink: Thomas Yates, Mavis Irvine.

The early pictures soon morphed into Thomas and Mavis Yates. Faded colour began to creep into the images, then tiny Polaroids. With each new image, the subjects changed their hairstyles and their fashion sense. Then, with no warning, a picture with children.

I was surprised that there were no pregnancy shots. Children's photographic lives begin from their first scan nowadays, every moment is recorded, from all angles, on every occasion, special or not.

It's hard to remember the time when you got twelve photos from the cheapest reel of film, thirteen if you got lucky and squeezed an extra image out at the end. It would take a week to get the film developed, that's if you didn't mess it up when you took the film out of the camera, and even then you'd have to save up for weeks to be able to afford the costs of development.

No wonder there were no pregnancy photographs. These pictures were taken in the late eighties or early nineties, at a guess, when you could scratch your nose in peace without somebody recording the event on a smart phone.

There were two teenage girls, about the same age, probably fourteen or fifteen. One was quite obviously Meg. She and her companion had appeared from nowhere. I shuffled through the pictures faster now. There they were again, two girls growing up. School photos, class trips, days out, everything that you'd expect to see in a family photo album. But this was only a selection. There were no sets of photographs in this box, only individual images, as if they'd been picked out from a larger collection.

As the girls grew older, it became clear that there was an age difference. It was easy to see that the younger child was Meg. I could recognise her face straight away from the first image, her beautiful spirit shone through. It was lovely to see her like that, in a flowery dress, wearing a terrible shirt with the most flowery collar I'd ever seen. Then came dungarees, crop tops and grunge, this was a life that Meg had never shared with me, one that I didn't know had existed.

As far as I was concerned, Meg's life, as I knew it in any detail, began when she was at university. We never really talked about anything before that. I'd get the odd reference to things she'd read or played with as a child, but very few specifics. It wasn't that I lived in the past, but since I had brothers and sisters, family gatherings inevitably involved anecdotes and memories from when we were kids. Maybe only children didn't have that.

As suddenly as the two girls appeared in the photographs, the visual history stopped dead. No graduation photos, no leavers' parties, nothing. It was as if the plug had been pulled. We were well clear of the eighties, that decade was so distinctive, these photos began and ended in the nineties. Meg would have been a teenager then, maybe as old as seventeen or eighteen, perhaps a bit younger. It was difficult to date the pictures exactly. The carefully written notes on the back of each picture had become less common as the years went by and photography became cheaper and a more disposable commodity. Imagine having to caption every image that we take these days? I take so many shots that I leave them with the numbering straight off my smart phone.

This was a mystery. Meg's maiden name was not Yates, she'd told me it was Stewart. That must have been true – if it wasn't, we wouldn't have been able to get married. Who the heck were these people? And why had Meg never bothered to share her stories and memories about them? It looked like a family grouping, it had to be that, but I'd never heard mention or caught sight of any of these people.

I dug my hands deep into a larger box, hoping to pull out more documents or photographs which might offer some explanation. Meg must have loved Enid Blyton, there were twenty or so Famous Five books in there, but nothing else to help to throw any light on her past.

Who was this woman that I'd been married to? When we got married, there were no name issues. She'd been Megan Stewart on the marriage certificate, I'd only ever known her as that. My journalistic senses were raging, something wasn't sitting right here. Why would Meg not tell me about these people? I'd always accepted that her family had died in a car accident; Meg never told me exactly what happened, or when it happened. She got all prickly about it whenever I cautiously mentioned the topic, so I backed off and we never talked about it.

Maybe it was something to do with meeting each other later in life. If you meet somebody young, your family life is pretty well all you've got to talk about. When you meet in your late twenties and early thirties, as we did, well, there's a lot more water under the bridge by that stage. Family life seems less important then, you've long since flown the nest and made your own life.

I used the elastic bands from the shoebox to wrap around the photographs. I decided to take them with me. I'd have a dig around, maybe see if Alex had any contacts that she could call upon. I wanted to know who these people were. Meg's family life had become much more interesting to me and I was beginning to wonder how well I really knew the woman that I'd been married to for seven years.

I finished packing the boxes back into the storage room, and by the time I was done, there was quite a lot of room to move around inside. I turned off the light, pulled down the door, and locked it, giving the padlock a shake to make sure that I'd fastened it securely.

I thought that it might be the last time I'd ever go in there. There was nothing that couldn't be thrown out. I'd shredded or retained anything private or confidential. When Meg let me know what she wanted to do, when she finally decided to reappear in my life, she could either take all that junk herself or I'd get it taken to landfill. I had no expectation of ever having to go back to that warehouse again. In fact, I was looking forward to the day when I could cancel my standing order and be done with the place.

As I handed the key back to the guy at the office, I had no idea that I'd be back there in a matter of days. And it would be after a meeting with one of the girls in those photographs. The one that wasn't Meg.

My early shift on the Friday was the last stint I had to work for several days. I'd had a bit of a long run covering other people's shifts, so I didn't have to book any leave. It would be fun, a chance to forget about Meg and have a laugh with an old friend. I was due back in the office on the following Wednesday, that would give me and Alex plenty of time for some R&R.

I hadn't realised how ready I was for it. I'd been in a state of tension ever since my fling with Ellie in the Newcastle hotel. I had only myself to blame, that ill-judged night had come back to bite me. Not only had it messed up everything with Meg, it had also resulted in the deaths of my best friend and his wife and two other completely innocent people. And Tony Miller, of course, Ellie's stalker.

I'd wrestled a lot with my conscience over the past six months. I knew that Jem's death was partly my fault, but I hadn't shared that with anybody. Nobody would ever blame me, there would be no suspicion, but the simple truth is, I could have saved him. I didn't, because he was supposed to be my best friend and he'd betrayed me. Worse still, he'd used sexual violence against my wife. I was furious with him, but I could have saved him from a terrifying and brutal death instead of rushing out to help Meg.

I was carrying Meg's secret too. The official report had got the whole thing wrong. She had walked away as a victim, and Sally had taken the blame for everything, but Meg had stepped beyond self-defence. She'd repeatedly stabbed Tony Miller.

It was the way Sally had been judged which bothered me the most. Her kids had spent some time in care, and it seemed that the grandparents would secure a parental responsibility order to look after them permanently. They would grow up learning that their mother had been a killer. Only she hadn't been, not really, she was no murderer, she'd had a mental illness, depression, and she was pushed to act that way by extreme events. None of us was without blame.

On a bad day, I wondered who I'd been married to. Did I really know Meg that well? And now, having found the photographs in the storage unit, there were even more questions bothering me. Eventually I'd see Meg again. There was nothing I could do until that time. But I was certainly going to dig into her past a little more; it seemed that our whole relationship had been based on lies about her family. I had to know, I couldn't wait until she finally decided to get back in contact with me.

My last day at work went pretty much as usual, except for one troubling incident. I'd arrived in the office shortly before 5am feeling in a good mood. I made a round of teas and coffees for the early team and started to work through the news stories for the day. It was the usual crap: councillors accused of wasting tax payers' money; the chief constable being hauled over the coals over stop and search; a local charity under threat because its funding had been pulled. It was time to shake things up, I'd been doing this local drudgery for too long.

I took my breakfast break immediately after the nine o'clock news and passed my boss, Diane, in the corridor, going into her office.

'Morning, Pete. Everything okay?'

'Hi Diane, yes, all good thanks, nothing too taxing going on today. Only that strike by the lecturers at the uni. The early reporter has been dispatched to get some audio.'

'Great, great, a nice quiet Friday then if we're lucky. Have you got a minute, Pete? I need to run something by you.'

My stomach was rumbling. I was desperate for my egg and bacon butty, but when the boss wants to call you in for an early morning chat, you don't say no.

Diane unlocked her office door and placed her bags on the table.

'Take a seat, Pete. Won't be a minute.'

'Door closed or door open?' I asked. The seriousness of the chat would be determined by the answer.

'Yes, close the door if you would, Pete. I want a quick word with you in private.'

I closed the door. Diane moved her bags under the table, placed her phone on charge and started her PC chugging away with the login process. The office routine.

After a few moments, she pulled in her chair, sat up and looked directly at me.

'We've had another crank letter in, Pete. I'm sorry to have to tell you, but I think it's important that you know.'

She saw my face drop. I thought the crank stuff had stopped.

'Is it the same guy again?' I asked, not really wanting

to know the answer.

'Yes, JD again. Initials only, same scrawl. It has to be him.'

'Damn it! Sorry, Diane, excuse the language. I thought it had stopped.'

'I said the same thing myself, Pete. It's been a month since the last one. I thought he'd got fed up. I'm so sorry, I know how this makes you feel.'

I'm not sure that she did. It made me feel exposed, threatened and unsafe, as if the nightmare would never be over. There had been a flurry of weirdos and nutters once the reports of the events of six months ago came out. It was all over the national press, I'd even seen it on a few foreign websites. Apparently, the nutters love a good murder story. I got a police liaison officer filling me in on the details. I had become a bit of a celebrity, I'd been bang in the middle of a national murder case. Cue the weirdos.

They'd had problems with vandalism at Jem and Sally's grave. It had become a place of pilgrimage for people who got off on the macabre. They'd visit the graveyard, the cathedral and our house. Some of them even booked viewings, to get 'the tour'. I tried not to let it get me down. The liaison officer advised me that the letters were unlikely to lead to anything, it would be some strange little man getting excited by the contact with me.

There was no address, not even a local postcode. Only initials, no hint of a name and nothing to track him by. This idiot had me by the balls, he could shatter my peace of mind in an instant. Screw him. I'd been all teed up for a nice weekend and now I had this to contend with.

'What does he say? Are there any threats this time?'

I was terrified of the answer. I was beginning to understand what Ellie had gone through with Tony Miller. At least she could see him and put a name to him, he was known to the police. It didn't give her any consolation, but she knew who he was and where he lived.

It was not knowing that made this guy so scary. As far as I knew, he could be following me or watching me. He was faceless and nameless. I didn't know if he was some puny saddo or a madman. The only consolation was that the letters were postmarked Newcastle. He was local to where Tony Miller had been when he killed the poor lad at the OverNight Inn. It didn't look like he would be bumping into me in the street.

He had the advantage. He knew exactly what I looked like – my mugshot had been all over the papers. They'd used my studio shot from the radio station. I'd asked Diane to stop making my presenter postcards available, they'd had a run on them when the case was all over the papers. She'd agreed to that one immediately and apologised that they hadn't thought about it before the problem arose.

'Are you sure you want to know, Pete? I'm going to send it over to the chief constable for a look, see what he can do about it.'

'I don't think there's anything the cops can do, Diane. This guy is trying to rattle me. I have to hope that he'll lose interest eventually. What does he say this time?'

Diane leant across her desk and retrieved the letter from her briefcase. She'd obviously been holding onto it, deciding whether or not she needed to inform me. She put on her reading glasses.

'You sure you're okay with this, Pete? It's not a nice

one.'

'Red ink and capital letters again?'

Diane nodded, looking over her glasses like a doctor about to deliver bad news.

'Show it to me,' I said. 'It's only a letter. I have to keep telling myself that.' I took the paper from her.

PETER BAILEY. I KNOW WHERE YOU LIVE. I'M WATCHING YOU ALL THE TIME. I KNOW YOUR SECRET. ONE DAY YOU'LL SEE ME. J.D.

'He's printed this out via a PC, he doesn't seem to know how to remove the caps lock,' Diane said, attempting to lighten the moment, 'although his communication skills are better than some of the young reporters we get in here nowadays. What do you make of it?'

'The guy's a nutter. It's the same old thing, he's trying to rattle me. It frightens the life out of me to think he might be out there. But what can I do? Until he shows himself or gives his location away, I'm shafted.'

For a moment I considered telling Diane about my thoughts of relocation. A job move and change of city would probably shake off this guy. I'd thought the letters had stopped, I'd begun to feel more confident, but he was back messing with my mind again.

'I'll pass it straight onto the police. I'll lean on the chief constable a bit, maybe offer to go a bit easier on him about stop and search. At least this guy hasn't figured out where you live, they're still being sent to the radio station.'

She was right. All the time the letters were being sent to the radio station, he knew no more about me than any other listener. This JD guy had been a pain in the arse. I wasn't going to let him ruin my weekend. He was probably some silly man in an anorak getting the only bit of excitement that he could in some sick power game. Well, screw JD, he wasn't going to mess up my weekend with Alex, I wouldn't let him get to me.

I headed back into the office. I'd lost my appetite for that egg and bacon butty.

Chapter Four

They'd been disappointed when they visited the cathedral to see where she'd jumped. You could still tell where a few paving slabs had been changed. The local council had been unable to remove the stains of blood. There were ageing wreaths resting against the cathedral walls marking the spot. Even six months on, people came to visit, they had to look. The thought of her jumping from that height onto the ground below. She must have been in a right state.

The woman knelt down to get a closer look at the messages which were attached to the flowers. They were alone, so she bent over further than was necessary, giving him a glimpse of her bare behind. She parted her legs slightly so that he could get a good look. He clocked it immediately, he knew what she was doing, and a surge of lust flowed through his body.

She had him completely on a chain. When she tugged on it, he came running. Willingly, too. He'd never met a woman like her. Sexy, on heat, and definitely not missionary position. She liked it a bit messed up. He'd never been with a woman like her before, it was intoxicating to him, he couldn't get enough of her. It suited who he was.

He knew that, soon, he'd have to let her go to him. It was part of her plan, but he thought he was okay with that. If it made her happy, he'd get the benefit of it. She'd be insatiable once she'd got what she'd gone for. And when she felt that way, she'd come back to him again.

She returned to her kneeling position, allowing her short skirt to cover everything up again – there were a couple of people walking through the cathedral grounds. She'd given him just enough to keep him hungry. She picked up one of the tags which was loosely attached to the flowers.

It read, *Why?*

Why not? she thought. What a stupid thing to write on a wreath of flowers. She placed it back contemptuously, picking up another card. The ink had run, it had been exposed to the rain for some days, but she could still make it out. Another generic platitude straight off the pages of social media: *God has a new angel. Sleep tight, KL & VB xxx*

She considered the initials. Probably a couple of voyeurs, not one of the family. The flowers had been left by people who'd heard the story and felt the need to express their horror in some way. They were the lowest level of vulture, getting off on the horrific events yet ashamed enough to feel the need to leave some flowers. They were lightweights.

'Shall we try our luck with the bell tower?' she asked, noticing how closely he was watching her.

'I don't fancy our chances during daytime, but we could give it a try.'

They walked through the heavy wooden doors. She knew every detail of what had happened there. She could see the light patch on the stone slabs where they'd had to scrub with bleach to remove the blood left from the wound on the verger's head.

He'd died soon afterwards, not from the superficial wounds that he'd received, but from the shock of it all. Two months later, going about his business in the cathedral, and he died. Heart failure, apparently. But it was attributed to the terrible events that had taken place there. He'd been up early, preparing for the 7am service of morning prayer. He'd got more than he'd bargained for.

She'd already studied the layout of the building online, so she knew where to head. They traced the steps that Meg and Pete would have taken. She pictured every move and sensation. Fear, terror, exhilaration. It was a delightful mix of all human emotion, and it had happened in that place.

They neared the door leading to the bell tower. They would first have to access a narrow staircase to reach the higher levels, it was quite a climb to get there.

'Damn it!' she muttered. There was no access to the bell tower where Jem had been decapitated. It was strictly out of bounds, they'd never get up there. There was a security guard, of sorts, positioned by the entrance. He didn't look as if he could have chased off a Chihuahua, but they couldn't draw attention to themselves by causing a scene. The staff would be used to the morbid sightseers at the cathedral, they'd probably had to stop several people already. She had thought that by visiting so long after the events, their path would be clear. But it wasn't, she'd have to return to this place later, wait for things to blow over a little more.

But now they were at the heart of the nest, the place

where the main players had lost their lives. She closed her eyes and took in the sacred silence of the place, the echoing footsteps and the hushed voices, the vastness of the ornate roof.

She pictured them running up the staircase, Jem being tied to the bell wheel, and then forcing Meg up onto the highest turrets, Pete running up the winding staircases, out of breath, exhausted, desperate to save his wife. Then the moment when Sally jumped. The ringing of the bells when 7 o'clock came. The thump of Jem's head on the old wooden floor as the heavy wheel ripped through his neck and tore it away from his body.

It had been well worth the wait. She'd read every newspaper story, scanned each word of the magazine articles and watched the reconstructions on TV. She'd used online translation services to scour the foreign reports; they were often less sensitive about sharing the full gory details. She knew every part of this story.

They'd even stayed in the hotel, the OverNight Inn, the place where it had all started. They couldn't get either of the two rooms that they wanted. The hotel chain had had to make that last block of rooms on the ground floor out of bounds to customers, it had become a bit of a freak show. But they managed to get part way along the corridor where it had all happened. She could touch the doors, walk through that part of the building, picture everything that had gone on there.

She couldn't take it anymore. She was wild with excitement and desire. He was watching her, knowing that the combination of frustration and location would drive her crazy.

She began to look around for a place where they would not be seen. The old man sitting in front of the door to the staircase seemed to have dozed off. She ducked into a side chapel, a place that was normally used for prayer and quiet reflection.

Sensing her intention, he followed her, making sure that they were alone. She had moved behind the altar, out of sight. He took out his smart phone and placed it where it could record what they were about to do. As she hitched up her short skirt for the second time that day, all that she could think of was that she had to do this for real now. She had to find Peter Bailey.

———————

As I drove into the entrance of the caravan site, Vicky gave me a wave from her office window. I pulled over in front of the shop and she came out to meet me. I was happy for the distraction. The letter from JD had been troubling me all day, it was souring my plans for the weekend.

'Hi, Pete, luv. Sounding good on the radio today, as ever!' she smiled. 'I'm in a bit of a fix with the family bar this evening. Would you mind helping out?'

There was all sorts of entertainment available at the site and the family bar was my favourite. I had never been keen on traditional pubs, where guys take refuge from their wives and kids, nursing pints and bemoaning their lot. That was never really my thing. I preferred female company or, at the very least, mixed company. I've never been keen on groups of men together. Maybe it's a throwback to caveman days when a gang of men meant you were about to get raided and beaten up; depending on where you live, it can mean the same thing nowadays.

The family bar was where I tended to have all of my luck with the single mums. Every night it would start at six thirty with family entertainment: magicians, people dressed up as furry mascots, kids' entertainers, kiddie discos and so on. At eight o' clock they'd line up all the kids on the dance floor, then start playing the Nighty Night song. What a great wheeze that was. All the kids would be singing their hearts out, and then they'd all exit the building leaving the adults to get smashed and cop off with each other.

Maybe it wasn't quite like that, but it's true that as the final lyrics faded away, the kids would file out, ready to be met by their parents and taken off to their static caravans. They'd be put to bed, listening systems activated, and the parents would be back in the family bar by nine o' clock.

Nighty Night!
Sleepy Tight!
Wake up nice and bright!

I loved that part of the evening. Nine o' clock was when the single mums filed back in, pleased to have packed the kids away for the night, and ready to let their hair down for a few hours. It was sacred adult time for them. Vicky had scored a winner when she had the camp-wide listening system installed. Any peep out of the children, and the parents would be texted immediately.

I was quite happy to work a shift in the family bar. I was always delighted when Vicky asked me.

'No problem,' I smiled, 'although I have a friend staying over for a few days from tomorrow morning. This will have to be the last shift for a day or two, is that okay?'

'No problem, luv. We've been hit by a bit of sickness today, but it'll all be fine by tomorrow. Do you want me to get towels and sheets sent around to your caravan …

or won't you be needing them?'

Cheeky cow! She was trying to find out if I had female company.

'She's an old TV friend, Vicky. Yes, I'll need extra bedding and towels please. Knock it off my wages, is that okay?'

'Have these on me, Pete. It's about time you had some friends around here. You've been lonely ever since … ever since … well, you know what. Is she anybody I know?'

'Can you keep a secret, Vicky? You must keep this to yourself – she's coming here for a break. You know her already, we've discussed her before. Promise to keep it secret?'

'Promise!' said Vicky, sensing that celebrity gossip was afoot.

'It's Alex Kennedy, she's staying with me for the weekend.'

'You mean *the* Alex Kennedy – off the TV? That Alex Kennedy? Ooh Pete, you know all the important people!'

Vicky looked ecstatic at the news. She'd moved up several notches, from meeting a local radio newsreader to a national TV show presenter.

'Please don't make a big deal about it, Vicky. If you promise to keep it quiet, I'll make sure that Alex joins us for a drink over the weekend. Deal?'

'Ooh Pete, I can't wait! I do like you being on the site. I watched Alex on the telly last night, and you say she'll be here at Golden Beaches tomorrow? I can't believe it.'

Vicky was one of those people who think that celebrities somehow have lives that operate completely separately from theirs. They're surprised to find that they shop in supermarkets and occasionally have to frequent public conveniences.

'She's travelling up on the train tomorrow morning, Vicky. She's got a break now the TV series has ended. For some reason, she thought it would be a great idea to visit me.'

'I won't say a word, Pete. It's going to make it really exciting seeing her on the telly from now on!'

After I'd finally got Vicky to calm down, I found out the time that she needed me at the bar and returned to my caravan. Vicky had sent the cleaners over after I'd moved out all the boxes, and it was spotless. I took a shower, changed into some more suitable clothes and opened up my laptop. A Facebook message from Ellie. We'd kept in touch since that fateful weekend in Newcastle, the one that started everything. We got on well, she'd send me jokes and gossip from her part of the journalistic world. We never talked about what had happened, but I was pleased that we were in touch. I liked Ellie, I'd have liked her if we'd been working in the same office together as colleagues.

I was pleased that she'd finally ditched her dodgy bloke. It had taken a while for her to shake him off, but she was writing to tell me that he'd got a new girlfriend.

Dave's got a new woman! She's good-looking too! Check out his Facebook profile, he doesn't know how to lock his settings down, you can see all their pix :-)

I checked out the profile. There was aggressive, muscular Dave with a new girlfriend. He'd even changed his relationship status.

Does that mean he's out of your life forever now?
Hope so! Good riddance, she's welcome to him :-)
You okay Ellie? Everything fine at work?
All good thanks. Busy at work. We have a job coming up in

the TV team. Ever thought about TV?

I'd avoided TV all of my career, but I was so bored with what I'd been doing that I was ready for a change. Ellie's timing was perfect.

At your place? What grade? Is it on or off screen? Will I like it?

It's off screen. You'd be great. Grade above yours, you'd get a pay rise! You can buy me lunch when you get the job :-)

I'd been putting off the job-hunting, but six months after the deaths, with no word from Meg, I was fed up and ready to move on. This latest letter from JD had unsettled me even more. I could leave the house on the market and let the estate agent handle everything. I was on a month's notice at the caravan park, my stuff was in storage. I felt like a single man, there was nothing stopping me from starting afresh. And if Meg decided to show up again? Well, I'd deal with that when the time came. She could take a train to London, after all, even with a baby in tow.

Send me the details will you? Sounds interesting!

Will do :-) Would love to see you working down here. Let me know how you get on, Ellie x

Would it be difficult for me if I ended up working in the same office as Ellie? I could see no reason why it should. If I'd stayed with Meg, it would have been a no-no. I couldn't have risked it, regardless of whether or not she knew about Ellie and me. It would be playing with fire.

Ellie and Alex were lucky to have escaped the fallout after the deaths. Nobody really knew about Alex, not the public anyway, and Ellie had been portrayed as a hostage. Like Martin, our marriage guidance counsellor, she'd been a bit player. The public didn't know what Ellie and I had done that night, and there was no way I was going to tell anyone about it.

Five of us knew what had happened, and each one of us had our own secret to hide. Martin Travis probably knew too – I had to assume that Meg had told him in her counselling sessions, or however it was that she was now communicating with him. It made little difference to anything, but I wanted it to remain private. It was nobody else's business.

I had a couple of hours to kill before my shift in the bar started. I decided to take a look through Meg's photos once again to see if there were any names or locations that I could use to make a start on some research. I hadn't got a clue where to begin, but I was anxious to find out more about my wife. We'd been married for seven years, not that long I suppose, but surely long enough to know who you're married to?

I thought back to how we'd met. It was, perhaps, not the best way to meet your spouse. But nobody plans this stuff. You get what you're given. We first ran into each other while I was doing an interview at her offices. We slept together the first night we met. Should I have held back a bit, got to know her better first? Not a chance, we couldn't wait to tear each other's clothes off that day. Temperance and restraint were not words that figured too much in our relationship.

It probably wasn't a good sign that everything started with a lie. Not a lie so much as an oversight. Meg had forgotten to mention her boyfriend. It was all but over between them, that was clear from the row that followed when he walked in on us. But it was the first example of Meg not telling me the whole truth. I didn't give a toss at the time. I'd bedded a hot and beautiful woman. I wasn't the wounded party. But I was beginning to wonder if Meg left victims wherever she went.

Take Daniel, Meg's spurned boyfriend, for instance. He cursed and yelled when he found us naked in bed, that was understandable, but he seemed an alright guy. He'd met somebody after Meg, and they were doing well. Meg was the guilty party there. I'd assumed that she was a free agent, but it turned out that she wasn't.

It was looking like she hadn't told me the whole truth about her family either. As I held the photographs in my hand, I wondered what untruths would be uncovered. I was a journalist, for God's sake. I was paid to ask probing questions. If I'd been interviewing Meg for one of the news shows, what would I have asked her?

'Why did you neglect to mention your existing boyfriend when we first met and slept together?', 'Why have you been so vague about your family history?', 'Have you told lies about your past?', 'Why did you conceal the fact that you were responsible for the death of Tony Miller when you were interviewed by the police?', 'Who is the father of the child that you're carrying?', 'Has the child been born?'

I'd never asked those questions of Meg, but they were the questions that needed to be answered if we were ever going to pick up our relationship again. And there were a few questions which she would want to ask me if the positions were reversed. I'm not sure how I'd have fared when it came to rigorous questioning.

'Did you know that your best friend Jem was a sexual predator?', 'Did you suspect that he might have been using the date rape drugs that you came into contact with as part of your radio investigation?', 'Why did you have an affair with TV reporter Ellie Turner on your fortieth birthday when we were trying for a child through IVF?', 'Why didn't you tell me that you had lived with TV celebrity Alex Kennedy for five years, a woman with whom you would have had a child if the pregnancy had not ended in miscarriage?'

I removed the elastic bands from around the photos and started to sift through them, trying to identify locations. There were some holiday shots in there, it was definitely a UK seaside resort. There it was, the Blackpool Tower! There was no missing that as a landmark. It featured twice: once in a picture with Mavis and Tom, in their courting days I assumed, and once on the beach with the whole family. If they even were a family.

Carefully, I ran through the other photographs, those taken at home and in the garden. The colour was washed out and the images nowhere near as sharp as we've become used to with digital cameras. But there it was, faint in the background of one of the pictures taken in the garden, the Blackpool Tower.

Whatever the make-up of this group of people, Blackpool featured in their lives heavily, either as a holiday destination or, if I'd got lucky, it was their home. That gave Meg a geographical location, a part of the country that she came from.

I opened up my laptop and began typing random guesses into the search engine. First the names: Mavis Irvine, Mavis Yates, Thomas Yates, Megan Yates. Every now and then I'd be rewarded with some results, but they'd be about other people, not the ones I was looking for.

I tried inserting Blackpool into my search to see if

that might pull up something of more interest. It did. There was nothing about Megan, but I got a result on Thomas and Mavis in Blackpool. It was an article from a newspaper, the Blackpool Courier, dating back a couple of years.

It took some digging to find the article itself, it was buried deep. The trigger for my search had only been a couple of lines of text. Meg had been telling the truth when she'd told me that her parents had died, that had been no lie. Well, it confirmed that one of them was dead, at least. But she'd been deceitful about what had caused the death. I read the words twice through, keen to be certain that I'd got the right people. I'd made no mistake. There it was, right in front of me, one of many parish updates from 2015.

(Blackpool Central) 03/05/2015 Friends of the late Thomas Yates, husband of Mavis Yates, formerly of Great Marton, Blackpool, gathered for a memorial service at Scott Road Methodist Church, marking twenty years since the tragic death of Thomas in their home. Donations totalling £123.67 were raised from those attending. The contributions are to be sent to Happy Siblings in memory of the couple and their children.

Meg had deliberately deceived me about her family. Why would she do that? I could understand if she was too distressed to speak about it, but surely she'd have mentioned it at least once in the time that we'd been together? Or perhaps the lie had become too well worn. Once she'd begun the deception, it might have seemed impossible to reverse it.

These newly discovered photographs and the old newspaper article made one thing very clear to me. Meg had told even more lies than I'd first thought. She'd been completely dishonest about her family. And now it looked like she had a sister and a mother, both of whom may well be alive.

Chapter Five

She had to look around the house. She needed to get a sense of what had gone on and figure out if this was history repeating itself.

'I'd like to arrange a viewing of 11 Ashbourne Drive,' she'd asked, speaking to some intern or work experience teenager. His phone manner hadn't been very impressive so far.

'Oh, you mean the murder place?' the young man had replied. 'Yes, we can sort that out for you.'

She hoped that whoever was monitoring his progress at the company would give him some guidance on his telephone technique. Referring to a property as 'the murder place' was likely to put somebody's commission in jeopardy. Most houses carry a history, much of it happy, but some of it sad. It's best to focus on the nice views, the lovely garden, the airy rooms and the excellent local school. This young intern would need a pep talk if he was going to make it in estate agency.

'What name is it, please?' he asked.

Should she use her real name or go by a pseudonym? It might get tricky if she used her real name. She'd keep a low profile for a while, get a feel for the lie of the land. She'd only recently flown in from Spain; she'd never have known anything about the latest developments if she hadn't read that article from the newspaper. And to think it was wrapped around her fish and chips.

She'd come out in a cold sweat the minute she saw the news story. Her Spanish was getting better, but she saw it was Meg. After all these years there was Meg again. It wasn't the first time Meg had been involved in a 'terrible business'. She'd looked through the article, digging deeper and deeper, uncovering all the press coverage that she'd missed. The local papers were best, they had more information about the people involved.

Meg Bailey. That's what she called herself now. No wonder she'd been so hard to track down. Married. A good-looking husband too. She worked for the probation service. There she was, bang in the middle of a shit storm. *Another* shit storm. But she still looked good.

It's what had prompted her to return to the UK for a few weeks. Not to see Meg, not yet at least, but to tread in her footsteps, to try to work out what had really gone on. Whenever Meg was involved, things were unlikely to be as they seemed.

'Hannah Young,' she replied. 'Mrs Hannah Young.'

It would do for now. She'd tucked herself out of the way, miles from the UK. It suited her, nobody would recognise her there. She'd changed a lot since Meg had last seen her. Meg probably wouldn't even recognise her now.

'Contact address?' the young guy had asked.

'I'm staying in a hotel and looking at property in the area. I'm in the Pine Trees Guest Lodge at the moment. It's probably best if you catch me on my mobile, is that okay?'

She'd managed to be specific enough to get the

appointment, yet vague enough not to give anything away. The intern might have needed to finesse his phone manner, but he'd been trained well enough in screening out the loonies and voyeurs.

She arrived about five minutes before Glenn Elliot. It gave her time to walk around, look at the exterior and try to get a sense of Meg's life in that place. Her husband was a local radio personality; she'd done well for herself, she probably enjoyed the prestige of that. The house was modest, but still required a couple of decent salaries to buy it. Meg was doing okay.

The house was in a state, neglected and sad. What you might expect from a property that had been left in a hurry and which was now haunted by so many ghosts. A BMW turned off the road and into the drive faster than it should have.

A middle-aged man with fast-greying hair and a stomach which pushed at the sides of his shirt stepped out. He wore a suit and tie. Most professions had ditched wearing ties. He looked old school.

'Hello, Mrs Young. Glenn Elliot, pleased to meet you. Apologies for being late, I had something that I needed to attend to before our meeting. Are you ready to take a look around?'

Hannah shook his hand and exchanged pleasantries. His hand was sweaty, as was his forehead, although it wasn't a hot day. He seemed flustered, as if he'd rushed from something to be there. He opened up the door and collected the post.

'More post!' he said, placing the letters to the side. 'It never seems to stop coming.'

'Didn't they redirect it?' Hannah asked.

'No, we collect the post on their behalf. I think it suits the owners better.'

She glanced at the envelope on the top of the pile as she walked through the doorway. *Mr P. and Mrs M. Bailey.* Meg. There she was. Everything came back to her, she could feel Meg's presence, even though she hadn't lived in the place for over six months.

Her eyes scanned the hallway. She was quick to see where initials had been carved. The house was cool, damp and very much unlived in. She took her tour, observing everything, trying to get a sense of what had gone on there.

'Has anybody placed an offer yet?' she asked.

'We have a couple very interested. They're from out of town, like you. They've placed an offer, it's in the right ballpark. I think that if you offered the asking price quickly, you'd stand a good chance. If you like it, that is ...'

She had no intention of making an offer. She wanted to soak up the place, listen to the echoes of the lives that had been lived out there. She could hear Meg's voice, picture her moving through the rooms. She knew that it would all be founded on lies. Wherever Meg went, the trouble followed.

From what she had read in the papers, this Peter Bailey looked like a decent bloke, she could see why Meg had fallen for him.

'I think I've seen enough,' she said. 'I won't be putting in an offer on the place. I'm sorry to have wasted your time. I think this house is too unhappy, it's going to struggle to shake off its demons.'

She was right too. There were many more demons still lurking within those walls.

■■■■■■■■■■■■■■■■■■■■

I looked at the clock on the wall. No battery still, thank goodness for mobile phones. I needed to go to the supermarket and get some bits and pieces before I began my shift in the bar. Alex and I would be eating out most of the time, but it would be good to get some booze and snacks in. We used to play a lot of Scrabble together too, I hadn't played in years. I'd buy a set if I could find one, it would be a good time-filler if we got stuck in the static caravan because of rain.

I wondered if Alex would be up for a trip to Blackpool. I looked up the train timetable. We'd be drinking over the weekend, and there was no way I was driving with all that alcohol floating around.

It would take an hour to an hour and a half, depending on when we went and which train we took. That wasn't too bad. It would be a fun day out. Marton was walking distance from the tower. I wondered if Alex would be up for it. I wasn't sure if I could wait until she left, I was desperate to dig deeper into Meg's past. Alex had been caught up with all the terrible events that weekend, she'd want to know too. But I'd pick my timing, I'd let her get her feet under the table before I asked.

The thought of Alex's imminent arrival, an evening working in the bar and a weekend away from work had put me into a good mood, and even my worries about JD had faded into the background. I picked up my keys and wallet, left the caravan and walked over to the car.

I was completely preoccupied on the drive to the supermarket. I arrived there and realised that I hadn't registered any of the journey. Google gets so excited about driverless cars, but I invented them years ago. I'd been remembering the years I spent with Alex.

I think that my hopes of a reconciliation with Meg had begun to fade after the third month of her disappearance. The immediate horror of what had happened to us had begun to subside, the shock of what she'd revealed to me before she left had had time to sink in, and the money problems were beginning to bite. My concern and sense of loss had been replaced by questions, anger, frustration and resentment. I was desperate to find out about the baby.

I locked the car, grabbed a trolley, put my mind back into neutral and started my walk along the aisles of the supermarket. I remembered that Alex liked grapefruit for breakfast and headed for the fruit and veg area.

'Peter? Peter Bailey?'

I heard a voice behind me. I recognised it but couldn't place it. It was deep and self-assured. I'd once been stuck in the same room as that voice for a couple of hours. My mind whizzed through its memory files. There it was, I'd worked it out before I even turned around. It wasn't a listener or a friend, it was Steven Terry, clairvoyant to the stars.

He'd warned me of the trouble that was about to come my way and all I'd done was to scoff at him. Yet everything he'd said had come true. At the time, Steven Terry didn't know me from Adam, and it was uncanny how accurate he'd been. I hadn't seen him in ages. Since the release of his book, he'd got a gig on a TV station. I hadn't taken much notice, I was used to people moving onward and upwards in their careers and his rise to relative fame was no big deal. It was some daytime show, I think, tucked away where it could be safely tested. He hadn't quite hit the big time yet.

'Steven Terry, good to see you!' I lied. 'Congratulations on your TV show.'

'Hello, Peter, nice to see you too.' He shook my hand, then placed his other hand on top. Is this how he sensed my vibes or read my mind or whatever it was he did? His posh title was precognisant, he could see things in the future. He'd been spot on with Meg and me. I wondered for a moment if I should pick his brains. I scolded myself. It's all a load of bollocks, he got lucky last time.

He looked at me as if he'd seen something. I'd seen that look before. I didn't want to know, I was looking forward to my weekend. All Steven Terry was likely to do was scare the wits out of me.

'It was a terrible business last year, Peter. Are you alright now? I read about it in the papers, and I couldn't help but remember our conversation at the radio station. I wanted to reach out to you, but I didn't know how it would be received. Are you any less cynical now about what I do?'

'I've got to admit it, Steven, you got it dead right last time. But you know me, I'm a journalist. I'm always sceptical about these things.'

I smiled at him, hoping to be able to laugh it off.

'You know, we start to film the second series next month, Peter. I wouldn't have dreamed of asking you beforehand, but how would you feel about us filming at the house? Has it sold yet? I drive by from time to time, and last time I looked, it was still unsold.'

'I can't shift it,' I replied. 'It attracts all sorts of weirdos. I'm not sure I want to fan the flames anymore. Besides, I had an offer in from a couple this week, they seem keen. They beat me down on the price, but I'm thinking of taking it. I want rid of the place.'

'I understand that, Peter. You must have very mixed feelings about that house. Of course, it might help to sell the property if it's featured on TV? I'll leave the offer open to you, may I give you my card?'

I thought about the job that Ellie had mentioned and of the fresh start that was long overdue. If this couple went flaky on me and didn't follow through on the offer, I would be back where I started. I took Steven's card and decided to hang onto it this time around.

He was looking at me, staring intently into my face. He'd done something similar last time I met him, it was very disconcerting.

'Peter, I hope you don't mind. Last time we met I told you that I can't help what I see. It can be a huge burden, a big responsibility. I'm seeing more things coming in your future. I'm sorry Peter, I'm so sorry, but I need to share these with you. I have to tell you what I can see. You must trust me, after what I told you last time?'

The truth is, I did trust him. I'd thought he was a charlatan before, a trumped-up showbiz mind-reader who had his eye on a book deal and a TV follow-up. Well, he'd got that now. He had no vested interest in leading me up the garden path.

'Please tell me it's happier this time, Steven. You're not exactly a good-news kind of guy. I only came here to buy bog roll and grapefruit, I didn't expect to get a vision of my future thrown in for free.'

Steven looked deadly serious. Did the guy ever smile?

'Peter, your house is not yet finished with the killing. There is more evil waiting there. Take care, the danger isn't over.'

'Can you see who it is or what it is?'

'I don't see things that clearly, Peter, I'm sorry. But

there is evil in that house. Be careful if you go there.'

'Fortunately I keep well away these days. Do you see anything else?'

I had to ask. I didn't really want to know, but I needed to understand what it was that he saw.

'The lies have to stop, Peter. This is all happening because of the lies. Only the truth will break the hold of this evil. Somebody is not telling the truth.'

He could say that again. We were all a bunch of liars. I'd already decided that the lies had to stop, but it would be easier said than done.

'There's one more thing, Peter ... '

Did he always see things in threes? He gave me three warnings last time. It was this sort of thing that made me sceptical. Still, I wanted to hear it.

'The women you choose to be with are what determines your path, Peter. There are some poisonous people coming into your life. You will need to decide who to trust. Your choices will determine the outcome, Peter.'

His face was dead straight. He was totally serious.

'I don't suppose you can give me any clues?'

'I'm sorry. That's what I see. I don't know who these people are unless I meet them and can see the intersections in between your lives. It's as much a curse as it is a gift. Take care, Peter, there are still more hazards ahead.'

'You don't mean more deaths, Steven, do you? Surely you can't see any more of that?'

'It's difficult to interpret. I can't be entirely sure, but there is evil, I see it very clearly. And it's close to you, Peter. Take care. Be very careful. Not everybody is who they seem to be.'

My meeting with Steven Terry might have gone better, but as I drove back from the supermarket, I tried once again to focus on the positives. There was no way that Alex was a bad influence in my life. And Ellie too, she'd found a great job for me, she could help me break out of my present situation and move on.

He must have been referring to Meg. She was the main problem in my life. I wanted a reconciliation, and I was prepared to work to achieve it, but she seemed to have made her views clear on that one over the past six months.

As for the house, well, forget that. I had no intention of going to the place ever again. The estate agent could handle the sale, my stuff was all out of the property and in storage, I'd washed my hands of it. Almost.

Steven Terry tended to talk in riddles. I still wasn't entirely convinced that I hadn't conveniently fitted events around what he'd told me the last time. There was no way anybody was getting killed. The house was empty, I was well clear of it. I dismissed Steven's warning as hyped-up nonsense and resolved to make sure that he got nowhere near 11 Ashbourne Drive for his TV show.

As I arrived back at the holiday park, I could see that people were beginning to get ready for a boozy Friday night out. Saturday was changeover day, so Friday was everybody's last night to get drunk before the holiday was over. It would be work again on Monday for most of the holiday-makers, and we'd be shifting a lot of booze as they all had a last fling.

I pulled up outside my caravan, opened up the boot of the car and grabbed as many of the supermarket carrier bags as I could in each hand. There were three steps leading up to the front door. I put the bags down, found my key and walked up the steps. The door opened as I tried to push the key into the lock. It hadn't been wide open, it was pulled to, but it wasn't locked. My static caravan had a weird circular turning mechanism for opening and closing the door. It wouldn't be the first time I'd cocked it up, but I was sure I'd locked up properly.

I investigated the door's mechanism in search of some malfunction. It seemed fine. I picked up the bags and walked into the lounge area. I took a good look around. My laptop was where I'd left it. I didn't have much in there that was worth stealing, but nothing looked like it had been disturbed.

I walked through the caravan – there weren't that many places to go. The kitchen was as I'd left it, the toilet and shower seemed fine. The two small bedrooms were as I'd left them, no further towels or sheets had been put out for me, so it appeared that Vicky's staff hadn't been in while I was out.

The only signs of life were in my bedroom. The quilt was ruffled where someone had sat on the corner of the bed. That was probably me when I'd been changing earlier after work. As far as I could see, it had been my own mistake, I must have left the door unlocked. Nothing had been stolen, so no harm done. I'd take more care in future, try to keep my mind on what I was doing.

I brought the rest of the shopping in from the car, checked that everything was ready for Alex the next day, and got ready for my shift in the bar. I freshened up with another shower and made sure that any cups and glasses had been dried up and put away. It would be a late night. I'd sleep in until 10 o'clock or so, get some breakfast, then head off to the station to meet Alex.

I was feeling extremely positive as I walked across the caravan park to the entertainment hub at the centre. I even popped into the arcade on the way into the bar area and ventured a pound in the slot machines. I won a fiver. I'd never won anything in those machines before. I was quids in before the evening had got underway.

I had a good feeling. Alex was visiting, Ellie had mentioned a decent job in TV, and I wasn't going to be back at work for a few days.

'You look happy!' said Jane, one of my co-workers in the bar that night.

'I feel it!' I replied. 'Things are looking good. If I can sell the house, I think that life could be looking up for me, Jane.'

She smiled at me, and we got to work stocking the shelves, bringing packets of crisps up from the storeroom, making sure that the spirit bottles were wiped down and ready to dispense drinks. Soon the first arrivals came, a couple more bar staff joined us and things started to get busy.

Bar work is very similar to working in radio, I think. That's why I enjoy it so much. It has set times, it's busy and never boring, and once the show is finished, we all go home until the next day. That's how I like my work, busy and self-contained.

So I'd barely taken my eyes off the beer pumps when eight o'clock came and the Nighty Night song started to play. That always meant a slight lull at the bar until nine o' clock or thereabouts. It was a chance to have a chat with the other bar staff, take a half-hour break and recharge the batteries ahead of the post-bedtime rush.

I was still feeling perky after my run of good news,

so I decided to pour myself a shandy and chat at the bar with Jane, Tom and the other guys. They were a good bunch, younger than me, but nice kids, really nice people.

They'd have to serve the occasional customer, but I was able to nurse my drink. I was on my break and I had another ten minutes before I'd be back serving. They'd all had to leave me, the bar was beginning to fill up again, so I surveyed the room, looking at who was in there.

Fortunately, the caravan site tended to attract family groups, pensioners and single parents. Occasionally we got groups of lads or girls in, and they could sometimes mean trouble. Groups of lads seldom ended well, groups of women were fine, but they could be hard work sometimes. We didn't have any large same-sex groups in that night. It had all the makings of a pleasant evening.

As I scanned the bar area, assessing the clientele for the evening, my eyes returned to a single woman sipping a glass of white wine and sitting on her own. I hadn't served her earlier, neither had I noticed whether she was there with kids. I thought not; most single parents could be identified by their mobile phones on the tables, ever alert to a call from the child-monitoring service.

I looked around for signs of her bloke. Perhaps she had a boyfriend or a husband with her? There was no sign of anyone and no second glass sitting on the table to suggest that somebody else might be joining her.

She had striking red hair and a small tattoo at the side of her neck. Normally, I wouldn't have looked twice, but there was something about her that made her stand out.

Her name was Rebecca and meeting her would make the nightmare start all over again.

Chapter Six

The simple headstone was covered with initials, messages and dates. The council had long since stopped trying to clean it. Things would settle down, eventually. The stonework would be scrubbed and she would be granted the peace that she'd craved when she jumped to her death in the cathedral grounds.

There was no headstone for him. His family had tried to put one up, but it had been repeatedly vandalised and defaced. People had actually defecated on the grave. His parents had been shocked to see that. They knew that their son was despised for what he'd done to those young women, but did his children deserve this? He'd been a father too, a much-loved one at that.

His children didn't understand what was going on. They'd heard the rumours of course, and the older children understood enough to know that many people were very angry with their dad. But they missed him. All they wanted was their parents back together, in the family home, the way things used to be.

The woman hadn't expected to see anybody at the grave, and she waited in the distance, watching from afar. They'd assume that she was another grieving relative come to tend the grave of a loved one.

It was the grandparents visiting with the children. The older youngsters were still dressed in their school uniforms, it looked as if it were a Friday ritual.

The children were well drilled. They'd been doing this every week for half a year. They removed the old flowers and placed them in the bins. The new flowers were unwrapped, cut to size and placed in the metal vases. The children filled a watering can at one of the taps placed around the cemetery, then carefully added water to the small pots.

Once the flowers had been arranged, one bunch on each grave, the children bowed their heads and said their prayers. She wasn't religious, the time for that had passed long ago, but it still made tears well up as she watched the children and their elderly grandparents standing in front of the two graves, praying for the people that they'd lost. Did the children know that their father had had his head torn from his body? She hoped not, although how long could that be kept from them at school was anybody's guess. Did they know that their father was a predator, grooming young women for sex and drugging them when they rejected his approaches? They'd understand it one day. Would they put flowers on their father's grave then? Or would they grow to despise him, hating the man for what he'd done to their family, cursing the day he'd brought such shame on them?

It was hard for the grandparents too. He was their son. They'd loved Sally like their own daughter, they'd adored their grandchildren from the moment they were born. How could their own son have done those things? They found it hard to believe.

Their moods could change several times within a

day, from hate, horror and shock to a massive sense of loss, the terrible emptiness of never seeing their son again, of never being able to ask him why he'd done those terrible things.

The small group lingered, they were in no hurry to move on, even though they'd repeated this ritual many times now. The smallest child, a girl, burrowed deep into her grandfather's legs. She was crying, distraught, still not comprehending that she would never see her mother again. Forever is a concept children struggle to grasp. Only now was this child beginning to understand what it meant.

At last the group moved on. She couldn't begrudge them that time, although she was impatient to make her way to the graves. She waited, watching, allowing them to leave the cemetery before she walked over to where they'd been.

An elderly lady threw some withered flowers into the bin behind her. The woman smiled, but didn't linger to pass the time of day. She wasn't here to make friends. The elderly lady returned to the grave that she was tending – her husband's. He'd been 78 years old when he died. The headstone informed her that they'd recently celebrated their fiftieth wedding anniversary when he passed away.

Eventually she reached the place where they lay. The children had written messages on small cards which were resting against the graves.

To Mummy, I'll love you forever and ever and ever, Gracie xxxxxxxxxx

The words had been carefully copied from a pencil outline, with flowers and butterflies drawn in crayon to decorate her work. She was not prone to emotion, the events of the past had helped to strip that away from her, but she couldn't help but cry for the tiny girl who'd lost her mother.

She hadn't come here to mourn or to join the scores of sightseers who flocked to the cemetery to take selfies in front of the graves. She was here because it was finally time for her to return, to step out from the shadows. It was time to stop hiding and deal with the past.

I hadn't intended to get pissed that night. I wanted to have a clear head for when I picked up Alex the next day. I always had a drink or two, it was thirsty work in the bars on the holiday camp. But over the course of an evening, I wouldn't get sozzled, I was at work after all.

After the mid-evening lull, the bar area started to fill up. In between pulling pints, mixing cocktails, chatting to punters and enjoying the music from the resident band, the evening whizzed by.

If anybody had asked me what I thought of British holiday camps before I went to live on the Golden Beaches Holiday Park, I'd have burst out laughing and said, 'Where do you want me to start?'

I was wrong about that. It was middle-class snobbishness on my part. I'd assumed that I'd have nothing in common with the clientele, but as with all prejudicial views, my assumptions were easily blown away by the smallest amount of scrutiny.

Take Vicky, for instance. On first appearances, you'd think she was common as muck, a bit brassy and probably left school with no qualifications. When I got to know her, it turned out that she was a sharp and astute businesswoman, cleverer than her deceased husband had ever been, and pretty affluent as a result. And here's the big surprise. She was studying part-time for a degree at the local university.

I'd met all sorts of people on the campsite. One guy had experienced a nervous breakdown after working in the City, bought himself a static caravan for cash – a fraction of the price of a house in London – and had happily retired there at the age of 39. That's a year younger than me. Lucky bastard. Another couple had rented two caravans, one for themselves and the one next to it for their two teenage boys. They'd been having rows when they lived in the same house, and the arrangement suited all of them. That campsite was a permanent and temporary home for such a variety of people, it had turned out to be a great life experience for me. Sure, I'd never move in permanently, but it had worked out extremely well for six months.

I couldn't keep my eyes off the woman with the red hair and the small tattoo. She was definitely on her own. Every now and then I'd see some sozzled single father – and probably a few married ones – try their luck. It's the curse of the single female, no peace from the eternal hounding of randy men.

She was striking. Noticeable. She stood out in that crowd. She was in the thick of it, but not part of it. It must have taken a lot of courage to sit there alone, nursing her drink, enjoying the tunes of Repartee, the resident Friday night band. There's another thing I loved about the campsite. It wasn't sophisticated, it wasn't hi-tech, but the entertainment was lively and great fun.

Repartee belted out all the favourites from the eighties and nineties with the occasional seventies cover version thrown in for good measure. Everybody knew every song that they played. The dance floor was packed, the place hummed with the smell of fresh sweat, and Vicky's bar takings were through the roof. It was good old-fashioned family entertainment and it suited me better than I'd ever have expected.

So far I hadn't managed to serve the woman with the red hair, but it was only a matter of time until she got to me at the bar. Repartee were playing a ballad at the time so it made it easy to speak. She was very forthright; it took me by surprise.

'I've been watching you,' she said. 'You're the best looking bloke in here tonight!'

'Aren't you going to at least order a drink first?'

I smiled at her. A bit of light flirtation went with the territory. She smiled back. I hadn't got a good look at her all night, just a view of her smooth back, slim arms and narrow neck, as well as that incredible hair. She was attractive, very sexy, and not in a way I'd normally go for. I'm a brunette guy through and through, with terrible consistency. But this woman had caught my attention.

'Can I buy you a drink?' she asked. 'And I'll have a Climax please ... if you think you can manage that?'

This was staple fare on the campsite, and it had taken me some time working behind the bar to pick up the names of all of the cocktails. Their double-entendre names were often used suggestively by tiddly women ordering drinks. Buttery Nipples and Silk Pantie Martinis were my personal favourites.

'I can certainly deliver you a Climax, it won't take more than a couple of minutes.'

'Promises, promises!' she laughed, leaning over slightly so that I could see her breasts nestled in her bright red bra. There was no hiding it under the tight white T-shirt that she was wearing. I'd already clocked the unbelievably short skirt from afar.

'Here's your Climax,' I announced, placing her drink on the bar. 'Let me know if you want another, I'll be happy to help.'

'What are you having?' she asked. 'Take whatever you want, it's on me.'

It had been some time since I'd felt quite so horny. The single mums that I'd copped off with in the past, I'm almost embarrassed to say, were more motivated by loneliness. On their part too, not only mine. But this woman was something else. I hadn't felt like this since ... since ... Ellie. Look how that ended up.

My brain was telling me 'No!' but my boxers were crying 'Yes! Yes! Do it, Pete, do it!'

In a rare moment for me, I decided to follow my head. I graciously accepted her offer of a drink, thanked her very much for the kind thought, and then went about my work at the bar.

I was so busy that she slipped my mind for most of the evening, but every now and then I'd see her. I'd catch a glimpse of those long, smooth legs and that incredibly short skirt, and have to fight off the urge to approach her, flirt some more and move things along to a crescendo at the end of my shift.

I'd had more to drink than usual. It hadn't helped that a couple of the punters had put money behind the bar for us that night. I was relieved and a little disappointed that she was nowhere to be seen by the time it came to collecting glasses and wiping tables.

'You can go now, Pete, luv,' Vicky said. She'd come over from her house to collect the night's takings. 'Thanks so much for stepping in, you really helped us out tonight. And your friend is coming tomorrow, isn't she? Best get your beauty sleep!'

'I haven't forgotten, Vicky,' I said, winking at her. 'I'll make sure Alex says hello while she's here.'

I said my goodbyes to the other bar staff and stepped outside into the fresh night air. Across the campsite I could hear people settling down for the night. They all had to be up and out at 10am the next day, there were no Saturday lie-ins for this lot.

'Hi, I thought they'd never let you out!' came a voice in the darkness. She'd been waiting for me on one of the benches outside the arcade area. She walked into the light. I could see the thin red bra straps on her shoulders where her T-shirt had dropped down.

'Hi, you surprised me!' I replied, knowing exactly why she was waiting for me.

'I'm Becky,' she said. 'I don't know your name yet ...'

'Pete,' I said, looking into her eyes. There was no doubt about what she wanted.

'I felt we didn't have time to get to know each other in there,' she picked up. 'Fancy a nightcap?'

I thought back to Ellie. This is how it had begun last time. A casual fling with a woman I'd only just met. A hot, sexy woman at that. Becky was something else. She was much younger: 27, 28, something like that, and nothing like the kind of woman I'd normally go for. But she seemed so confident, it was obvious that she wanted to sleep with me, there was no chatting up or dancing around. Becky had sex on her mind.

I thought about Ellie and how badly that had gone. I recalled Steven's warnings in the supermarket earlier that day. And I considered Alex, whom I'd have to pick up the next day. I also gave a fleeting thought to Meg. We'd been married when I'd slept with Ellie, and there was no doubt in my mind that I'd been wrong. But now we were separated, permanently as far as I knew. I considered myself a free agent.

Becky would be on her way to wherever it was she lived the next day, out of my life forever from 10 o'clock on Saturday morning. I could almost see her knickers, her skirt was so short, even though I had only the light of an outdoors lamp to guide me. The way she was looking at me, it was a wonder she could restrain herself. I'm not used to that with women, not ones who barely know me. Women usually need to get more familiar with me before their lust is unleashed.

I thought about Meg, Ellie, Alex and Steven one more time, eyeing up Becky's beautiful smooth breasts, which she'd made very little effort to conceal in that figure-hugging T-shirt. Then I thought 'Sod it!' and decided to sleep with her anyway.

It took me a while to open my eyes. It was light in the room, I must have slept in late. Outside the caravan I could hear the sounds of car boots being slammed shut and vehicles driving off. It had to be before 10 o'clock. At least I wasn't too late for Alex.

Then I remembered. It had been one hell of a night the night before. She was still in my bed, asleep. I played dead, replaying what had happened after we'd headed back for our nightcap.

There was no nightcap, of course. We'd kissed by the arcade, leaning against the large glass window, the machines still flashing, and our hands began to explore under each other's clothing. We walked over to my caravan, chatting and flirting. The minute I'd got the caravan door open, she walked over to the curtains and drew them.

'Close the curtains in the bedroom,' she ordered.

I walked along the short corridor, entering the main bedroom at the end and drawing the curtains as Becky had instructed. Then I walked up the corridor, excited by what was coming.

Static caravans have wide semi-circular settees in their lounges, they're made to seat several people at once and double up as beds. Well, Becky had discovered a new use for mine.

Her small handbag was sitting on the edge of the sofa, open. She'd removed her bright red lacy G-string and it was sitting to the side of her, together with her bra. I could see her nipples through her white T-shirt. She parted her legs slightly and I caught a glimpse. She was almost completely shaved. There was a touch of shaving rash there still, it looked like she'd prepared for this night out.

I could feel the bulge in my boxers. Whatever the rights and wrongs of this, it was too late for me, I was in too deep.

I knelt by the sofa and began to kiss her. We immediately gelled, there was no awkwardness, it was as if we had kissed before, it was sure, and confident, full of passion. My hand slipped up to her right breast, cupping it first, then gently caressing her nipple. I wanted to feel her flesh. I moved my hand up her T-shirt, hesitating a moment before touching. She was waiting, she took my hand and placed it there. It was smooth, soft, beautiful. Exciting. Our lips moved faster, our kissing became more frenetic, and I moved my hand down to her skirt. She ready for me. Moving down to lick her nipple, still gently rubbing her, she sat forward and removed her T-shirt.

'Fuck me!' she said, and I unbuttoned my trousers, pulled them halfway down, then my boxers. I was still kneeling and had no intention of standing up to take them off.

She hitched up the rest of her tiny skirt and I entered her. She raised her legs up, so that her feet rested on the sides of the sofa, and it allowed me to move closer and push deeper. We kissed again, our tongues caressing, my hand sliding down to the curve of her buttock as I thrust gently. She tensed and let out a cry as I exploded inside her.

I held Becky as we slowly relaxed. I awaited her cue for what would happen next, and I was surprised when she said, 'I want you to take me again.'

I wasn't sure that I could, so soon. She might have been in her late twenties, but I generally needed a bit of recovery time. I slowly moved away from her, and she lifted her legs up, so I could see where I'd been. I moved towards her once again, she sat back pushing her hips towards me. I began move my tongue lightly, she moaned with pleasure and I felt myself begin to harden again. I breathed a quiet sigh of relief. For a moment I'd been concerned that I might let myself down.

She reached into her bag and brought something out of it. I was still busy with my mouth and tongue, the top of her skirt resting on the tip of my nose. She'd brought out masks. Venetian masks. This was about to get kinky.

'Put this on,' she said, gently placing her hand to my head to indicate that I should move away.

I'd seen these on the TV. They were on sale all over the place when Meg and I had gone to Venice. I'd had a secret fantasy then, wondering if Meg would go for it. I'd always wanted to make a porno to upload to one of those sites. There was no way I was doing it with faces exposed, but how sexy would that be, your own porn video online and nobody knowing it was you?

Now here was Becky wanting me to place a masquerade mask on my face. I followed her lead. Her mask was brightly coloured, mine with black and white chequers. This was the stuff of fantasies.

Becky stepped up and picked up her bag.

'Get properly undressed, join me in the bedroom,' she said.

She walked away, sliding her skirt down as she did so, leaving it there on the floor.

I took my clothes off as quickly as I could, following her through to the bedroom. There's no elegant way to enter a room with an erection, but it didn't matter much since Becky was lying front down on the bed, looking up towards me.

'Use the oil,' she said, looking over towards the baby oil that she'd left on my small dresser unit. This woman came well prepared for a night out. I thought for a moment about whether we should have used a condom. There was no way I was interrupting this encounter with one of those things. The single mums always made me wear one, they were probably afraid of getting pregnant again. Becky seemed to have no such worries.

I took the oil, warmed it in my hands, and began to rub it on her back. My hand moved around her shoulders, along the base of her neck and by her tattoo. Gradually I moved down to her buttocks, tentatively exploring around her cheeks and wondering how far she'd let me go. There was no resistance, just a quiet sensual moaning. The masks were turning me on big time. I couldn't believe that within a matter of minutes I was ready to take her again.

She turned over, I trickled the baby oil between her breasts and with smooth strokes, caressed her nipples.

I worked my hand between her thighs, trickling more baby oil onto her breasts, then moving my hand to gently massage it into her smooth skin. The sheets were going to be a mess. I'd have to do something to hide them from the cleaners. I'd work it out later.

Now completely covered in baby oil, her smooth skin looking even more sensual, she took me in her mouth and I closed my eyes, luxuriating in the feeling, as she expertly kissed and gently sucked. When she felt me about to come again, she gently pushed me down to the bed.

'This way,' she said. 'I want to watch in the mirror.'

My head was resting at the end of the bed. I could see the mirror of the dressing table. She slowly straddled me. She began to rock slowly backwards and forwards. I placed my hands on her breasts, they were oiled and sensuous, my fingers glided around her nipples as she continued her slow rhythmic movements. She was looking in the mirror. I could see myself moving in and out of her.

'Take off your mask,' she said, moving her hand to my face and pulling the mask so that it dropped to the ground. At that moment I didn't give a damn what she wanted to do, my fingers had moved around to the curves of her arse and I was past the point of no return. It only seemed to fire her up even more, she was moving faster and faster as I felt my own orgasm become closer, nearer, more urgent. I'd come before, it took longer for me second time around, so I could relax, make sure that she was fully satisfied before finally releasing myself inside her. Our bodies were tensed, ecstatic in the moment, not wanting the sensation to end.

I fell asleep like that. I was aware of Becky moving off me, doing something with her phone, going to the bathroom. My neck was uncomfortable. I turned around and, somehow, we ended up the right way around in a bed that was covered in baby oil and semen. I wasn't complaining.

It was the sound of the pigeon that had woken me.

'Becky? Becky?' I said.

She stirred. Like me, she was awake already, dozing.

'Hi,' she replied, turning over and smiling. 'Now that's what I call a good Friday night out.'

I knew what she meant. The lovemaking had been hot. We'd clicked immediately, there was none of the usual awkwardness of a first-time encounter.

'Do you have to be out of your caravan?' I asked. 'It must be nearly 10 o'clock.'

'No, it's fine. I'm here for two weeks, there's no rush.'

Now that might get awkward with Alex around.

'Which zone are you staying in?' I asked, anxious to see how close we were. It wasn't that I hadn't enjoyed the previous night, but I hadn't expected it to be an ongoing arrangement.

'Red,' she said. 'It goes with the underwear.'

I smiled. And what hot underwear it was too. I'd need to manoeuvre carefully here, I had to pick up Alex from the station, but I didn't want Becky to feel that I was casting her aside. I also had to do something about my sheets. I couldn't let the cleaners get their hands on those. Vicky might find out.

I explained to Becky that I had a female visitor coming, a friend, not a romantic attachment, and that I'd need to keep her entertained for a couple of days. She seemed to have got the message.

'When does she leave?' Becky asked.

'Wednesday,' I replied. 'I'll be able to see you again before you go.'

I meant it too. If there was a chance of spending a couple more nights in bed with Becky before she left, I was well up for that. But I didn't want to complicate things with Alex.

'I need to sort these sheets out too. Any ideas?'

'I'll let you have the sheets off my bed. I'll say that I had my period and threw them away. I'll pay the fine on my breakage deposit, they'll probably let me off anyway.'

'Good idea,' I said. 'That'll save us any embarrassment. You certainly came prepared last night.'

I looked at the discarded masks on the floor and the baby oil bottle opened at the side of the bed.

'I'll admit it,' she said. 'I spotted you earlier in the week, and I've been watching you from afar. You're a nice guy, you're kind to people. You're hot too, although I don't think you know it!'

I was quite flattered by that. What a nice thing to say.

'Are you here alone? It's unusual to see somebody on their own like this.'

'Yes, we used to come here when we were kids. I needed a break, I fancied my own company for a couple of weeks. I like it here, it's simple. Shall I go and get those sheets – what time is your friend coming?'

'I need to leave here at midday,' I replied. 'Alex is here until Wednesday. How about we exchange mobile numbers and I'll keep in touch?'

Becky jotted down her number and took mine too. We then bundled up the sheets into the supermarket bags that I'd saved from the day before. She retrieved her clothing and underwear from around the caravan and I checked for any evidence that Alex might spot. The bedroom stank of sex and baby oil, I opened the windows slightly to encourage it to waft away.

As I was opening the curtains to the lounge area, I saw a couple of coppers walking towards my part of the park. Not unheard of. They got trouble every now and then, the occasional break-in or skirmish, but they seemed to be heading in my direction.

I kept watching until it became a sure thing.

'That's odd, the police are here,' I said to Becky.

'Shall I keep out of the way?' she asked.

'Might be a good thing.'

Becky went into the bedroom and I opened the door to see two uniformed officers outside.

'Mr Bailey?'

'Yes,' I replied, waiting to see what bad news they'd got for me now. I rapidly scanned through the possibilities. A break-in at the house. That wouldn't be so bad. Maybe my mum had had an accident. I hoped not. Perhaps news of Meg? I didn't know.

'Can I help with anything?'

'I'm sorry to have to inform you, sir, that there's been an incident at your property, the one that you own at Ashbourne Drive. A body was found there this morning.'

Chapter Seven

What was it Steven Terry had said?

'Your house is not yet finished with the killing. There is more evil waiting there.'

His words came back to me as the police officer indicated that he'd like to come into the caravan. I could see Becky standing at the end of the corridor. There were two doors in my static, one that brought you directly into the lounge area, the other at the far end of the unit, which was the equivalent of the back door.

Becky pointed to the second door, asking if I wanted her to go. I looked at her, gave a slight nod, and as the two cops entered at one end, she nipped out the other. She'd got the sheets too, that was great. She'd no doubt pop in the replacements later.

The police officers seemed serious. It was probably a crappy way to start a Saturday shift, the usual drill would have been releasing pissheads from the cells where they'd have had a night to cool off.

I sighed, not really in any mood to hear the news.

'So what's happened? Can I get you both a tea or a coffee?'

They took me up on the offer, so we spoke as I worked in the kitchen. Static caravans are mostly open-plan in nature; the kitchen adjoined the lounge, so I was able to hear what they'd got to tell me straight away.

'A neighbour telephoned the station to say that a car had been parked in the drive overnight. The driver's door had been left open and they thought that the property was presently unoccupied. A couple of beat officers called in in the early hours of this morning. They discovered the body of a single male.'

'Do you know who it is?'

I asked the obvious next question, thinking through who it might be, panicking in case the horrors of what had happened previously had come back to haunt me. But who was left? Everybody was dead.

'We're not at liberty to reveal that information yet, sir. The body still has to be identified.'

'What car was in the drive? You can tell me that, can't you?'

'It was a silver BMW.'

I couldn't think of anybody who drove a silver BMW, nobody that I knew well. All the broadcasting team were far too poor to drive BMWs. There's this strange idea that if you work on radio or TV you're instantly rich, due to the perceived glamour of the job. Well, journalists work on pay scales like everybody else. And like everybody else, those pay scales continually get eroded. The HR department are usually in the vicinity when it happens.

I couldn't think of anybody who drove a car like that. My boss, Diane, maybe? No, she had something much more modest. I couldn't think what it was, but I'd have noticed if it was a BMW.

'Have you had any access to the house recently, sir?'

'No, I never go there. I haven't been there in six months, not since the original murders. It's all handled through the estate agents now. I've got one local agent on the case and two of those internet sites listing the property. There are three boards outside. Elliot's is the local agency managing the property. Did they break in or cause any damage?'

What had happened? I'd had a few communications from the police, mainly relating to weirdos and sightseers. They'd had the same problems at Fred West's house, and it was demolished in the end. Cromwell Street is forever engraved on the consciousness of the UK population; my house was in danger of following suit.

There had been vandalism in the property, nothing major. Either I'd have to put it right before the house was sold or I'd knock a small amount off the price to allow the new buyers to fix it. Nothing that a bit of wood filler and sandpaper wouldn't solve.

'The property was unlocked, sir. There was no forced entry. I'm sorry, sir, I know that you've had to go through this before.'

What has life come to when you know the name of the company which will remove the fleshy debris and bloodstains from your living room floor? They hadn't told me how he'd died yet. Maybe I was jumping to conclusions.

'Where did he die?' I asked, realising that it might not have been in the lounge. Why should it have been?

'The victim was found in the main bedroom. I'm unable to share any more details at this moment in time, I'm afraid.'

I had a sudden burst of inspiration. Glenn Elliot, the estate agent. Did he drive a BMW? He'd be the sort of person who did. Glenn's office had emailed me to let me know that there was a viewing the day before. We'd had a couple that week, but I was learning not to get excited, most people were only there to take a snoop around the local murder place.

'It wasn't Glenn Elliot in the house was it? The estate agent? Doesn't he drive a BMW?'

The two police officers shuffled nervously and looked at each other.

'As I say, sir, we can't discuss any details at the moment. But we do need to ask you some questions, if we may?'

I was used to this drill. I looked at the clock on the kitchen wall. I was mindful of Alex's arrival, and I needed to get those sheets sorted out too.

'Can we do it here? It won't be long will it?'

'It won't take long, sir. We need to get an idea of your whereabouts and who has access to the property.'

The sooner we did this the better. I was never going to sell this bloody property now, not with another death there. I'd have to investigate those 'we'll buy any crappy house' websites, there had to be some fool out there who'd take it off my hands.

The copper used an electronic device to take my statement. I expressed an interest in it – surely the police hadn't moved to cool electronic notepads? No such luck. The poor guy had to click the letters on the keypad one by one. It was slower than a pen and paper.

There was nothing much to worry about in there. Who had keys to the property? Me, the estate agent, presumably Meg still had a set. Had I been to the property? No, not since I cleared my stuff out. Had Meg been to the property? Ask Martin Travis, our marriage counsellor, but I assumed not. Had anything suspicious happened recently in relation to the house? No, nothing other than the usual oddballs. The police would have their own records on that. Had I met anyone suspicious? I mentioned JD, my weirdo letter writer, but they knew about that already. There was nothing more to tell as far as I was concerned.

Eventually they went. I was tighter for time than I would have liked, but Becky had clearly been keeping an eye out and she returned with fresh sheets about ten minutes after they left.

'What was that all that about?' she asked. 'Everything okay?'

'Yes, yes, just a bit of a problem I've had in the past. They needed to follow up on something. Nothing to worry about.'

She paused a moment after I answered, as if she was deciding what to ask next. As far as I was aware, Becky knew nothing about me. She wasn't local, I was some guy that she'd met and shagged on a holiday park.

'I brought my sheets,' she said, handing them over. 'They're not entirely clean, but then that shouldn't bother you too much after what we did last night.'

She smiled and I returned the gesture, thinking about what we'd done together. That had been hot. I felt a slight stirring in my boxers, looking over to the sofa and picturing her with her bare legs pulled up, everything on view.

Alex. I had to focus on Alex.

'Thanks for the sheets. Okay if I look you up when my friend has gone? I had a great time last night, it would be nice to take you out for a meal maybe, get to know you better.'

'That'd be nice,' she replied, touching my arm. 'I'd love that, Peter ... Pete.'

That was strange. She knew I was Pete, why had she used Peter? I was only Peter on the radio. I let it slide, maybe she knew another Peter, I didn't have time to ask.

'You've got my number, text me when your friend leaves. Have a nice time!'

She was on her way. I was pleased that it wasn't going to be messy. No clinging, no asking if she could tag along with Alex and me. She'd taken it at face value, a very nice and sexy encounter. But she wasn't acting like my wife.

I hurriedly put the sheets on the bed, made a pig's ear of getting the cover on the quilt and tried to make it look as if nothing had happened in that room. The smells of the night before had gone, so I shut all the windows and did a final check. When I'd slept with Ellie, I'd been embarrassed by a discarded bra. It wouldn't be a tragedy if Alex found any evidence of my encounter with Becky, we were only pals now, after all. But I didn't want her to feel uncomfortable about it. I was forty, we weren't teenagers accidentally-on-purpose leaving evidence of our conquests so that all our pals knew what we'd been up to.

Happy that the house was clear, I checked that Becky had locked the rear door before I left. It was still open. I was pleased I'd checked that, after my previous incident with the unlocked door.

I set off through the campsite, driving over the regular speed humps at the prescribed 10mph. As I passed the office, Vicky spotted me and waved me down to stop. I looked at the clock on my dashboard, she'd need to be quick.

'Morning, Pete luv, everything alright? The police were here earlier asking for your pitch number. Did they find you okay?'

She was snooping. Fair enough, she wouldn't want

the cops around every five minutes. It was supposed to be a holiday camp after all.

'It's all fine, thanks Vicky. It won't happen again. A problem up at the house, nothing to do with me.'

If only I'd known when I said those words. How wrong could I have been? It was only just beginning. And the next time the police visited the Golden Beaches Holiday Park, the problem would be closer to home.

⸻

Alex was waiting outside the station when I got there. I was annoyed with myself about that, I'd wanted to meet her off the train. By the time the cops were done, Becky had gone on her way, and Vicky had got her fill of gossip, I was ten minutes late.

'Hi Alex, I'm so sorry I'm late. I got delayed.'

'No worries,' she said, standing up to embrace me. 'I got recognised by some old couple, they were very nice.'

We hugged for a moment. It felt comfortable, natural, as if we'd never left off. It was well over twelve years since Alex and I had been together as a couple. In the meantime, I'd had a relationship with Meg – a marriage. It seemed so long ago. Yet standing there, holding each other, it felt like no time at all.

'It's good to see you, Alex, really good. You look amazing!'

It's difficult to tell how people really look when you usually see them on the telly. There's lighting and make-up at work, and for all I'd known, Alex might have really aged. As it turned out, she'd barely changed. She'd discovered the secret of eternal youth. I wasn't so sure how I was faring on that front.

'You look tired, Pete,' she said, giving me a searching

look. 'Is everything okay?'

I didn't really want to get too deep in too soon. Would I mention the body at the house? The newspaper boards would carry the story from midday, maybe not quite so fast on a Saturday, but there would be no hiding it.

'Shall we grab a coffee?' I said.

'Yes, I'm gasping for a drink. Why does everything go to pot at the weekends? Travel any other day and there's a buffet service, travel on a Saturday or Sunday and it's post-apocalyptic. You have to scavenge for resources.'

I laughed at that and picked up her bag. It was heavy.

'You planning on staying long?' I asked. 'This is quite a weight!'

Alex shrugged it off, and we made for the nearest coffee shop.

Having navigated the complex menu of coffee options, most of which I'd never even heard of, I settled for a white coffee, no sugar. Nothing fancy.

Alex went posh, she had an espresso Ristretto.

'What on earth is that?' I asked, taking the mickey out of her. 'You posh London types, that's a month's mortgage payment in the north!'

'You've got to enjoy your coffee, Pete. Look at you, you'd still be supping Nescafé instant if you could!'

'That's what I've got at home. Should I have employed a barista for the weekend and invested in some coffee-making equipment?'

'No, I'm not that posh! I need a shot of strong coffee, it's been a busy week at work, I'm ready for this visit. It's great to see you, Pete. I really mean that.'

She squeezed my arm. It was great to see her too. We'd already slipped into that easy way that we'd always had. Our relationship had moved online since I'd met Meg. I'd not thought that much about Alex since Meg and I got together, why would I? But when you share five years of your life with someone, you don't just switch them off.

In days gone by, people married the first person they met. These days, we have all sorts of relationships: flings, affairs, marriages, living together. We carry debris along with us, the remains of failed relationships. When you fall in love, those relationships don't just go away. Feelings remain, memories linger. Often you can't recapture something that you loved about an old relationship with a new lover. Maybe you crave that feeling sometimes. It's only if you've never been with somebody else that you don't experience that.

It was all coming back to me with Alex now. I felt as if I'd travelled back in time. It was always so easy, so uncomplicated with her. Yet, we'd drifted apart, it was never meant to be. Had she settled down? Did she have a new partner? I hadn't got a clue. She'd tell me if she wanted me to know.

'How are you now, after what happened?'

Well, she was a journalist by profession, there was no reason for me to expect her to make small talk for much longer.

'Crikey, you don't hang around, do you?'

'I want to know, Pete. I was part of it too, remember. It was me who got Jason killed … '

She blamed herself for that. It wasn't her fault, how could it have been? She was helping me, watching my back. She'd sent Jason to keep an eye on the house when Meg had been abducted by Tony Miller. She'd told him not to intervene, but he had after he heard shouting. It was not Alex's fault that Jason died. It was his mistake, he was the one who went into the house and got himself pounded by a baseball bat and his throat cut.

'It's not brilliant, to be honest with you, Alex. It could be better.'

I was welling up, getting emotional. I'd had nobody to share all these upheavals with, except for my counsellor, Blake Crawford. I'm British, I keep my feelings hidden.

I went on to tell Alex everything: my money worries, my frustration over not being able to talk to Meg, my dislike of my job, and my feelings of being completely shafted and trapped. I went on to talk about the body that had been found at the house and the complete mess that I was in. I neglected to mention JD, the single mums and Becky. It was good to get it all out, but I wasn't opting for full transparency. Some things could wait until later.

'Jesus, Pete, that's quite a shit list. I didn't realise everything was so messed up.'

'How is it you never swear on TV?' I asked. 'You've still got a mouth like a sewer.'

We laughed at that. I know I'm the same. I'm sure the strain of having to watch what you say on the radio or TV makes journalists swear more than the average person. It has to work its way out somehow.

'Look, Pete, let's try and enjoy this weekend. I've got stuff going on that I want to talk about too. No dead bodies, you'll be pleased to hear. But life stuff, career things. I want to talk to you ... you always were my best friend, Pete. I've missed you.'

Then she said it. We hadn't talked about it for years.

'You know, we could have a teenager now, Pete, if things had been different. Can you imagine that? I wonder what our lives would be like.'

I felt as if I was on the Jeremy Kyle Show. Tears came into my eyes again as I thought about the baby that we'd lost to a miscarriage. How long ago was it now? She was right, we'd be the parents of a teenager. How weird would that have been?

Her eyes were red. She'd got emotional too, thinking about what we'd been through together. It was a difficult time and eventually resulted in us drifting apart. I thought I'd got over it, but I guess that never happens. We put the bad stuff in a box and only bring it out occasionally, a bit like all the crap I had in storage. But sometimes, when you bring a box out, it can trigger something new – Meg's secret photos, for instance.

I was ready for this weekend with Alex. I sensed that we were both ready for it. I took her hand and squeezed it gently. It was so good to see my friend again.

Alex and I picked up where we'd left off. She loved the static caravan. She'd never been in one before.

'This is amazing!' she declared when we walked inside. 'How do they fit everything in? It's like the Tardis!'

'I know, I know, they cost nothing to rent and it's very much like a house. You have to keep them heated in winter, but look, I've even got radiators.'

Alex walked through the caravan, commenting on the built-in units and space that I'd got.

'I think it's amazing, Pete. I love it. I didn't think they were as good as this. I assumed they were like regular caravans, but without the wheels. What a great place to live.'

I pointed out the entertainments complex in the distance, pointing through the window across the park.

'They've got everything you need here, Alex. There's even a swimming pool if you want to use it. Do you still swim?'

'I do, actually. Got to keep in shape for the telly. Ever since everybody got HD TVs, you can't get away with a trick! Where's my room, by the way? I'll get rid of this case.'

I showed Alex to her room. There were towels laid out on the bed, wrapped in plastic, as the cleaners had left them.

'Wow, you even get room service!' Alex laughed. 'I could get used to this.'

Alex's career had rocketed since we'd gone our separate ways, but I was pleased to see that she was exactly the same woman that I'd known before I met and married Meg. There was no edge to her, she didn't look down her nose at how I was living my life or how my career had barely progressed. She took everything as it was, with no judgment. I felt instantly nourished by her presence.

'What do you fancy doing today?' I asked. 'Are you knackered from the journey or are you up for a night on the town?'

'I'm good,' she replied. 'I'm tired, but I've got some time off work. Let's have a good time, it's been far too long since we did this.'

She was right. But how could I have ever gone away for a weekend with Alex, my former lover and the mother of our child, the child that was never born? It would have been too dangerous for Meg to accept, and that's fair enough. She always saw Alex as a threat, so we'd cooled off, reduced our relationship to online chats. There was barely a day that went by when I didn't hear from Alex. I'd never really thought about that, I accepted it as how things were.

But now I was a free agent again. I didn't have to conceal my history with Alex from my wife. I hadn't a clue how things would work out with Meg, but after so many months of being incommunicado, I'd begun to accept the possibility that she no longer wanted me in her life.

'How do you fancy a night out drinking and hitting a club? Nothing too noisy, but I can't remember the last time I went to a club.'

'You're on! It'll be nice to spend an evening away from the celebrity pool. Some of them can be complete wankers!'

So that was it. We spent the rest of the afternoon chatting and catching up on old times. We didn't dwell on the sad bits, we had enough time together, we'd catch up on all that later. We even fitted in a game of Scrabble on the new board that I'd picked up at the supermarket in honour of her visit. The evil cow still beat me, I could never match her word power.

We got changed. I booked a taxi and we walked over to the shop and office block to await pick-up. It was a bit of a hike into town. The taxi would cost over thirty quid, but I wasn't going to ruin the night by not being able to have a drink.

There was no sign of Vicky when we got to the office area, and I was pleased that Alex would get a night off from her before she had to do the celebrity thing. As we walked through the campsite, a couple of people did a double-take.

'Is that that Alex woman off the telly? You know, the crime one?'

'Wasn't that Alex thingamajig from the police programme?'

'Don't you get pissed off with all that, Alex?' I asked. It was one of the reasons why I'd avoided telly. I like my anonymity. I'd written a letter to Blue Peter many years ago, hoping to become a presenter. By the time I'd reached the age of thirty, and had some rudimentary experience of what was involved, I was pleased that I'd stayed on radio.

'Sometimes,' she replied. 'It can really mess up an evening if you run into a weirdo. And ever since Jill Dando died ... well, it worries me sometimes, you never know who's out there. But it kind of goes with the territory. It pays well. Not that I have anybody to spend it with.'

This was my cue. It was none of my business, but I wanted to know what Alex had been up to since she moved to London.

'So you haven't met anyone yet? I thought I'd seen you photographed with Johnny Richardson recently. Didn't it work out?'

'Johnny Richardson is gay!' she laughed. 'Don't tell anyone that, please. He hasn't come out yet. Not in public anyway. His family knows. But he's the hard man on Colchester Road, he can't let on he's gay. He's good company, it keeps the press at bay and it suits us both. He's a nice guy. It stops all the lesbian conjecture. It's pretty horrible being a woman in the spotlight, actually.'

I didn't watch Colchester Road. Soap operas aren't my thing, but I knew of Johnny. I'd never have guessed that he was gay. But then, I was the guy who thought Martin Travis wanted to shag Meg and completely missed that he swung the other way.

'To be honest with you, Pete, I never really found

anyone else after you and me. I know it's long over now, but part of me wishes ... Well, part of me wishes that we hadn't lost the baby, that maybe we'd stayed together and things had worked out for us. Do you know what I mean?'

I'd never really thought about it like that. Perhaps I'd been lucky, I always felt like the one who'd been left behind. While my career had ticked along, Alex had achieved amazing things. I'd been happy with Meg for almost a decade, I'd barely glanced in the rear-view mirror. It was only now that I was questioning my choices. Part of me wanted to patch things up with Meg. I wanted my old life back.

I didn't know how to reply to Alex. Fortunately, I was saved by the taxi. Uber hadn't yet reached us, so #AAATaxis it was. They'd added the hashtag for online use. The marketing strategy was advanced, but the bigoted opinions of the driver were not. We smiled at each other as he recognised Alex, told her he loved the programme, and then shared his views on crime and punishment with us for the next twenty miles.

All we could do was laugh when he drove off into the town.

'Does Uber give bigotry ratings to drivers?' I asked Alex. 'Can you choose the political leanings of your driver to create in-car political harmony?'

'I can't believe how bad normal taxis are,' she laughed. 'They all bitch and moan about Uber, but they need to up their game. It's a long time since I had to sit through a load of bollocks like that. He wouldn't survive five minutes on Uber. Have you ever thought about London, Pete?'

I had. I was thinking about it all the time. Since I'd chatted with Ellie, I'd done that thing where you go through all the options in your head. You try to picture what it would be like. So far, it was looking good. Life was much more civilised in bigger cities.

We worked our way through a couple of pubs, and then headed for the safest nightclub that I could think of. It was the gay club, the one where the younger guys went from the office. Fanny's this one was called, after Julian Clary's famous dog. What a great name for a gay nightclub. We'd be able to spend a night in there without testosterone-fuelled outbreaks of violence and drunk fat guys hitting on Alex.

It was early in terms of nightlife, so the music was at reasonable levels. It was wall-to-wall great tunes. I'd neglected this side of my life. Meg and I would never have gone out to a club.

'Shall we do cocktails?' I asked. 'Mix it up a bit?'

'Why not?' Alex laughed. 'It'll make a change from white wine.'

The night moved on, the club got more crowded, we became increasingly drunk, the music got louder. We got up and danced. I'd forgotten that Alex loved to dance. I hated it, but she'd always dragged me up and I always had fun when I got there. I was a disgrace on the dance floor, like a cack-handed MC Hammer without the trousers. Alex didn't seem to mind. We even got up on the dance podiums. I was larking around pretending to do pole-dancing moves, and at one stage we had most of the nightclub clapping us, urging us on. I love gay clubs. I'd forgotten what a great laugh they could be.

'I've got to pee!' Alex shouted over the music. 'Which way to the loos?'

I pointed out where I thought they were. She had to walk right across the dance floor; it was a long way to go to reach a toilet. She was gone some time and I'd begun to wonder what had happened to her.

While I was waiting, I went to get us a couple of soft drinks. It was time to start the dilution process if we were going to see anything of Sunday. I'd managed to buy the drinks and return to our seats by the time Alex returned.

'I just met a friend of yours!' she yelled at me over the music, which was getting far too loud for old gits like me.

'Oh yes, who was it?' I asked, intrigued to know who she'd met. The younger reporters came to Fanny's, but I hadn't spotted any that night. They usually arrived when the pubs were throwing everybody out.

'He's not a journalist, said he knows you personally as a friend. He must have seen us together. He knows all about you: where you live and work, where you're living at the moment. Sounded like a close friend to me.'

'What did he look like? Did he tell you his name?'

'Dark hair, gaunt, quite cold eyes actually. Balding, he'd shaved off his hair, down to a number one or number two blade. Not the type of person I'd expect to be your best friend, sorry about that.'

I was intrigued and getting a little unsettled. This didn't sound like anyone I knew. I tried for a name again.

'Did he tell you his name? Surely he told you who he is? Can you see him in here now?'

Alex looked around, then turned back to me. She shrugged.

'I can't see him now. Said he'd be seeing you soon, though. What did he say his name was? It was something short. Jeff … Joe … no, Jay! That's it, he said his name was Jay Dee! You know him?'

I knew him alright. His name wasn't Jay Dee, it was JD, the nutcase who'd been sending those letters to the radio station. And now he'd decided to show his face at last. Just as a new dead body had turned up.

Chapter Eight

JD's sudden appearance screwed up the evening for me. We'd had a great time and I didn't want Alex to worry. I kept the truth from her, I didn't want her to know whom she'd been talking to. I'd tell her later, the next day. I'd also be speaking to my boss Diane. If the coppers came round about the murder, I'd be telling them straight away that they needed to find this JD guy.

Alex and I took the taxi back home. It was a fair drive back to the campsite, and fortunately we had a lovely Asian guy driving us. He opened the doors, drove considerately, and didn't chat once the pleasantries were out of the way.

Alex fell asleep with her head resting on my shoulder. It was all I could do to rouse her again when we finally reached the static caravan. I paid and tipped the driver, thanked him for dimming his lights as he drove through the site, and accompanied Alex to the door.

As I placed the key in the lock, the door opened again.

'Bloody hell! There's something wrong with this damn door. I know I locked it this time.'

Caravan doors aren't the most impregnable barriers

on the planet. Tom Cruise and the MI boys would have no trouble getting in, but this was ridiculous. I'd have a word with Vicky the next day. She could have her VIP meet-and-greet and I'd ask her to send around Len the maintenance man.

I helped Alex up the steps and into the caravan.

'You okay? Do you want a drink of water or something?'

'I'm fine, Pete. I'm knackered. I need some sleep.'

'No problem, let's sleep it off.'

'Pete, don't take this the wrong way … can I sleep with you tonight? Not sex or anything, can I be in the same room with you? I want the company tonight. Tell me no if you don't want to.'

Truth be told, I was pleased she made the suggestion. After so many years of marriage, I was finding it hard coming back home to an empty bed. And she was right. It wasn't anything to do with sex that night. It was the companionship that I wanted too, the presence of somebody next to me in the bed.

I checked through the caravan, making sure that the doors were properly closed. There didn't seem to be any problem on the inside, the doors were shut fast. Maybe the problem was with the outside mechanism. I resolved to start using the door at the back of the unit until Len had checked things out.

I went ahead to the bedroom while Alex was brushing her teeth. I pulled back the quilt, which was looking more ruffled than I remembered. The bottom sheet looked as if someone had had sex on it. They were Becky's sheets. She'd told me that they weren't clean, but I'd assumed she meant that she'd slept in them. Surely she hadn't been shagging in them?

She was a grown woman, after all. If she'd picked me

up in the bar, there was no reason why she shouldn't have picked up someone else earlier in the week. She was a hot woman and I wouldn't be the only one lusting after her, but I was pretty certain that the stain hadn't been there before. The light was a bit dodgy in the room, with only a single lamp I'd probably missed it. I didn't want Alex spotting it, so I pulled over the quilt and took out a couple of spare blankets from the wardrobe.

She walked into the room, still looking tired.

'I need to sleep!' she said. She took off her shoes, lay on the bed and did exactly that. She was asleep in moments. I checked the doors once again, then turned out the lights and joined Alex on the bed. We were both fully clothed, I'd even left my socks on.

It took me a while to drop off. I'd been rattled by JD's appearance. I remembered Ellie telling me about her stalker, Tony Miller. He'd turned out to be a proper psycho. There was no way I was ignoring JD's appearance. It had to be connected in some way with the death at the house. Were the police calling it a murder yet? Glenn Elliot might have had a heart attack, I suppose.

I wondered if I could call the police there and then. It wasn't a 999 call. I tried to remember the other number that they gave out, the one for non-emergencies. I couldn't remember it. 911 was the American number. We'd done it on the radio, what was it? I'd Google it as soon as I got up in the morning. I was too tired now.

I thought about Steven Terry and his warning to me. He'd got it completely right last time. What had he said this time around? He'd already said that there was more death to come in the house. Well, that was Glenn Elliot.

He'd warned me that the lies would have to stop. I'd been honest with Alex, I was going to tell her everything in the morning. I'd tell Meg too, everything. If she ever showed her face again.

He warned me about the women in my life. Who were they? Meg. Alex. Ellie was over, we were still friends, but we'd had our fling.

Meg and Alex. Did Becky count? And the single mums? Surely the casual encounters weren't important, they were all back home by the end of each week. It wasn't as if we sent each other postcards.

I thought about Becky for a while. She'd been prepared for an intimate encounter the previous night, right down to the masks and oil. Even down to the pubic pruning – she was freshly trimmed, ready for sex. There were signs of sexual activity on the sheets, there was no reason to suppose that I was the only bloke she'd slept with that week. But she had suggested that we see each other again.

She'd set out specifically to get into my pants the night before, she'd said as much. And the masks and oil, that wasn't something that was whisked out of a handbag during a regular one-night stand.

I'd need to make sure I chatted to Becky again, there was something about our encounter that didn't ring true. I fell asleep with Alex's hand draped across my chest, thinking about all the things I would have to do the next day.

We woke early, considering our previous night of booze and dancing. As I lay awake in the bed next to Alex, I started to itemise the things that I would have to get done that day. Her arm was still draped over me from the night before, she'd barely moved since we fell asleep.

'Hi Pete, my mouth tastes like a sandpit. I should have drunk more water before I crashed out last night. Do you want a cup of tea?'

It was nice to have somebody else to put the kettle on. A simple thing, but I'd grown used to doing it myself every morning. Even if you're only sitting there in an early morning haze, it's still nice to have someone else around.

We'd had a good night. Until JD had spoiled everything. This is how they get you, like a tick burrowing into your skin and feeding off your blood. Now the guy had shown his face, I'd get the police on the case. In fact, this was a positive outcome in a way. Now he'd surfaced, he would have to stop hiding in the shadows.

I thought about weaponry and protection. Was there anything I could carry with me, legally, in case he did a Tony Miller on me and turned into a psycho? Sally had been waving an air pistol around when she decided to get to the truth about Meg and Jem. It had been extremely effective in scaring the living daylights out of us. I wondered if I'd be able to get one locally and maybe carry it around with me. Sally had used one that Jem had bought to shoot at targets in the garden with his oldest two kids. Ironic that – it was Jem himself who became the target.

It's fine being in a country with gun laws, but when there's a nutter on the loose, it would be handy if you could invoke a bit of USA constitution and get yourself tooled up. The nutters never seem to have any problems getting their hands on proper guns, it's the rest of us who are left with our pants down when the violence begins.

I'd maybe keep that to myself, not mention it to Alex. I didn't want to frighten her. I also didn't want the cops to catch me with a weapon. That would make the local papers, they'd love a story like that: *City Murder Man Gun Shock*.

I brought Alex up to speed about JD over our first cup of tea of the day.

'How tall was this JD guy, Alex? Could I take him in a fight?'

I smiled at her, trying to lighten up the question, but wanting an answer.

'He was one of those small guys, lean and fit. Not a muscle man, but he looked like he was in good shape. He had a lot of tattoos on his arms. They call them sleeves, don't they? They looked quite good actually.'

'What was he like? Friendly? Aggressive?'

'Look, Pete, there's no point fretting about this guy. At least he's shown his face now. I'll keep an eye out for him, and if I see him again, we'll call the police. Maybe even take a picture. You should have told me about him earlier, I could have done something about it if you had. I hope you're keeping that phone of yours charged now, after last time?'

I'd changed my phone since the killings six months ago. It had a decent battery life and I made sure that it was charged. If any crazed killers started abducting people again, I'd be ready for them. I could Snapchat my way out of trouble.

Alex and I finished our drinks and then took it in turns to shower. We decided to get a newspaper. I wanted to know if there were any more details about Glenn Elliot's death, I'd forgotten to turn the radio on for the hourly bulletin. I wasn't even entirely certain that it was Glenn who'd died.

'We may well run into Vicky. She's a fan of yours. If you want to hide in the caravan, you're welcome to. I'll get the paper.'

'No, it's fine, I'm used to it. She sounds okay and she's done you a favour letting you rent this place and giving you the bar work. Let's get it over with.'

Vicky deserved her success at the caravan park. We could see her through the office window processing the takings from the Saturday night. She jumped up when she saw Alex and me approaching.

'This is Vicky Walters, Alex. She's a huge fan!'

For the first time since I'd met her, Vicky didn't know what to say. Alex was great, putting her at ease, being really nice to her. She got the real celebrity treatment that morning. Alex shared a few insider secrets, signed Vicky's copy of the TV listings magazine, which had a picture from the TV show inside, and made her feel really special. No wonder everybody loved Alex so much, there was no edge to her at all, she made Vicky's day.

Eventually it was time to move on. I wanted to ask Vicky a couple of questions before we left the office and moved over to the campsite shop.

'You won't forget to ask Len to look at the lock, will you Vicky? I had another problem with it last night. I'm getting really concerned.'

'No luv, don't worry, I won't forget. He's in at 10 o'clock on a Sunday, I'll send him straight over. Are you in or out today? Is it okay if he lets himself in? I don't want him disturbing you two.'

I knew what she meant by that. But Alex and I were just friends. Len might have got a surprise if he'd walked in on me a couple of nights beforehand, but he was safe with Alex around. I didn't want to mess things up with her, I'd done enough of that with all my other relationships already.

'It's fine, Vicky. Send him over whenever. We'll be going out today, we'll get some breakfast in town then go on and make a few visits.'

I hesitated over the next question. I didn't want to tip Alex off about what had happened with Becky. Part of me was ashamed to admit it to her, it was my idiot side, which I had difficulty controlling.

'I know that you can't tell me about other guests, Vicky, data protection and all that, but you don't know if there's a lady called Becky or Rebecca on the site, do you?'

I probably gave more information than was needed.

'She was talking to me in the bar the other night, seemed like a nice lady. She was on her own, no kids or hubby in tow. She hadn't been left any fresh sheets in her room, I suggested that she pop in to see you. She was a bit embarrassed to ask. Do you know her?'

Alex gave me a knowing look. Vicky flicked through some papers on her desk.

'Single occupant, luv? Initial R. Can't see anything here. Becky, you said?'

'Yeah, she's here for two weeks.'

Vicky looked at a different set of papers.

'We've only got three families staying on from last week, luv, and they're all big groups. It's funny you mention sheets, though. We did have a set taken from a caravan on the far side of the site. I didn't believe them actually, they probably stole them or something like that. I let them off, gave them the benefit of the doubt, but they swore that someone must have come in and pinched their sheets. Double bed too. Usually it's kids pissing in the bed that causes sheets to go missing.'

Vicky looked at Alex again.

'I'm sorry, luv, I should mind my language.'

Alex smiled, put her at her ease again, and we said our goodbyes.

———

That feeling was back again. The one that I had when Meg had gone AWOL in the hotel.

First JD had turned up in the city, seemingly following my movements. Now something wasn't quite right with Becky. Had she lied to me about her name? As a single woman sleeping with a strange bloke on a one-night stand, maybe that was a sensible thing to do. Vicky said that there were no single females, only family groups staying on the site for a two-week period. Had Becky been lying about her name and her family situation? Maybe she was in one of those open marriages. I'd look out for her on site. I had her number, I'd try and contact her later, when Alex wasn't around. But Alex was onto me already.

'You slept with that woman, didn't you?'

It wasn't accusing, it was more taking the mickey.

'They train you well on that Crime Beaters show. What was it? The DNA evidence, the forensics investigation?'

'I'm not your mum, Pete, but after what happened with Ellie, maybe you ought to be a bit more careful? Perhaps get to know these women better. You don't even know her surname, do you?'

There was a bit of tension in the air, only for a moment. I wasn't used to being told what I should and should not be doing. But I needed the casual flings, I'd have gone mad without them. They blocked the memories of what had happened in the house and at the cathedral. I'd stop them later, when I had things under control.

'I know, you're right. I will, honestly.'

It was a flimsy promise, but I didn't want to fall out with Alex. We'd made our way past the buckets, spades and inflatables and had got to the newspaper stand in the site shop. It was still early, and a Sunday morning too, but the papers had been virtually wiped out already.

'And they say nobody buys newspapers anymore,' I said. 'These holiday-makers have cleared the shelves. Can you find a local paper in there, Alex?'

We sifted through the carnage of discarded advertising inserts and forgotten TV magazines. Assembling a Sunday newspaper is like doing a 5000-piece puzzle. Eventually, Alex found one. She read the headline and I could sense immediately that she was hesitant to share it.

'What is it?' I asked. 'Go on, you can tell me. Although I might shit myself, so be warned.'

She looked at the headline again, then looked back at me. She turned the paper around so that I could see the front page. There it was, a picture of my house taken from the road, with the three For Sale boards artfully placed for dramatic effect. But it was the headline that told the real story: *Bloody Horror at Murder House – Estate Agent Throat Slashed.*

———

It took another cup of tea back at the caravan before I was ready to talk about the news story. I needed some processing time. Alex sensed that I wouldn't want to be subjected to an inquisition about it straight away.

'What is going on, Alex? First this JD guy, then Glenn Elliot being killed at the house. And Becky too. It feels like it's all happening again.'

Alex moved closer to me and took my hand.

'I'm sure it'll be weirdos, Pete. A house like yours attracts nutters all the time. They become shrines if you're not careful, it's all the TV coverage. It seems to excite them. Glenn Elliot probably walked in on somebody. It might have been a break-in gone sour. And as for JD, we should pop into the police station this morning before we do anything else. I'll give them a description. The sooner he's out of the picture, the better. I'm sure this isn't about you, Pete. Try not to get too jittery, we'll sort it.'

She was right. It helped to have Alex there, calming the more extreme thoughts that were shooting through my mind. How was I ever going to sell the house? I felt angry with Meg, disappearing like that and leaving me in limbo. I resolved to give Martin Travis a piece of my mind. I had to get a message to Meg, we needed to sort things out, and he was my one link to her.

'Do you mind if we go to the cop shop straight away?' I asked. 'I know it's not quite the leisure activity you expected, but if I know that the local police are keeping an eye out for this JD fella, then at least I'll feel a bit safer.'

'Of course, Pete. I'd want to do the same. Did you get Becky's number? Can you call her? That would help put your mind at ease too. Be discreet, she might have some tough guy as a husband.'

Alex could read my mind. She'd said the same as Steven Terry. I needed to make better choices about the women in my life, and the lies had to stop. I'd stop lying to Alex, she wouldn't judge me. It would feel good to stop covering up. But could I tell her everything? Even what Meg had said to me before she left? Yes, I would. Not all at once. I'd let it drip out over the weekend. I needed to tell someone this stuff. I'd try to be honest.

As it turned out, we didn't have to go to the police station. They came to us. There was a knock at the door and I assumed it was Len. It was two police officers, one I recognised from the day before, the other was new.

Len turned up five minutes later, as I was handing out the brews to the officers.

'Can you come back a bit later, Len? I'm sorry, this is a bit sensitive. And please tell Vicky there's nothing to worry about, everything is fine here.'

Len went on his way. I was annoyed about the timing, I wanted that door looked at as soon as possible. I also wanted the cops to get a description of JD, and the sooner they were all out there looking for him, the better.

I don't do this often, but very occasionally I use my position at the radio station to lean on people. Not in a heavy-handed way, but when you're in the public eye, when you have such a big stage to shout from, it can help to get the outcome you want.

I dropped Diane's name into the conversation, and also let the bobbies know that I was on first-name terms with their boss the chief constable. I wanted this issue to go straight back to the station, not sit on someone's desk until they felt like doing something with it.

It helped to have Alex there too. They recognised her immediately and were starstruck straight away. She did a good number on them, as she had with Vicky earlier on. I knew that Vicky would be getting jittery about the police calls to my static caravan. I resolved to buy her a gift to try to smooth things over.

The cops had come to inform me about what had gone on at the house. It was crawling with police once again. The press were camped outside on the street, and they'd need me to head over there as soon as possible to talk to the investigating officer and make sure that the property was left secure.

We explained what had happened with JD. We had to go through the tortuous process of one of the officers typing, letter by letter, Alex's physical description of the man that she'd met in the nightclub. I'd forgotten what a lovely voice Alex had, although everybody I work with has a lovely voice, they wouldn't get far without one in my industry. But the second bobby looked as if he was ready to bang one out there and then as she slowly and clearly gave information about the man that she'd seen.

Eventually, we were done. The cops assured us that the description would be circulated at the station and the chief constable informed of their progress. It would be a good chance for them to earn some brownie points with the high-ups, so I didn't feel so bad about abusing my position and leaning on them a bit. I promised to make it over to the house that day, but I'd get in contact with the estate agents, they were dealing with property issues for me. I had no intention of chasing around after a locksmith or whoever it was I needed to make the house secure.

It felt as if we'd made some progress at last. I'd be much happier when JD had been warned off. Maybe he'd killed Glenn Elliot, that would get everything sewn up quickly.

One thing was for certain. After the visit from the police and the news about this latest killing, I was putting in an application for that job Ellie had mentioned to me. I was fed up of this way of living and tired of all the terrible things that had happened. It was time for a change. I'd get rid of the house, at any price, and move down to London. It was time to put it all behind me and make a fresh start.

I didn't know it then, but it wouldn't be quite so simple. More people would have to die before I could leave that place. There was still worse to come.

Chapter Nine

As Alex and I drove out of the campsite, I was annoyed about having had to chase off Len. I wanted that lock fixed. I didn't want to be delayed by another chat with Vicky, and she wasn't sitting at the window to wave to as we passed by. I'd pop in on the way back and make sure she'd remembered to get my door checked.

I'd got Alex to witness that both doors were locked from the outside. We'd left via the rear door, it felt safer that way, then we'd both tried the two doors. They were locked, there was no doubt about it this time.

I'd been looking at the faces of the women we passed as we drove through the site, but there was no sign of Becky. I'd texted her before we left, but so far, no reply. If she was hitched with a hubby and kids, she'd need to be discreet. I didn't want to land her in any trouble if she'd cheated on her bloke, and I certainly didn't want some hairy guy chasing me through the campsite if I'd slept with his wife. Alex and Steven were right. I needed to take more care over the women I let into my life. But it's hard to stop. When I thought back to my night with Ellie and the night I'd had with Becky, the sex was addictive. It was the consequences of my actions that I wasn't so keen on.

I was nervous. We were going back to the house. I'd called the estate agent to speak to Glenn's number two, Melissa Drake, and she seemed particularly keen to meet me there, at the property itself. She'd known about it overnight; the police had rung the office for Glenn's contact details, so she'd had some time to adjust to the shocking news. Turning up at the place where her boss had been murdered still showed a high degree of professionalism. She'd be earning her 1.75 percent commission, that was for sure. Not forgetting the VAT.

'It's ages since I've been here,' I said to Alex, as we entered the outskirts of the city and drew near to the area where Meg and I had once lived.

'I can't blame you. I know this is horrible for you, Pete, but I really want to see it. I was stuck on your laptop talking over Skype for much of that night, it'll be good for me to see where it all happened. I still feel guilty about sending Jason over to the house. It'll help to fix things in my head.'

'We can go to see Jason's grave later, if you want. Jem and Sally are there too, there's only one cemetery used in the city nowadays. We can avoid their graves, if you prefer. Jason was cremated, he's in a different area.'

'You sure know how to show a girl a good time!'

Alex was attempting to lift the mood. She could see that I was grinding everything that had happened over and over in my mind. I decided to lighten up, I needed to have a bit of fun. We'd do the crappy things that we had to, then have some Sunday lunch and try to enjoy the rest of the day.

We drove into a media storm. There were cars packing the drive and vehicles parked all along the roadside. The guys from the radio station were there in the satellite van, as were various teams from TV. At least work hadn't phoned me for a comment. Diane must have leant on the weekend team to prevent them from calling me. They'd have been itching for some inside information.

'I'm going to park up the road and walk down,' I said. 'Let's see if we can get to the police tape without being spotted.'

'Some chance!' Alex replied. 'If they don't spot you, they're certainly going to recognise me. They'll think I'm here for Crime Beaters. Maybe I should hang back in the car?'

'No, screw them, Alex. I'd like you there. With me. If you're alright with it, I'd like you to come with me. It'll be good for you to see the house too. You were involved in the murders as well, it'll be the last chance you get to see where it all happened. We'll do the "no comment" thing. People have done it to me hundreds of times, it'll be good to turn the tables for once. Besides, I know most of these media guys. It's a murder investigation now, they'll know there's only so much that we can say.'

We parked quite a distance from the house. I checked the drawer in the car. I had two pairs of sunglasses in there. One of them had been Meg's. I really needed to clear out all that junk.

'Let's use these, they should get us to the front of the crowd without being spotted.'

It wasn't raining for once, so we wouldn't look too crazy if we turned up wearing sunglasses. It worked too. We sauntered right past my colleagues from the radio station. I kept my head down, and we made it as far as the police tape before I lifted my glasses. The officer who was guarding the entrance to the drive was well briefed. He let me in and didn't challenge Alex's presence, as she was clearly with me. We looked like The Blues Brothers with our shades on. Alex remained anonymous until we got to the front of the house and then there was a ripple of excitement from the people working inside. Melissa had already arrived. I'd spoken to her several times on the phone and we'd met once or twice before.

'I guess this means that offer is off the table?' I smiled, then thought better of it. She'd lost her boss. She looked okay, although a bit rattled, mostly distracted by the police activity. We couldn't go into the house; they hadn't finished the thorough sweep that would need to be completed before they were entirely happy that every scrap of evidence had been collected.

'It's going to be a devil of a job to get anything useful in there,' said a capable-looking woman as she walked out of the front entrance to meet us.

'DCI Kate Summers,' she said, extending her hand to me.

'It must be serious if you're here,' she smiled at Alex. 'What next, Kate Adie?'

'Pleased to meet you,' Alex replied, the sunglasses now off. She'd worked with enough police officers to know that there would be excitement but no nonsense around her presence there. And some ogling from the guys, and the occasional female too.

The DCI shook Melissa's hand. She seemed completely no nonsense. As we spoke, we'd occasionally be interrupted, and it was immediately obvious that she had the respect and obedience of her team.

'Normally we'd assign a constable to go through the basics with you, but I want to ask you myself as I'm on site. This is interesting, we think Mr Elliot must have disturbed someone here.'

'Was it a break-in, or did they have access already?'

'There are no signs of a break-in. Glenn Elliot had opened the door. We understand from Ms Drake that Mr Elliot had an appointment here, and for some reason he stayed back for a short time after that initial meeting. It looks like he was making some phone calls or filling in some paperwork.'

Melissa began to cry. Kate Summers looked at her disapprovingly, as if she'd let her gender down.

'I can't believe that Glenn is dead,' Melissa sobbed. 'I only saw him yesterday, I was at the house myself earlier in the week. It's unbelievable ... '

'You've heard that I have a stalker I take it, DCI Summers?' I interjected. I've always been fortunate not to have female figures in my day-to-day life who are prone to tears. I wasn't quite sure how to respond to Melissa.

'Yes, I've received that update, it was called through to me about half an hour ago. We're taking this very seriously, Mr Bailey. I'm aware of the unhealthy attention that your property has been attracting since the murders that took place here.'

Alex had worked her magic calming Melissa down. I surveyed the officers who were doing a painstaking search of the overgrown grass in the garden at the front of the house.

'Any idea what went on?' I asked, fully understanding that DCI Summers would not share anything too important with me. I knew the score, I had a key to this place, they'd at least need to consider me as a potential suspect. The cops had seen it all, and even as a journalist I'd seen most of it. It wasn't out of the question for Glenn Elliot and me to have been having a gay liaison at the house, but in a lover's tiff gone bad, I slit his throat, mimicking the events that had taken place in the house six months beforehand. Ludicrous, I knew, but I'd put money on the chance of that crossing somebody's mind. They had to exhaust all possibilities, and that was fair enough.

'Nothing yet,' DCI Summers replied. She had long hair tied back tightly in a ponytail, making her look severe. That's probably how she preferred it. As a woman, she'd have to make sure she didn't give an inch to the guys working for her or they'd see it as a weakness. I'd not encountered her before in my work as a journalist. I liked her, even though she wasn't what you'd call friendly.

'Do any of you have any keys missing? Are you aware of anybody else having access to the house?'

Melissa and I shook our heads.

'Did you recover Glenn's set of keys?' Melissa asked, wiping her eyes with a tissue, conscious that her tears had messed up her eye make-up.

'We'll need to check that with you, Ms Drake. You have an inventory of the keys held by the estate agency, I take it?'

'Of course.'

'And you, Mr Bailey, are all your keys where they should be? Everything accounted for?'

'Yes,' I replied, taking the small bunch out of my pocket. 'I haven't been here for several months. I avoid the place, you know.'

DCI Summers nodded.

'I can understand that,' she said. 'I saw the pictures taken here after the murders, it was gruesome stuff. It's going to be difficult to shake off the interest in this house now Mr Elliot has died here. I'm sorry about that, Mr Bailey, I know that you're trying to move on.'

She paused, and I knew it was coming. DCI Summers looked at me.

'And what about your wife, Mr Bailey?'

She looked at Alex, perhaps wondering how much I'd moved on.

'Does she have a key, Mr Bailey? Are you still in contact with her? Is it possible that she might access the property?'

It took us a while to get away from the house. We weren't allowed to enter, and I was advised to get the locks changed and be careful about how the keys were distributed. Strictly speaking, I should have included Meg in that circulation list. Her name was on the deeds, but she'd left me to pay the mortgage. Without a word. She'd have rent to pay, wherever she was living now, but it was making life difficult for me financially.

'You know, if things are a bit tight, Pete, I'm happy to help out. They pay me far too much for what I do. I've got a lot saved in the bank. I can't spend it. I have nobody … I have nothing to spend it on anyway. It's yours, if I can help. You might be able to get yourself a posher caravan!'

I laughed at that. There was a time when Alex and I had shared household expenses. Before Meg came along. I suppose we were never meant to be, we didn't graduate from single bank accounts. It had been very modern, we'd paid our way fifty–fifty. Alex would pay the rent and I'd reimburse her by standing order. We lived like students. We had two kettles, two toasters and two microwaves from our college days, and my stuff even had my name written on it in black indelible pen, a hands-off warning to anyone thinking about nicking my stuff. I'd never really thought about that.

We'd spent five years living together, almost had a child together, but never even merged our finances. Did we sense it at the time? Did we know that Alex would move on? Perhaps it was inevitable, bearing in mind the transitory nature of our careers.

I was so busy moving forward with my life, especially after I'd met Meg, that I never thought about how Alex was feeling. I'd assumed that she was carried away by the excitement of her career. But already she'd said a couple of things that hinted at some unhappiness in her life. Loneliness, even. I'd always thought she would be immersed in a constant whirlwind of celebrity fun. Maybe that wasn't the case.

We answered more questions from the police. I gave details of my comings and goings and Alex was able to confirm all of it. Who'd question a TV celebrity? After all, it was impossible for the presenter of Crime Beaters to tell a lie.

Not for the first time, I found myself withholding the full truth from the police. I missed out on what had happened with Becky when giving details of my movements. My account to the police ended with me finishing my shift in the bar and going back to my caravan. To sleep. I missed out the bit about Becky, the baby oil, the masks and the hot lovemaking. They didn't need to know about that. Just as I'd concealed the details of my night with Ellie before my nightmare began the last time. It was none of their business. I wasn't a suspect, I was truthful about where I'd been, it wouldn't mess up the investigation.

This death felt different. I'd met Glenn Elliot when I put the house on the market, and I spoke to him occasionally to get an update about why it hadn't sold. But he wasn't connected to me in any way. If he'd been killed in my house, it was a gruesome coincidence. It would be connected to what had happened in the house, but it was probably a case of wrong place, wrong time for Glenn. I was a bystander this time around.

No need to mention the sexy night with Becky to the police. If Vicky had been mistaken, and Becky was genuinely a single female staying on the campsite, I'd be coming back for a rerun after Alex had left. I'd felt like I was in a porno with Becky, even the thought of it was exciting me. Best not to leave the crime scene with an erection. Not with the TV cameras outside the house.

At last we were able to leave. DCI Summers promised to keep in touch. I'd be assigned a police liaison officer. Again. I thought about the vacancy that Ellie had mentioned. I resolved right then that I was going for that new job. If there had been any doubt in my mind at all, it was gone. I had to shake the shit off my shoes.

This house had to go too, at whatever loss, and it was time to move on. I ran the numbers in my head, wondering what the price drop would have to be to shift the place. I reckoned that I could walk away a few thousand pounds down after all the costs. I'd make that up soon enough if I lived in a shitty flat for a year.

'You know, you could have a room in my house if you take that job in London. I'd love to have you there. I know what you're like already. Only, don't leave a stink in the bathroom like you used to, eh?'

Alex could read my mind. Was she Steven Terry's love child? How had she managed that?

'I was thinking about that job in London, mulling over the practicalities. But I need to shift this house.

You see that, don't you?'

Yes, Pete. This house is an albatross. Especially now Glenn Elliot has died here. It's got to go. You have to move on. I can see how it's wearing you down. You make light of it, but I know you, Pete. You haven't changed. You make the jokes, but I can see it's bothering you.'

She was right. Meg and I had always been more of a physical connection; with Alex it was more ... spiritual. Somebody shoot me, I can't believe I'd even use the S-word. I'd be lighting joss sticks next and getting my aura read. But it was true, Alex and I were in tune with each other. And it was still the case, more than a decade after we'd gone our separate ways.

'What did you do after we split-- after we parted? Was there anyone else for you? Did you meet someone?'

I was sounding like Martin Travis, my former gay counsellor. The one I thought wanted to shag my wife.

Alex shifted uneasily and put her sunglasses on. We had to make our way through the press pack again, they'd know who we were by now. I suspected that sunglasses wouldn't be much use this time around.

'I had a few relationships you know, tried them out for size. My biggest mistake was dating a footballer. I won't tell you who, I'm too embarrassed to admit it. I think he was more used to being with his mates. It felt like he preferred male company every time we went out together. Too much time spent in the communal bath!'

I laughed, but even I could see that she was evading the question. Even me, with my carefully calibrated antennae, finely tuned to detect every nuance of female emotion.

'We'd better make a run for it, see if we can get

through this lot without being noticed. Can we head for the cemetery next? Is that okay?'

We'd pick up on Alex's love life later. She hadn't told me everything. We needed to get pissed again. Blackpool would do the job. We'd go on Monday, maybe stay overnight and hit the town. Try and find out more about Meg's former life there.

The radio and TV guys were all over us the minute we started to approach the police tape. We kept walking, heads down.

'What's going on in there, Pete?'

'What can you tell us about the police investigation, Mr Bailey?'

'How do you feel about there being another murder in your house? Are you a suspect?'

'Would you ever consider doing a topless photo shoot in Ballz! magazine, Alex?'

The tabloids had turned up. Good to hear that they'd saved their best and most probing journalistic question for Alex.

We rushed by, but it was only the small team from my own radio station that I felt guilty about spurning.

'Come on, guys, you know it's not appropriate for me to be talking about this stuff. Go through the police, talk to DCI Kate Summers, tell her I sent you. She's the best person to talk to, she'll share what she can with you.'

Finally Alex and I got into the car and drove off. I checked the rear-view mirror to make sure they weren't doing a Princess Diana on us. It seemed fine.

'Fuck! Fuck!'

'What have you done, have you hurt yourself?'

'No, I saw someone in the crowd while we were rushing by, I didn't recognise him at first. Bollocks, I'm sorry Pete!'

'What is it, Alex? Who was it?'

'He was wearing a cap to hide his face, but it was JD, Pete. I recognised the jacket. He was there, he was watching us. We could have got him!'

DCI Summers had given me her business card. I was straight on the phone to her.

'That bastard JD was outside in the crowd. Move your arse out there now, he's standing out there, metres away from your own fucking police officers.'

I'm not proud to admit it, but I'd sworn at her in my fear and frustration. There are some people you never swear at or hassle. Never give a waiter a hard time while you're eating your dinner. Be an arsehole and you might find a secret ingredient in your salad.

The same applies to DCIs who are trying to catch crazy people on your behalf. To keep you safe. It's best not to yell down the phone at them telling them to do their job properly.

I was ashamed of myself. I liked Kate Summers, I could tell she was good at her job. I did not want to get on her bad side and I immediately regretted it. Unusually for me, I made amends immediately.

'DCI Summers, Kate, I apologise for that comment unreservedly. I'm so sorry, I should know better. I'm sorry.'

There was a brief silence on the line. DCI Summers must have been called every name under the sun in her line of work. Still, she seemed to appreciate the apology. It was the equivalent of catching the waiter moments before he spat in my Caesar salad and added his own unique dressing.

'That's alright, Mr Bailey. I appreciate how stressful this is for you. We'll check the crowds outside your house and see if he's there. If he is, you have my word, we want to talk to him, we'll bring him in for questioning.'

I calmed down and pulled out of the bus lane where I'd stopped to make the call.

'Everything okay, Pete? Are they going to look for him?'

'Yeah, yeah, they're onto it. Was I a real wanker there?'

'You did right to apologise. She'll understand, the cops know what's what. Kate Summers knows the score; she'll get worse every day from the guys in her office. But you were right to apologise, she'll appreciate that. She won't hear it very often.'

'Do you want to go to the cemetery? Go and see Jason's grave? We can get some decent flowers from the supermarket on the way round.'

I didn't particularly want to go to the cemetery, I still didn't know how I felt about things. The last time I'd been there was the funeral. It was where I saw Meg before she did a runner.

I didn't feel the same guilt as Alex did about the death of Jason Davies. He was an ex-Special Forces guy that we'd known through our radio days. Alex had asked him to watch the house, but he was supposed to monitor it from afar, not stick his hand into the hornet's nest.

Well he did and he screwed up and got himself killed. He knew the risks, he was Special Forces. It would be like Bear Grylls taking a dump on an anthill, he should have known better. Maybe it was right that I was going with Alex, laying flowers was the least I could do. He did get bludgeoned to death and his throat slit in my house, after all.

I hate cemeteries. A kid died once, when I was still at primary school, and I can remember going to the cemetery to see his grave. They're such depressing places, there's so much sadness there. Every headstone marks some miserable story. The death of a child. The loss of a parent. A car crash. Cancer. Even murder.

I hadn't got a clue where Jason's ashes were located. Alex and I worked out between us, investigative journalists that we are, that there would be some dedicated area for the people who'd been cremated. It was easy to find, as it turned out. There was a sign. Imagine us not thinking of that.

Jason had a plaque marking his name. He was forty-four when he died, not that much older than me. Of all the deadly tasks he would have faced in Special Forces and it was Jem's wife who whacked him over the head with a baseball bat which I'd found on a beach while on holiday. Then she slit his throat to make sure he was dead.

Alex peeled off the price tickets from the supermarket flowers that we'd bought. We'd gone sober on the colours, nothing fancy. Alex laid them as close as she could get to his plaque and we stood there for a few minutes, in silence.

'I wanted to come here,' she began. 'I feel so guilty about Jason. He was only doing me a favour, and look what happened to him.'

'It was a paid job, Alex. You offered him a couple of hundred quid to do it. I know it all turned sour, but it wasn't as if you asked your granny to watch the house. He was the right person for the job, you were paying him well. You told him not to interfere, he was a grown man, it was his decision to go inside the house.'

'I know, I know. But I can't help feeling responsible for it.'

'I've gone through this a million times in my head. We all made mistakes that night, but neither you nor I slit anybody's throat or hit somebody with a baseball bat. Even my counsellor, Blake, agrees with that one. "We can only change our own decisions. We can't alter those of others." That's what Blake told me. It's true. We didn't kill anyone, Alex.'

It wasn't entirely true. I could have released Jem from his precarious position tied to the cathedral bells, or at least allowed him to move his neck from the wheel mechanism. He'd lost his head as a result. What a way to go, I still couldn't think about it without flinching. It had crushed his neck, torn through his spine, ripped off his head.

The police had got to the bell tower in time to save him, but they couldn't untie him because of health and safety regulations. They had to risk assess the rescue first. It was too late. While they were still working through a checklist, it turned seven o' clock and the bells rang anyway. Too late.

Was I to blame? It was both my fault and the fault of the police. I could have helped Jem. The police could have helped Jem. He died anyway. In truth, it was the fault of the person who tied him there in the first place. His own wife. With a bit of help from Meg, though she was looking down the barrel of a gun at the time.

'Do you mind if I go to see Sally and Jem's graves? I know it's a bit morbid, but I want to see them and understand. It was horrible for me being so far away when it was happening.'

'I'll come with you, it's time I went and paid my respects, to Sally if nobody else. And out of respect for their children, poor things, what must their life be like now? I should have thought ... we should have got flowers for Sally.'

We walked slowly through the graveyard, in silence. I knew exactly where to go, I remembered it clearly from the day of the funeral. At least it wasn't chucking it down with rain this time. There were fresh flowers by the graves, on Jem's too. It's hard when you knew someone and liked them, but then found that they weren't who you thought they were. Jem was a predator and rapist. He was also a father. How must the parents of a murderer feel? Do they still love their child? As humans, we have to try and reconcile this stuff. And it's complicated.

We stood for a moment looking at the flowers. They were fresh too. Reading the cards written by Jem's kids made me want to cry. I remembered Gracie being born, she was always a lovely little thing. She'd left a beautiful card for her mum.

There was one bunch of flowers which particularly drew my attention. They didn't look as if they'd been bought from a supermarket or a petrol station, these had been assembled by a florist. I hunted around for a card. It had come unstuck and fallen onto the ground.

I picked it up and read it out aloud, so that Alex could hear.

'This is interesting,' I said. 'I've never heard of this person before: *To Sally & Jeremy, a love torn apart by hate, I'm so sorry for your beautiful children. You have your peace now. With so much sadness, Hannah Young.*'

Something had been scribbled out, it was hard to work out what it said. The morning dew had loosened the tape on the card and begun to blur the ink.

'Can you work out what that says?' I handed the card to Alex. She scrutinised it for a moment.

'Yates,' she said. 'It says Yates. She wrote it as her surname, then scribbled it out and changed it to Young. Maybe she's a recent divorcee, something like that?'

That wasn't the issue that was occupying my mind. Yates was the name of the people in the photographs. It was what I suspected Meg's last name had been originally. It was too much of a coincidence. This had to be connected with Meg.

Chapter Ten

After reading the card on the flowers, I was desperate to get to Blackpool. Alex's visit had long since stopped being a leisure break, we were both in deep now. We'd have to wait until Monday morning and catch an early train. Alex wasn't due back in London until Wednesday, so we could stay overnight in Blackpool, try to make it more than a day-trip.

We ate out before returning to the caravan, then got back in the early evening. I explained to Alex what I'd pieced together from the photographs that I'd discovered in the storage unit. We'd been chatting about the possibilities, trying not to let our minds soar with ridiculous ideas. This woman – Hannah Young, or Yates – could be anybody. Yates is not an uncommon name. For all we knew, we were grabbing entirely the wrong end of the stick.

But it felt like too much of a coincidence, there had to be a connection. The flowers stood out. They'd been placed there by someone with a different agenda. They weren't from Sally or Jem's family, I knew that much.

As I drove past the main campsite complex, I could see Vicky hard at work at her desk. She was preoccupied and didn't look up and see us drive in. As we pulled up to the static caravan, I could see that the door was open.

'For God's sake!' I exploded. 'I asked Vicky to get Len down here to fix that thing. I might as well hang up a banner saying "Steal My Stuff!" Sorry, Alex, but I'm driving back up there now, I'm going to have a word with Vicky while she's in the office.'

I put the car into reverse and drove through the campsite slightly faster than the permitted 10 mph. I was annoyed, it wasn't much to ask to get my door looked at. I tried to calm myself down before I went to the office; Vicky had been good to me, she'd given me a place to stay and a second source of income. I needed both.

'My caravan door is open again, Vicky. Did Len get to it?'

'Oh, hi luv, I was getting on top of my paperwork. He said the police were around again earlier today, and you chased him off. I asked him to make sure he went back and had a look. We need to talk about the police, Pete. I've had a couple of the punters asking me what was up. Did Len not get to you?'

'My door is wide open, Vicky. We've been out all day. I'm sorry, I didn't mean to raise my voice, I hoped it would be fixed by now.'

'That's unusual, Pete. Len stayed on late to sort it out. He was about to clock off, then remembered that he had to check out your unit. He'll have gone straight home again afterwards. He's a reliable guy, I'm sure he must have got to you. That was some time ago now. Did you go inside? Was he still there?'

'No, we didn't go in. I came straight here. Will you drive over with me now and take a look? Maybe you can work out why it keeps coming open. I got Alex to check that I'd closed it properly, so it's not just me going crazy.'

We drove back to the caravan, sticking to the 10 mph speed limit, with Vicky in the back seat. She'd looked a bit shocked when I'd had my outburst, I didn't want to be a problem for her. The police were becoming a nuisance, it wasn't good for Vicky's business, I could see that.

Vicky examined the locking mechanism from the outside, turning the rotary handle and looking for damage.

'It looks okay from here,' she said. 'Alright if I go inside, luv, see if I can see anyth--'

She was halfway through the door when she stopped suddenly and let out a gasp.

'My God, poor Len!'

I could see the shock on her face. Len was lying on the living room floor, completely still. Alex rushed over with me. We felt for signs of life.

'Have you got a mobile, Vicky? Here, use mine. Call the police.'

As Vicky explained to the emergency services what was going on, Alex and I tried to figure out if Len was still breathing.

'I don't know how much more of this I can take!' I cursed, as Alex undid the buttons on Len's shirt to get a proper feel of his heartbeat.

'Oh jeez!' said Alex. 'He's been strangled.'

There was a red bloodied line all around Len's neck. We'd not seen it before since it was concealed by his clothing.

'He's dead, Vicky. Tell them he's dead. We need the police.'

Len was an old guy, one of those people who probably should have retired years ago. He wouldn't have been able to put up much of a fight, poor chap.

Alex and I sat on the floor, resting, exhausted by what had happened. Vicky was being spoken to by the emergency services, her face was white, she looked like she might faint.

'I'll handle it, Vicky,' I said. 'You sit down. Can you put the kettle on, Alex? I think we could do with a cup of tea.'

I made a face to her, passing on a silent message that we needed to look after Vicky. I picked up on her phone conversation, gave my name and explained once again that Len was definitely dead. I worked through the checks that I was asked to do, but there was no bringing Len back.

Alex gasped. What was it now?

'They strangled him with the iron lead!' she said. 'It's got blood all over it!'

One thing was for sure, Vicky was seeing an entirely different side of TV personality Alex Kennedy that day.

'I know this is bad for you, Vicky,' I began, deciding to pre-empt the inevitable. 'I can see it's terrible for business. I'm sorry, but you know I'd end this if I could? I want it over too.'

Vicky squeezed my arm.

'I know, luv, I know. Poor old Len, what did he walk in on? He should have retired ten years ago. He loved it here, said he wanted to keep working here till he died.'

There were the inevitable processes and procedures to work through. I was pleased to see that we got a visit from DCI Kate Summers. She looked as if she'd broken off whatever she'd been doing at home to join us.

'Good evening, Mr Bailey. Twice in one day, this is becoming a habit.'

'What do you think DCI Summers? Is it this JD guy? Did you find him in the crowd outside my house?'

'No, he'd gone. He left when you did. We got some extra information about him, but he's clever, he's changing his appearance. Most people notice the big stuff, like hats and sunglasses. I think he's changing his outfit intentionally, making sure people notice the wrong things. It's what magicians do. Misdirection. He seems to have a good idea what he's doing.'

That was disappointing. It wasn't as if I lived in a huge city like London, surely they'd find him soon.

'We pulled some CCTV footage from the nightclub. That was interesting. Nice dancing, by the way.'

'Oh hell!'

Alex chimed in this time around.

'Please tell me you didn't get footage of us on those dance podiums. It will remain confidential, won't it?'

'There were some pretty nice moves in there,' DCI Summers smiled. She looked much nicer when she smiled. She must have been called in from home. She probably had a hubby and kids, she hadn't had time yet to fully adopt her hardened exterior for work. I liked her more like this.

'Did you see JD, though?' I asked, anxious to dwell on the important stuff.

'Only glimpses, it was so dark in there, nothing we can use. Now, if it was you two we were looking for, we got some lovely clear footage there!'

I was mildly annoyed with Alex for fixating on our performance on the dance floor. On the other hand, I could see that a video like that would go viral on YouTube or Facebook. Alex was the host of a serious current affairs show. We'd been careless.

It felt as if the questions went on forever. All three of us got the third degree. We weren't really suspects. DCI Summers knew there was no way we'd killed Len. The cops kept pushing and pushing. Had I seen anyone other than JD? Any arguments or threats? Again, more questions about Meg and her whereabouts. We were going around in circles. The whole thing was crazy, they were clutching at straws.

There was no CCTV on the campsite, only in the slot machine areas. There was nothing to go on. The police would question holiday-makers the next day. DCI Summers agreed with Vicky that they'd set up an area in the main complex and ask if anybody had seen anything – or anyone – suspicious. But it was a holiday site, nobody knew anybody.

'Are we free to do as we please?' I asked DCI Summers. 'I mean I assume we're not suspects or anything? I want to go to Blackpool tomorrow, is that okay?'

'More dancing, Mr Bailey?'

She smiled again.

'Are you allowed to call me Pete, or does it have to stay formal? No, we're going … we want to have a night away.'

I decided not to mention the bit about Meg and the family that she may have been hiding. It wasn't relevant to Len's death or the death of Glenn Elliot at the house. All that stuff seemed to have nothing to do with what was going on at the campsite.

I'd be pleased to get away from everything. An overnight stay in Blackpool with Alex would remove us from the possibility that JD might run into us. It would give the police time to find him. If we were lucky, by the time we got back from Blackpool they'd have found him.

'Yes, make sure that we have all your details and that you stay contactable. We'll be stepping up our hunt for this JD fella, although if we can't place him at Golden Beaches or inside your house, we'll only be able to question him about the letters he's been sending you. It will help if we can get a name and see if he has any form.'

'I'd like to retrieve a couple of things from the back of the caravan, if that's okay? Have your guys done their sweep yet? Is it alright to go in there?'

'What is it you're after?' DCI Summers asked.

I wasn't hopeful that I'd get the go-ahead.

'A box of photos in my bedroom, they're old family pictures. I'd like to take those with me if I can.'

DCI Summers instructed a member of her team to go through to the rear of the caravan and try to locate the box.

'We'll need to get them checked over, make sure there are no prints and no evidence there. I might be able to release some things to you tomorrow morning, but I can't promise.'

A guy walked up to us wearing plastic wraps on his shoes and one of those forensics suits that you see on the TV.

'There's no box there, ma'am. I've checked everywhere. No sign of them.'

'Are you sure?'

DCI Summers was using her 'I take no prisoners' voice again. I'd bet she was formidable in the office.

'Completely, ma'am. There are no photographs in any of the rooms.'

'Well, there's your answer, Mr Bailey. It looks like

whoever was in your static caravan took a look at those images. It sounds to me like they're more than just holiday snaps.'

We were standing on the platform at the station. Our train was due in five minutes and we couldn't believe our luck: there were no leaves on the line, no engineering works and plenty of staff to go around. We were heading for Blackpool.

It had been an interesting night. Vicky had found us a replacement static caravan to stay in and we'd made our way over there once the police had finally allowed us to leave. Our previous caravan was sealed off, a police officer assigned to watch it, and a complete cordon placed around the area.

The police would be interviewing campsite holidaymakers all through the following day, but we were free to go. DCI Summers made sure that we'd exchanged contact details and promised to let us know if there were any developments.

The story was running on all of the news outlets, but Alex and I chose to ignore it. All I cared about was finding JD. The police were onto that. I was grateful for the change in caravan location. I'd asked Vicky to keep it completely quiet; nobody knew where we were, and I thought it best to keep it that way. DCI Summers agreed.

Alex and I had shared a bed again. It was only for company, we both wanted it. We fell asleep with the light on. We lay down on the bed and started chatting about what had happened, then drifted off to sleep, exhausted.

We awoke shortly after 6 o'clock and decided to get up and catch an early train. If we got on the train without JD following us there – and we had no reason to suspect that he was actually tailing us all the time – we'd have two days in Blackpool. Enough time to do some research on Meg and have some fun. The police would surely have apprehended JD by then, and we could keep clear of it all.

Melissa had agreed to get the house professionally cleaned – for the second time – and to sort out new locks, front and back. She'd do that as soon as it had been released by the police. In the meantime, there was an officer stationed there all the time. They'd found that a back door key was missing. Melissa had her suspicions about who might have removed it from the estate agent's key ring, but they were not contactable via any of the details that they had left with the estate agency.

Alex went off to get us some drinks from the coffee shop. It was a rattling regional train and we'd be lucky if we could get a seat. My phone vibrated in my pocket and I looked at the screen. It was early for a text, I assumed that it would be work or some sales nonsense. It was Becky. She'd finally replied to my message; it had taken her long enough.

Sorry I didn't get back to you. Missed your message. Went to caravan to see you. Wtf? Hope you're okay? Where are you now? Becky xxx

She was still keen to meet up. I got a momentary thrill from the thought of it. Then my better judgment kicked in.

Steven Terry had urged honesty and caution with women. Vicky had mentioned the stolen sheets and the fact that there was no Becky booked in on the site. Things weren't quite right as far as Becky was concerned, I was keen to find out more about her.

Which caravan are you staying in? Are you alone? Couldn't find you. Nobody knows where you're staying!

Unusually, I got an almost immediate reply.

Becky is what I like to be called when I meet new blokes. Use real name for bookings. I'll come round to your new caravan. Where is it? When does your friend leave? Want to see you again xxxxx

Okay, so she used a different name, fair enough. It never did Sting any harm. But still no mention of a caravan location. Or a real name. She was very keen to know where I was staying, though. And, once again, there was the suggestion of a second meeting.

I decided to leave off sending an immediate reply and to mull it over. Alex returned with the drinks.

'Hope you don't mind spending a day with a girl who's wearing day-old knickers?'

We'd had to relocate to our new caravan without any of our possessions. DCI Summers promised to release our stuff as soon as possible, but it wouldn't be soon enough to get a change of clothes before Blackpool.

'My socks aren't too pleasant either. Let's get some new gear when we get to Blackpool, at least we were able to take shower this morning.'

'Here's your tea, it's got UHT milk. Sorry, no fresh.'

Alex smiled when she saw the expression of disgust on my face as she handed me the cardboard cup.

'At least it will distract you from my knickers.'

The train made its way into the station. It was one of those two-carriage affairs, the sort of train that's seen better days; it was about half the size of what was really needed to serve the number of people who used it.

'At least we're early,' I said to Alex, after my first slurp of the drink that claimed to be tea. 'We'll miss the big work rush.'

It was after seven o' clock, there were other people boarding with us, but we managed to get a seat. I surveyed the platform once again, looking for JD. He wasn't there. We stepped on board.

'You grab a table seat, if you can find one. I'm going to walk up and down the train to be sure he's not here.'

Alex knew I was jittery about JD, so she let me go ahead. There was a small ripple of excitement as she walked through the train. Her life must be punctuated by members of the public doing double-takes as they recognised her from TV.

There was no sign of JD. I did a thorough sweep. I was as certain as I could be that he wasn't following us. Good. We could relax for a day or two. Hopefully the police would find him soon.

'I hope you feel like a queen, travelling in this regional railways luxury?' I smiled at Alex as I sat down opposite her. 'Good table seat too, I'll get a bit of leg room.'

'No sign of him, I take it?'

'No, I'm sure he's not here. Maybe you should take a walk through the train. After all, you're the only one who's seen him.'

'Not sure about that, Pete. A few people have recognised me. I had to sign an autograph on a serviette while you were doing your checks. Let's drink our tea, I'm certain he wasn't on the platform.'

I tried to settle down. I'd been looking forward to this trip. The change of scene and location was welcome and I was keen to see what we could find out about Meg.

'Do you think we'll be able to make any progress without the photos?' Alex asked, reading my thoughts.

'Hopefully. I've got an area and a location from that online article. We have a place to start. I want to find out about her family set-up, if I can. We need to find someone who knew the family.'

A text came through on my mobile phone. It was Becky again, wanting to arrange a meet-up.

Hope you're not ignoring my text? Let me know, where are you staying now? See you soon. If you thought our first night was hot, wait till you see what I have planned for next time xxxxxxxxxx

I felt a slight movement in my boxers thinking about it, but I decided to ignore the message for a bit. It was tempting to fix up our next encounter there and then, but I opted for caution. I could hear Steven Terry's voice whispering in my ear.

'Anybody interesting?' Alex asked. I think she sensed that it was something significant, but she didn't push the issue.

'No, it's work bothering me about the murders.'

A lie. Another lie. But it was a white lie. I'd tell Alex more once I'd made up my own mind about Becky. I'd follow Steven Terry's advice. I would tell the truth. Later.

The train journey passed quickly enough. It got busier and more packed as the journey continued, picking up more commuters along the way. We stopped chatting once we were joined at our table seat by a middle-aged couple on their way to work. Fortunately, they were too well mannered to chat to Alex, although I could see from their not-so-subtle eye movements that they'd spotted her. We sat in silence for the remainder of the trip, not wanting to have eavesdroppers on our conversation.

'Okay, new knickers first of all!' Alex smiled as we reunited on the platform of Blackpool station. She'd had to deal with a couple of Crime Beaters fans as she was leaving the train. I'd made myself scarce.

'The shops will be opening now,' I replied. 'I can't stay in these socks all day, they're actually crispy now!'

'Nice,' Alex laughed. 'And to think I could have been spending the day with a Premier League footballer. *They* don't wear old socks you know. You'll have to up your game if you want to spend more time with a TV celebrity.'

Alex took my hand and we moved towards the exit. I loved the way she did that, it was so confident, so natural. Why wouldn't I hold a friend's hand?

I felt good about that day. I was convinced that we'd find out more about Meg. Someone in the Marton area had to know the family. We'd start with the church which was mentioned in the online article. We'd have some fun too, away from the worry of JD and what was going on at home. And we'd both buy some new underwear. Underwear first. I desperately wanted to put on a clean pair of boxers. But more important than anything, I felt as if I was finally getting closer to the truth about my wife.

Chapter Eleven

We got off the train within walking distance of the Pleasure Beach. It had been several years since I'd been to Blackpool, and I couldn't quite remember the layout. It was a simple enough place to navigate, and we could use the trams or take a taxi if we had to. It didn't take long to get sorted out with new socks and underwear. Alex bought herself a black *I Love Blackpool* T-shirt and cap, some cheap sunglasses and a five-pack of pants, so she was good to go. We located a traditional seaside café and were filling up on tea made with real milk and bacon butties in no time.

'So, what's the plan?' Alex asked, supping her tea. 'A ride on The Big One or over to Marton first?'

'I'm not going on The Big One on a full stomach, there's no way! How about we get the Marton visit out of the way to begin with and then have some fun. Are you fussed about where we stay tonight or shall we busk it?'

'Busk it,' Alex answered. 'Let's see where we finish up at the end of the day. I've never stayed in a low-budget B&B before. It might be an adventure.'

'Maybe not the kind of adventure you want!' I

laughed. 'It's a nice day, for a change. How about we walk to Marton and get a feel for the place? Are you up for that?'

'Yes, let's do it. We'll walk and talk. Can you track the church on your smart phone? It'll guide us there if we can get a decent signal. We should be okay in a place like Blackpool.'

Sure enough, thanks to the miracle that is modern technology, I was able to tap in the postcode of the church where the memorial service had been held and get step-by-step walking instructions to our destination.

We walked along the promenade, looking out towards the horizon and enjoying the sea breeze. We passed the fun park. We could hear the screams of excited youngsters as they worked their way through the plethora of terrifying rides that were on offer.

A couple of family groups had spotted Alex and were taking selfies, trying hard not to get noticed. One old chap came up with a traditional camera and asked politely if Alex would pose with him and his wife for a photo.

She launched immediately into showbiz mode, asking their names, finding out all about them, making them feel as if they were the most important people in the world. I was the guy appointed to take the photograph.

Once the selfie-takers realised that Alex didn't bite, they all stepped up, and I spent the next ten minutes taking pictures on smart phones. Finally we managed to dispatch the crowd and Alex took out her new sunglasses and placed them on her face.

'Better keep a low profile,' she said. 'We'll never get anything done if we keep getting stopped for impromptu photo shoots. Did you know I have my own hashtag now, by the way? #AlexKCrime. How cool is that?'

'Doesn't it ever get you down? Don't you wish that you could walk down the street without any of that nonsense? It must get a bit wearing.'

'To be honest with you, yes, I do get tired of it. I am tired of it. Do you want the truth, Pete? I haven't been completely straight with you.'

'Oh yes? What is it?' I asked, intrigued about what she was going to say.

'I've left Crime Beaters. That was my last show. It's not been announced yet, we agreed to wait until they find a replacement.'

'What will you do? Have you got something lined up?'

'Nope! Nothing. It all happened very quickly. The next series hadn't been formally commissioned so there was a narrow window in which to change it all around. I may live to regret it!'

'That's a brave move, Alex. What made you do it?'

'I want some peace again. I'm fed up with all the relationship speculation and the body-shaming trolls. I mean, I'm still quite hot for thirty-nine, aren't I? I don't know, I want something more. I thought that TV jobs were what I wanted. I love the work, but there's something missing in my life.'

I hadn't expected that. Not from Alex. I'd never really stopped to consider if she was happy or not. I'd assumed that because there was a perpetual smile on her face everything was okay.

'I think you're brave. I should have done the same after Meg left, shaken everything up a bit. But I was too scared. I couldn't face cutting off my salary. And as things turned out with the house, I did the right thing. How long until you have to find a job?'

'I have plenty in the bank, Pete. It won't be a problem for a while. The mortgage on my flat is paid off and it's gone up in value a lot since I bought it. I reckon I can survive for a year at a push. I'd have to start thinking about renting out a room after that, or moving to somewhere smaller.'

'Won't they forget about you if you're off the screens for a while? Or doesn't it work like that?'

'Well, I have a few things coming up that are pre-recorded: Celebrities in the Stew, Starstruck Celebrity Audience, and Celebrity Fast Food Takeout, you know the sort of thing. I'm good for maybe five or six months. The TV listings mags will have my mugshot in them for a while yet. Hopefully I'll get something lined up before everything finishes screening. My agent doesn't even know yet. She's going to be really annoyed. Crime Beaters has taken care of everything for a long time now, she's barely had to move her arse to get her ten percent cut.'

'I can't blame you. It must get very tiring all this celebrity stuff. What are your plans?'

'I'm going travelling for a bit, I think. Remember where we used to go in Spain? I've booked a place there for a month, and I'll figure it out from there. It has lots of happy memories. It seems like a good place to start.'

'Wow! Lucky you! Sounds fabulous to me, I'd love to take off and leave all of this behind.'

'You know, you're welcome to come, Pete. As a friend. I'd love to have you out there. You could do with a break too. It would be lovely to spend some time out there again. Together.'

I'd been thinking a lot about the job that Ellie had mentioned, in between watching my back for nutters and finding dead bodies. I needed a change, I had to move things on. In the back of my mind, I'd also resolved to force the issue with Meg. I might be the father of a child, she owed me that much, to tell me the truth.

'You know I'd love to, Alex, but I have to sort out my issues with Meg. If the child is mine, if she decides she wants to work at the relationship again, I have to give it a try.'

I could see the disappointment on her face, even through the sunglasses.

'It's fine, Pete. Of course it is. I thought it would be a nice thing to do. No pressure, I know you've got your own life to sort out. But if I can help in any way, and I mean with money too, you only have to say the word. You know what you mean to me, Pete. You're my best friend. You've always been my best friend.'

We'd arrived at the church and I was grateful for the chance to change the topic. It had been a long walk, a little short of an hour, further than it looked on the smart-phone map. I'd screen-grabbed the web article on my phone. I checked once more to be certain that this was the right place. It was.

It wasn't that what Alex was proposing scared me or offended me in any way. It had been remarkable how quickly we'd picked up as seamlessly as we'd left off. It was always so easy with Alex, we were like the old married couple who never married.

But I was married to Meg. We'd spent years together, most of them very happy. If I hadn't been so stupid, maybe we'd still be happy, and with a baby on the way, or possibly even born by now.

I'd begun to resent Meg more and more since the deaths. I wasn't even sure if we would be able to rescue our marriage. Not after what she'd told me about the murders, how she'd let Sally take the blame for Tony. But if I was the father of her child, we'd have to work something out.

I couldn't think about Alex yet, much as the thought of getting out of the country for a month really tempted me. Maybe I could negotiate a delayed start on the London job, quit my own job, take a break in between?

'This is it,' I said, taking in the building. It was one of those churches that's tucked along a regular street, rather than set on its own, surrounded by a graveyard. The front door was open and the car park almost completely empty.

Alex removed her sunglasses and we stepped inside.

'Hello,' I said, not really sure who my greeting was aimed at. There were three old ladies removing flowers from vases, ready to replace them with the splendid arrays which were adorning the pews. It took them a moment to tune into my voice, they were so engaged with what they were doing and immersed in their own chatter.

'Hi, my name is Peter Bailey, my friend is Alex Kennedy.'

I paused, waiting to see if they recognised her. There was no glimpse of it, so I carried on.

'We're looking for a family who live – or lived – in the Marton area. I've got two possible names, either Yates or Irvine. Do you know them, or have you heard of them?'

'Of course we have, young man,' one of the ladies began. 'They used to attend this church. Their house was down the road, five minutes' walk away. But you heard what happened, didn't you? You must know about the fire.'

The ladies at Scott Road Methodist Church were delightful hosts. They were Deirdre, Janet and Cathy, but I'm not sure which was which because they all talked so fast that I missed out on the introductions. However, by using one name at a time, somebody would always answer, so it didn't seem to matter too much.

They marked us out as a nice young couple and treated us to tea and biscuits as they obligingly answered our questions, albeit in a circuitous and anecdotal manner.

'So, what happened to the Yates family?' I asked, nibbling on my fourth chocolate cookie. The six-pack stomach would have to wait another day.

'It was a terrible business,' said the woman I thought was Cathy, but who may well have been Janet. 'It was a house fire, my darling. It destroyed the entire property. It brought everybody out from the surrounding streets. We were all there, weren't we ladies? It was a terrible affair.'

'Those poor girls,' Deirdre joined in, although it may have been Janet. I needed to work out which one was Janet, and then I'd have it figured out.

'Losing their parents like that. It was a terrible thing to happen. They were such sweet things too.'

'How long did the Yates family live in this area?' Alex asked. 'Were they here all of their married lives?'

'Yes, my dear, I remember them moving into the street on the day they married. Thomas Yates had bought that small terrace as a surprise for Mavis. He was a caretaker in the local council building. It's closed down now. Mavis was my best friend in those days, you know. I'd only recently married my Ted, we were newlyweds too, and it didn't take us long to make friends. There weren't as many cars on the streets in those days, you could stand in the street and chat all morning.'

'Did they have children?' Alex continued to steer her and keep the conversation on course. She was gentler than I was, I tended to forget sometimes that I wasn't grilling some politician in a live radio interview.

'Well, my dear, after Thomas and Mavis moved into the street, a lot of us began having babies. Mavis was desperate to have children too, but it didn't happen. I felt terrible for her, the poor dear. I'd had my Henry, Janet had her Davina not long after, and poor old Mavis was left all on her own.'

The woman whom I was almost certain was called Deirdre brought us into a huddle to share a secret. I'm not sure who was supposed to be listening in, there were only the five of us in that church, but we played ball. We'd hit the jackpot with these wonderful old ladies.

'I think she had problems *down there*,' she whispered, conspiratorially.

'We didn't talk about things openly like you do these days. It's all cocks and pussies now. I know, I've got the internet at home.'

Alex and I didn't know where to look. I spluttered on my tea, spitting it out onto the floor and had to apologise.

'Don't worry, my dear. We may look old, but we were young once, you know. I think she had a problem in her tubes, she never told us what it was. She might not have known herself. She became very quiet after the street began to fill up with children.'

The woman who was probably Cathy chimed in. I hoped that she wasn't as foul-mouthed as Deirdre. Alex looked as if she was about to wet herself as she tried to contain her laughter. It was a good job she'd bought a five pack of knickers, she might be needing another pair by the time we'd finished with these ladies.

'She told me once, it was a long time ago. She said, "Cathy, I've got a problem with my fallopian tubes. I can't have children. I'm never going to have children." She had a quiet cry. We didn't make a fuss in those days, we kept it all bottled up. There were none of those psychologists to talk to about your problems, like you have nowadays. We had to get on with it.'

At least I knew that she was Cathy now. I was getting there, slowly but surely. From out of nowhere Janet came up with some gold dust.

'When they adopted those two girls, it changed her life. They were her pride and joy, she suddenly got her old joie de vivre back again. It was lovely to see. I think she felt like she was one of us again.'

'Can you remember their names?' I asked.

'One of them was Hannah, she was older,' Cathy said. 'She was a lovely thing, so kind and gentle. She used to wear a yellow dress with bright flower patterns all over it. She wore that dress until it was falling off her shoulders, she loved it.'

'The younger child could be a minx, she was more mischievous than Hannah. She was called Megan. She used to like playing with the boys. Always getting into trouble, she was. But Mavis loved them both, they were her pride and joy, they made her life complete.'

'Were they sisters?' I asked. 'I mean, were they birth siblings, or had they come from different families?'

'No, they weren't related by blood. They were

adoptive sisters, my love,' Janet chimed in. 'They had quite a job adopting them both, but Mavis was adamant she wanted two children so she wouldn't have an only child. It happened so quickly too. One minute they were on the waiting list, the next they had two lovely teenage daughters. They gave her the run-around, but she got what she wanted in the end.'

Alex had composed herself once again.

'What happened with the fire?' she asked, anxious to reclaim her place in the conversation.

'It was such a terrible thing,' Deirdre began to explain. The women bowed their heads for a moment like an over-seventies version of a Mexican wave. We had to remember that these women went way back, we were dealing with difficult memories for them.

'I can still remember the screams from the house,' said Cathy. 'It makes me shudder to this day. The heat from the flames was fierce, it was so hot. How those girls got out, I'll never know.'

'They were standing there, out in the street, while their parents burned in the top bedrooms. We never knew how they escaped, but it was a blessing and a miracle.'

Janet was quite overcome describing the events. Alex placed her arm on her shoulder. These ladies were built of remarkable stuff. They must have carried these memories with them through their lives. We'd hit a nerve now, we would need to tread carefully.

'I saw Mavis at the window. She was desperately trying to shout to me, but the window wouldn't open. They were made out of wood in those days, they were always swelling in the wintertime, the darn things would get completely stuck. All I could see was her mouthing to me, pointing to the children.'

'What about Thomas?' I asked. 'Did he die with Mavis?'

It was Deirdre's turn to take up the story.

'He died in the house,' said Cathy, 'but Mavis didn't die, she got out. She was burned terribly. He was in a separate room, trapped in one of the children's bedrooms. They didn't know what had happened.'

She lowered her voice again.

'They think that Thomas and Mavis were having a fight and perhaps she shut him in one of the bedrooms to calm him down. The fire must have broken out and left them both trapped upstairs. Those poor girls, at least they managed to escape. Poor Megan and Hannah, I still remember them standing in the street watching the house burn. Meggy was so shocked, she couldn't even cry. She just stood there watching.'

There were a few moments of silence. All three women had been there that night, we'd brought back the ghosts of the past.

'What happened to the children afterwards?' Alex asked. Ever the journalist, she was making a clean sweep with the questions, making sure we got everything that we came for.

'That was sad too,' said Janet. 'Those poor girls. They didn't have any other family left. Both Thomas and Mavis's parents had died young, and neither had brothers or sisters. Mavis was in a nursing home after the fire, she was in a terrible state ... or so we heard. She needed special care and lots of operations. They took her down south somewhere, we never really knew where she ended up. There was no internet then, my dear, things weren't so easy to find out in those days. The girls went back into care for a short time until Hannah was old enough to look after them, but I don't know what happened after that. Those poor girls, what they went through.'

'It was a terrible business,' Deirdre said. 'We never saw the girls again. They used to be the life and soul of the street, but we never saw them after the funeral. I can still remember them there, in their black dresses and shoes. Poor Megan still couldn't find the tears to cry. It must have been so overwhelming for them.'

I decided that we had found out everything we could and started to make a move.

'I can't thank you enough for all of the help that you've given us today, ladies. You've been so kind making time for us and looking after us so well.'

This had been an excellent idea. We couldn't have had more luck. At last I knew that Meg had not told me the truth while we were married. She'd constructed a lie around her life as a child and a teenager. She'd fabricated a past. Had it been too painful for her to discuss? Had she airbrushed all those terrible things from her life story? I couldn't blame her if she had. Maybe she'd reinvented herself as an adult, it might have saved her the pain of retelling that story over and over again. It was even possible that Meg's mother was still alive, although it did sound unlikely from what our informants were telling us. She sounded like she'd been in a bad way.

We thanked the women once again and started to make our way out of the church. As we were walking away, Cathy touched my arm and leant in to say something to me.

'That's that Alex Kennedy from the TV isn't it? We recognised her straight away, but we didn't want to be rude. We knew she was in town today. I saw it on my feed while I was posting on Twitter!'

The great thing about Blackpool is that you're never far away from a café. We found a small one across the road, in a side street, and stopped off for a drink and a chat about what had happened in the church. It felt good to be laughing my head off again and, for a moment, I forgot about Meg, JD, the murders and all of the other troubles in my life.

The three old ladies had been great company and we couldn't stop laughing at the cocks and pussies comment. Alex howled when she realised they'd recognised her all the time. It didn't take long for us to get serious again. I'd learnt that Meg had created a complete untruth about her life before she met me.

'But was it a lie, Pete? Or more of an omission.'

'You know, Meg's sister has the same first name as the one that was on those flowers. It *was* Hannah, wasn't it? Hannah Young? Is that a coincidence?'

'Come on, Pete. You're imagining things. That can't be Meg's sister. Why would it be? It has to be a coincidence.'

'But what if she'd seen what was going on, like every other person out there? What if she was trying to find Meg? It's not so impossible is it?'

'I don't see how that could happen. We've only just learnt that she exists, and now she's popping up at the cemetery all of a sudden, putting flowers on graves. Unlikely, I'd say.'

I didn't share Alex's assessment, but I didn't push it any further. I'd seen enough things that had taken me by surprise already. I'd reserve judgment on Hannah, but I wanted to find her, I knew that much.

'I want to see the house, Alex. I know there won't be much there, but I'd like to see it. I want to feel closer to Meg. She never told me any of this stuff. Was she hiding it, or was she inventing another past for herself? I think I might do the same if that had happened to me.'

'I wonder how the girls got out of the house, Pete, and why he was locked in that room? It doesn't ring true to me. I wonder if I can get access to the case files. I know a few people in the Lancashire constabulary – shall I put some feelers out?'

'That's a great idea, Alex. It's a few years ago now, it'll still be on paper, I think, but you never know. I'd love to hear what the official report said. At least I'll know what really happened that way.'

Alex took out her phone and started to write some emails.

'Look at all these Twitter notifications. Those pictures that we took earlier have been shared all over social media. Apparently my tits look great in this T-shirt!'

I took out my own phone and searched for Alex on Twitter.

'I don't know how you put up with it, Alex. You're a serious journalist, they always reduce everything to tits. Although I see what they mean … '

I chanced the joke. Alex laughed, playfully punching me on the arm.

'Pervert, I can't help it if they make these T-shirts so small. Maybe I should wear a sack. It's a good job they didn't get a photo of us together, they'll be asking who my mystery suitor is next. Oh wait, there are a couple of us in here. They don't miss a trick.'

She was right, there were no posed photos of me, but a couple of tourists had spotted us together and posted pictures on Twitter.

Never guess who I just saw! #AlexKCrime and some bloke. In Blackpool!

It was hardly Shakespeare, but I guess it succeeded in expressing the author's thoughts in 140 characters or less. Alex moved back to her emails and fired off a few notes to her pals in the Lancashire police. I used the free Wi-Fi in the café to connect my maps app and work out where Meg's old house had been. The women had told us that we couldn't miss it and that it was easy walking distance from the church.

As it turned out, it was really close. It was also completely obvious which house it was, even after all those years. It looked as if they'd had to gut the house completely, replacing much of the front brickwork. It was as if somebody had dropped a new house right in the middle of an old terrace.

'It must have been some fire!' Alex said.

I was imagining a young Meg standing in the street with her sister, watching her parents burn in the house that was in front of us. Well, her father at least. Who knew what had happened to her mum? She must have been petrified. Would I hide something like that if I'd been the one standing in that street? For a moment I wondered if I was judging Meg too harshly. I was angry with her about what she'd done, screwing me over with the mortgage costs and disappearing into thin air, but she'd been through some serious problems in her life. Maybe I should have been listening a bit harder. Who did she talk to about this stuff? Maybe that was the problem, perhaps she needed to share her experiences more openly.

'Shall we knock at the door?' Alex asked. 'See if the neighbours can tell us anything?'

'They'll think it's This Is Your Life if they see you standing on the doorstep,' I laughed. 'Either that, or they'll crap themselves. Put your sunglasses on, I'll do the talking.'

We knocked at the door. Nothing. More knocking. Nothing.

'Bollocks, why do people have to go to work? Why can't they sit around watching daytime TV all day and be in the house when I want to speak to them?'

We were turning to walk away, when the door on the right-hand side of the house opened. It was an old guy, probably in his seventies. He used a walking stick.

'Can I help you?' he asked. 'The house is empty, has been for some time. It's rented out now. Sometimes I hear someone in there, but it must be the landlord. Who are you looking for?'

'We're doing some research into the neighbourhood,' I lied. 'Do you know anything about the fire that broke out in this house? Were you living here at the time?'

'See this stick?' he asked. We nodded.

'I don't use this because I'm an old git, I use it because I injured my leg that night.'

This was getting interesting. We didn't interrupt and let him continue his story.

'I've lived here all my married life. My wife is dead now, she's been dead for three years. I can still remember that night. I heard glass breaking, that's what woke me, and the roar of the flames, it was so loud. I looked out onto the street and I could see what it was straight away. Those two girls were standing out there, their faces lit by the light of the flames. I could see it was fire.'

He paused a moment, he hadn't thought about it for some time, and I could see that the memories still

172

haunted him.

'There were no mobile phones in those days. Well, we didn't have one, most people didn't. We couldn't even afford a phone in the house. We used to use the phone box that was on that corner over there.'

He pointed along the street, but there was no longer any evidence of a call box.

'I woke my wife and told her to get the kids out of the house and onto the street, well away from the fire. I told her to get the Yates girls further away from the house, they were standing too close. I was worried they'd get hurt.'

'What did you do?' Alex asked. It was the first time she'd spoken to him. He looked at her, searching beyond the sunglasses. I think he'd recognised her voice, but seemed unable to place it.

'I ran out the back and got my ladder. I put it up at the back window where there were no flames. We didn't have double glazing in those days, you could break the glass. I could hear Mavis in there, screaming, but there was no sound from Tom. I could see him on the floor of the back bedroom. He was out cold, a lot of black smoke was coming under the door. Mavis was in the front bedroom. I could only hear her.'

'What did you do?' I asked, completely captivated by this story.

'I messed up, that's what I did.'

His face dropped. He was still blaming himself for something.

'I climbed down the ladder as fast as I could to get a stone or a brick or something to smash the window and get Tom out. Only, I caught my foot on the bottom rung of the ladder and broke my ankle. Quite badly as it turned out. Hit my head on their concrete yard when I fell. I was out cold for a while, that's what the ambulance guys told me. The fire brigade had arrived by then and they took me away from the house. You know, I still blame myself for Tom's death.'

'I'm sure there was nothing else that you could have done,' Alex reassured him. 'It must have been horrible.'

'They said it was a tragic accident. I never really knew why Tom was stuck in that back bedroom. It was a spare room or one of the rooms that the kids used. I'd had to go round there earlier that night because there was shouting. They'd had a big row about something. It woke my kids up. I had to go round to make sure everything was okay. One of the girls answered the door. Little Megan it was.'

'You don't sound so sure that it was an accident?' I suggested.

'It was all suspicious, if you ask me: Tom dying in that room like that, Mavis being so badly burned. Who knows what they did with her after they carried her out of there? She was still alive apparently. There were local rumours that it was a childish prank gone wrong, but the police didn't say that. They reckoned it was a tragic accident. Some problem with the heater set the place on fire they reckoned.'

'Why do you think the police got it wrong then?' Alex asked. 'What did they miss?'

'I always wanted to know why it was Meg who answered the door to me. At that time of night. What was she doing up so late? And she screamed at me when I asked what was going on. Told me she hated her mum and dad. She slammed the door on me. It made me wonder what that row was about. And why she and her sister were the only people who got out of the house unharmed.'

Chapter Twelve

The old guy's name was Edward – or Ted as he preferred. He'd been the second brilliant find that day. We were lucky that it was still a traditional community where the older residents lived in houses that they'd occupied for years.

We chatted to Ted for a bit longer, but there was nothing else that he could tell us. We thanked him and moved on. It was quite a walk back to the seafront, but we had so much to talk and think about that it was welcome. There's something invigorating about being near the sea. I'd experienced it while living at the Golden Beaches Holiday Park.

Alex was looking at her phone.

'I've got two replies to my emails already. One of my contacts has moved on, he won't be able to help. The other can get access to the files, and she'll see if she can find them. They're quite old, there might not even be a record of the case. If it was written off as an accident, there won't be much paperwork, if any, but she'll do her best to see what she can find. What's the full address?'

Alex emailed the name of the street and the house number and even sent a photo, in case it was useful.

'Do you think there's anything in Ted's suspicions?

That's the second time that somebody has told us that Meg didn't cry during the fire or even at the funeral. She was always very straightforward at home, she never cried or got emotional about things. I never thought anything of it. While some guys at work had to deal with emotional wives getting tearful, I never had that with Meg. You never cried when we were together either. I assumed that was the kind of woman I'm attracted to. That and the fact I'm such a great guy that there's nothing to cry about when I'm around.'

'Ha, ha! Yeah, right, who gets sad when Pete Bailey is around? It's true, though. I don't get particularly emotional about things, I never have. Maybe that's how you like your women. Straightforward, hot, intelligent, sexy, sophisticated … '

'Okay, okay, I get it! But it is interesting, what they were saying. Do you know anything about being in shock? Would that make the girls behave like that?'

'Who knows?' Alex replied. 'Maybe you should talk to that shrink of yours. Martin Travis, is it? Or what's the name of the new guy … Blake?'

'Yes, Blake Crawford. Would you mind if we popped in to see them before you leave? I need to speak to Martin Travis. He knows where Meg is. I'm going to ask him to set up a meeting in a neutral place, with him there. Meg trusts him. That's not too pushy is it? It's not weird is it?'

'No, of course it's not, Pete. It's perfectly reasonable that you want to speak to your wife. You need to know about the baby too. I'd say it's more than reasonable. Besides, the police will be contacting her about Glenn Elliot's murder — and Len's. They'll want to speak to her, she owns the house. You should contact Martin. I'll come with you.'

Alex took my hand again as we walked along the street. I liked the way she did that. It didn't mean anything, it wasn't a come-on or anything like that. It was … nice. She was nice, she'd always been like that.

All the time, while we were at the church and outside Meg's old house, we could see Blackpool Tower. Just like in the photos. It was as if we'd stepped back in time. I was picturing what the streets would have been like then. Fewer cars. The same amount of dog shit probably.

We sat down on a wall outside a corner shop. Alex popped in to buy a couple of chocolate bars while I emailed Martin Travis. I tried to be as conciliatory as possible, I didn't want a row with him. Surely he wouldn't block me this time. I got Alex to Bluetooth me her picture of the house and I added it to the end of the email. I hoped it would intrigue Martin, but he probably knew all about Meg's past already. They'd hit it off straight away when we were in counselling, she seemed to tell him everything.

It wasn't long before we were back on the promenade. The sounds of amplified music, screaming teenagers and mobile phone ring tones filled the air. It was Bedlam, but that's what you get when you visit a British seaside resort.

'What do you fancy doing then?' I asked Alex. 'We can't progress anything until we hear from your mate in the police or Martin gets back to me. Shall we go on some of the rides?'

'Hell, yeah!' Alex replied. 'How brave are you feeling?'

'Well, I've been for a shit today so I should be safe on most things. If you want to go on anything too scary, let's do it now before I eat. I'd rather do it on an empty stomach.'

'How about The Big One?' Alex asked.

'What here and now? In public? And how nice of you to show the reverence my penis so rightly deserves.'

More laughs. Her face lit up when she smiled. I hadn't realised how worn out she'd looked when she arrived. Serious. We'd been laughing a lot over the past couple of days. I'd forgotten how much we used to laugh. Despite all the shit that was going on, Alex helped me to forget it.

Fairground rides seem to get bigger, higher, faster and scarier all the time. There has to be a limit to the fear that humans can withstand. Alex took it in her stride, but I wanted to get off as soon as we started the high climb. It was too late. It was three minutes of bowel-loosening discomfort for me. I'm pleased I did it, but it was only going to be a one-time thing. And the queues too. We'd had to wait almost an hour to work through the long line of people.

I was ready for food once we stepped off the ride. My legs were unsteady, I was exhilarated but delighted to be back on the ground again. We filled up on grey, greasy burgers, half-cooked chips and a bucketful of cola.

'What do foreigners make of our food when they visit Britain?' I asked as I slurped the over-sweetened drink. There was no way I could finish it.

'We eat rubbish in this country. If I was a visitor from abroad, I'd ask for my money back. Think of the lovely food we eat on holiday and all we can offer is this crap.'

We walked back to the promenade. There was one of those giant Ferris wheels on the central pier.

'You ever been on one of those?' I asked Alex.

'I've been on the London Eye, it's great. Shall we go on this one? They're not too fast, we won't throw up our lunch.'

'If I throw up my lunch, it'll have nothing to do with the big wheel,' I laughed, and we started to make our way over to the pier.

We got a carriage to ourselves. I was pleased about that. Alex was able to remove her sunglasses since it was unlikely that she'd be noticed up there. Everybody was too busy admiring the spectacular views. It was a great place to stick a big wheel.

'Do you think it was because of the baby that we went our separate ways, Pete? Do you ever regret it?'

'Shit! Where had that come from? As we slowly rose higher and higher, people entered the carriages below us. Alex had taken the stillness to hijack me with that question. It was the killer question. The one that struck to the heart of our relationship.

'I don't know, Alex. I really don't know. It wasn't until after the murders and Meg left that I realised what an impact it had had on me. I thought I was over it, but it was affecting how I felt about me and Meg having a baby. I was scared.'

I'd never told anybody that before. I'd only recently admitted it to myself.

'I was wrong to go to London, Pete. We should have tried again. Losing the baby affected me more than I thought. It was weird. If it had been born and died, we'd have got more sympathy, but it was as if nothing had happened, people expected me to get over it. I felt I should get on with things, I hadn't lost a real baby. But it felt like a real baby to me, Pete. It was a baby to us, wasn't it?'

I nodded. It had come as crushing news at the time.

Maybe Alex was right. Perhaps we shouldn't have drifted as we did. Maybe we let things go too easily. We should have tried harder.

My thoughts were suddenly interrupted. Alex jumped up as if she'd been stung by a wasp. We were in motion again now, the ride had started properly, we were moving around. It took me a moment to figure out what was going on.

'Look! There, over there! He's following us. Look, Pete!'

I couldn't make sense of what she was saying. Alex was pointing wildly, she seemed to have spotted someone in one of the carriages.

'What Alex? What is it? What are you pointing at?'

'Look down there, he's almost opposite us, on the other side of the ride. Straight ahead, two carriages down. It's him. I'm sure it's him!'

I followed her pointing finger, still not sure what was going on. I looked in the carriage. There was a bloke on his own in there. Close cropped hair and a hoodie. He was wearing a black *I Love Blackpool* T-shirt, the same as Alex's. I'd never seen him before, but I didn't need Alex to tell me who it was.

It was JD. He'd followed us to Blackpool. Somehow. How had he known where we were? He was only metres away from us. At last I was going to get my chance to have it out with him.

───────

'How do we stop this thing?' I shouted. 'Does it have an emergency button or something?'

'Don't think it works like that, you have to get the attention of the guy who's operating it.'

'Quick! Can you get a photograph of him on your phone? I'm going to try to get the guy to stop the ride.'

We were beginning to slow down, the ride appeared to be coming to a stop. The young lad who was supposed to be in charge was talking to a teenager with her midriff barely contained by a pair of tight trousers and a T-shirt, which had either shrunk badly in the wash or was designed to half-heartedly cover up her breasts. Needless to say, he didn't give a toss about me. He studiously ignored me as we whizzed past: some crazy bloke in a carriage shouting 'Mate! Hey mate!' while he chatted her up.

Reluctantly, he was forced to pay some cursory attention as he began to let people out of the carriages. I looked below to figure out the order in which we'd be let off the ride.

'Bollocks, Alex. He's getting off before we do. The bastard will be well away by the time we get out. I'm going to try to climb out.'

'Damn, Pete, you'll break your neck! These cages are locked from the outside anyway. You'll never get out. They'd get jumpers all the time if they weren't locked, can you imagine the mess?'

'I looked at the locking mechanism on the carriage door. She was right. I could squeeze my fingers through the metal grille, but there was no way I would be able to slide the bolt upward then out of its retainer. We were shafted. We'd have to sit there and watch, admiring the views of Blackpool, while JD exited his carriage and walked off into the crowds.

'Are you sure it's him?'

I'd never seen the guy before. I wanted a good look so I'd recognise him in future.

'I'm as sure as I can be, Pete. He's dressed the same.

Same height, hair and look.'

'What are your photos like? Did you get anything?'

'They're terrible, Pete. We were too far away and moving too fast. They're blurs, although I got a lovely shot of the promenade.'

I was frustrated and not feeling very playful. It only took a small thing and I was completely unsettled again. The thought of this JD guy watching me, following me, waiting for … who knows what? Was he some weirdo, excited by my connection with the murders? Or was it more sinister than that? Either way, I wanted him scared off by the police.

My phone vibrated in my pocket. I took it out to see that I'd received a couple of texts.

One from Diane at work. Strange.

Hi Pete, sorry to disturb on your holiday. We've had an unusual visit at the station. A lady called Hannah Young. Very keen to speak to you. Says she knows Meg. Please call when you can, Diane

'Now this is interesting!'

I forgot all about JD and handed my phone to Alex so that she could read the text.

'Hannah Young. That's the person who placed the flowers on Sally's grave. It has to be Meg's sister, it's too much of a coincidence.'

Alex nodded and handed back the phone.

'Has he got off yet?' I asked, resigned now to JD getting away. 'Is it worth phoning the police?'

Alex looked over the side of the carriage.

'He's getting out now. I can try for a photo, see what I can get on zoom. I'll do my best to follow him in the crowd. He wants to get under your skin, Pete. He'd have done something by now if he was going to. He's trying to rattle you.'

'He's doing a good job of it!' I said, opening up the second text. It was Becky again. She was sounding increasingly unhinged. Please tell me I hadn't hooked up with a nutter.

Pete. Where are you? Police still at your caravan. Need to see you. Becky xxx

The next one had a photo attached. A picture of her breasts. Alex caught a glimpse of it.

Remember these Pete? They're all yours. Meet me. Where are you? Becky xxx

There was a third text from Becky. This was getting a bit more intense than I was comfortable with.

Where are you Pete? Can't find you on the site. Want to see you. Has that bitch friend of yours gone yet? Call me. Text me. Soon. Becky

No more pictures with that text. Shame. We'd agreed to meet again after Alex had left, it all seemed a bit strange to me. And, all of a sudden, Alex was being referred to as a bitch. This had all the makings of jealous girlfriend material. Only, we weren't an item, we'd had casual sex, a one-night stand.

'Whose were the tits?' Alex asked. 'Not your mum having trouble with her mobile phone again?'

I burst out laughing at that.

'Look, I'm going to tell you something. Please don't book me in for a chemical castration when I do, okay? I slept with that woman from the campsite the night before you came, the one you asked me about when we were talking to Vicky, but you guessed that bit already.

'I got lucky, she was young and hot. It was a one-time thing, although we did arrange to meet again after you'd gone. Only, she's getting a bit heavy now. She's going crazy because I moved caravans.'

'Have you told her where we moved to?'

'No, not yet.'

'Don't. Not with the break-in and Len's death. She might be a suspect for all we know.'

'I doubt it, Alex. She obviously can't get enough of me and is desperate for more. It's the effect I have on women.'

Alex gave me a playful kick.

'Funny that, I don't remember it!' she said, then immediately apologised.

'Sorry, Pete, I didn't mean that, even in jest. I loved being with you when we were together. Funny thing is, I can understand why she's getting like that. You're a nice guy, you know. You're a bit of a prat sometimes, you need to keep that cock of yours zipped up a bit more often. But there aren't a lot of guys like you around. Don't underestimate your powers over women.'

I was a bit shocked by that. It was a very nice thing to say. Especially from a woman who'd spent several years living with me. She knew me, warts and all. She'd experienced all of my bad habits. She was right about my cock. It kept landing me in trouble, I was slow to learn for a forty-year-old. But it wasn't easy, Becky was hot and she wanted me. It was a challenge to say no.

'I think I should--'

'There he goes!' Alex interrupted. 'He's off into the crowds. Lost him already. I'm doubting whether it's even him now. He didn't even look back. If it was JD, he'd be watching us, wouldn't he?'

'Who knows?' I answered, frustrated by the whole affair.

'I'll tell DCI Summers when I speak to her next. How would he even know we were here anyway?'

'Twitter, that's how!'

'What?'

'He knows exactly what we're up to because it's on Twitter. People have been taking sly photos all morning. If he's following me on Twitter, he knows exactly where we are.'

'What time were those photos taken? You're right, he could have driven or trained it down here, and he'd have known that we'd eventually be somewhere near the seafront. But surely not. It seems a bit secret service to me.'

'Look at my hashtag.' Alex showed me her phone. 'If you follow me via my hashtag, it's like a tracking system. A nutter could piece that together – maybe not everywhere, but in Blackpool it's simple enough. You can see that we're at the front now. I'll bet that's how he did it.'

'We're getting paranoid. You're not even certain it's him, are you? This is how they get to you, Alex. I saw what it did to Ellie. Tony Miller messed with her mind. It's what stalkers do.'

'Maybe you're right, Pete. What are you going to say to the tits lady? Becky, was it? I'd give her some answer, but don't tell her which caravan we're in. Will you see her again?'

'I'm thinking twice about it now, to be honest with you. I know you won't appreciate this as a woman, Alex, but she was hot. It's hard to say no. But she's beginning to sound a bit psycho now, I think I need to put her off. What should I say? Any tips?'

'Tell her the truth. Tell her that we're away overnight and that you can't see her. Say that you can't remember which caravan number you're in as it was a last-minute change. Give her some general location on the campsite.'

'Good idea,' I said. 'I'll tell her I know where it is,

but can't remember the plot number. That sounds convincing. Should I see her again?'

'I wouldn't disappear completely, not if she's a bit intense. It depends how you feel.'

'Much as I'm tempted to see her again, she leaves on Saturday. If I can avoid her until then, she'll be gone forever. I can block her on my phone. It might be a problem if Vicky offers me any more shifts in the bar, but if I can survive until the weekend, I'll be clear of her. Might get that picture of her tits framed, though.'

'I've been thinking about staying a bit longer, if that's okay? Maybe until the weekend. I know there's some weird stuff going on, but I'm having fun. I haven't had fun like this for a long time. Would that be alright?'

I didn't need to think about it.

'Of course it would! I love having you here. It's been great, especially with all that's going on. Stay as long as you like. I'll mention it to Vicky, I'm sure she'll be fine with an extra tenant. It's not like you're staying forever.'

'It's going to annoy Becky. Especially if you promised her a rematch. Are you okay with that?'

'Yeah, yeah. Come on, Alex. I know I'm a dickhead, but I'm not going to chase you away because I've got a chance to sleep with some woman that I only met the other night.'

Alex slapped my arm.

'Bastard!' she said, then gave me a kiss on the cheek. I did like having her around. It was good to have company while all this weird stuff was going on.

'I'm going to reply to Becky. I'll maybe block her number tonight when I can download a decent app over Wi-Fi.'

Hi Becky. Can't remember where my new caravan is, somewhere over the far side now. Sorry, I changed my plans. My friend is now staying until the weekend. We won't be able to meet up again. I enjoyed our time together. Enjoy the rest of your holiday. Pete

'Should I add a kiss at the end? Too much?'

'Maybe not, Pete. Or how about one? That would be okay, she uses enough of them.'

'Okay, one kiss. How about a dick pic? Too much?'

'Do you have super-zoom on that camera of yours? If not, best give it a miss!'

'Cow!' I laughed, then sent the text to Becky. Minus the dick pic.

I thought nothing more of it. I thought I'd be able to dispatch Becky with that one text and it would all be over. We were consenting adults, it was a casual encounter, I hadn't made any promises to her.

Only Becky had other things in mind. For her, it wasn't a casual encounter. She'd been watching me for some time. For Becky, that night had been the start of something special.

———

We woke up next day in the small hotel that we'd booked into on the seafront. It had felt a bit odd checking in, as Alex had kept her sunglasses on, even though it was dark outside.

'I don't want anybody tweeting that we're here. That's all we need, to find JD with a meat cleaver in the next room to us.'

'Jeez, Alex, you know how to put a man at ease!'

We booked in as Mr and Mrs Bailey, there was no need for us to sleep in separate rooms, we were pals.

'Twins or double?' I asked. 'No pressure for either, I just thought as … '

We'd spent our first two nights curled up on my bed, fully clothed, but comfortable in the other's company. I didn't want to assume anything.

'Twins!' Alex answered straight away.

She must have seen my face drop.

'I'm only kidding, Pete. Get a double again. Only no farting like you did the other night. Bet you didn't treat Becky like that.'

We made our way up several flights of stairs, which were lined with a dingy deep red carpet which had seen better days. Each room had heavy fire doors, and occasionally we'd hear the sound of a tinny TV as we passed by one of the rooms. Not my idea of a holiday, but it would do for the night. If the sheets were clean and there were no rats, it would be fine. We were both knackered and in need of sleep.

We'd taken great care to make sure that JD wasn't following us, ducking in and out of the attractions, separating and then meeting up again at pre-agreed places. There was no way he could have kept up with us, and with Alex now wearing her black cap to conceal her long hair, we were no longer aware of the selfie-takers spotting her then capturing that special moment with their camera.

We slept in until 9 o'clock and had to shower and get ready fast to catch breakfast, a traditional British fry-up. As we waited for our food, we sat in front of the large picture window, gazing out to sea as we came round from a good night's sleep.

'What do you think about this Hannah woman?' I asked. 'Do you think it could be Meg's sister? Why would she turn up now?'

'I don't know, Pete. Stranger things have happened. Did you email Diane last night? Has she got back to you?'

'Yes, nothing so far. She'll only just have got into the office. We can't do anything about it until we're back anyway. How about you, any replies?'

'No, all quiet. It'll take a while, I think. Anything about the house fire isn't likely to be on computer, although it may have been transferred over into a digital format. It's a waiting game. Are you going to call Kate Summers today – tell her about JD or whoever it was?'

'Yes, I will. If I'm honest, I don't really want to go back to the campsite. I've really enjoyed it here. I can see why you want to go to Spain, though – get away from the selfie-brigade. It's horrible, I don't know how you tolerate it.'

'It wasn't like that in the olden days. I met Peter Purves once. He used to be on Blue Peter in the seventies. He was a nice guy, we had a good chat. He told me it used to be completely different. People still recognised you, but they respected your privacy more – and they weren't taking photos all the time, either.'

'Well, it's a pain in the arse. I think you're very good with the punters. I reckon I'd get shirty with them after a while. It's an invasion of privacy. You can't do anything without someone watching you.'

'Did you think any more about coming to Spain with me, Pete? Only for a while. It's not only me who has to disappear, you know. You could come too. We still get on alright, don't we? It's been like old times doing this.'

'I've loved it, Alex. It's been great seeing you again. But I have to sort out what's happening with Meg. You don't just switch that stuff off unfortunately. I might have a kid. I can tell you something, though, you have made me decide one thing. I'm sorting everything with Meg. It's time to put it to bed.'

'Well, you know what I want, Pete. I know you have stuff to sort out, but this feels to me like what we should have done a long time ago. I shouldn't have gone to London. I know it was great for my career and everything, but we should have worked it out. You could have come with me. We didn't have to drift apart like that.'

I knew what she was driving at. Alex had made no secret of the fact that she regretted what we'd lost. She'd got her fabulous, shiny career, but it hadn't made her happy. I'd met Meg, and we'd had a life together while Alex was experiencing her meteoric rise in TV land. Sure, it had all gone tits-up, but I still loved Meg. I still owed her something, even if we were over. I might be a father, after all. I'd have to provide financial support, if nothing else. I'd want to see my own kid. What a mess.

The fry-up arrived. It was huge, more than any single human could possibly eat. My phone vibrated as I started to chew on the first bit of bacon. It was an email from Diane.

Hi Pete,

Hope you're well, so sorry to hear what's happened at the house. We're covering the story, of course, but I've sent out a memo telling the news team not to bother you. The national outlets have been chasing us for an interview too. Maybe we can do what we did last time – record one interview and distribute to all of the outlets. You decide, there's no rush, I understand how this must be worrying you.

I dealt with Hannah Young when she came into reception. She was very insistent that she speak to you. She's well educated, not aggressive or anything like that, but she knew how to rattle Pam, and you know how good a receptionist she is.

She gave me her email address and she's staying locally. I've attached the details in a document so that you can print it out. I don't think she's a journalist, she assured me it was a personal matter.

Hope you're enjoying your break, so sorry once again that you're having problems over at the house.

Take care,

Diane.

Hannah used a Hotmail address. There were no more clues about her name in there. I was hoping to see Yates in the address, but it was written as hannahy and a load of numbers. The 'y' stood for Young, I knew that already. I sent her an email, dropping mushrooms on my jeans as I tried to do two things at once.

'Bollocks,' I cursed, wiping the greasy mark off as best I could.

'The papers are still going big on the murders, Pete, it's all over the place. They've reprinted one of those photos on Twitter. Everybody in the country knows that you and I are in Blackpool now, but at least there aren't any new pictures of us. There's no way JD can know where we are.'

I was keen to see Hannah and find out what she wanted. Was she Meg's sister? If she'd left flowers at Sally's grave, she had to be connected in some way. Perhaps she was part of Sally and Jem's family, or it might be a dead end, but I wanted to know, and she was keen to meet me too.

Hi Hannah,

Diane Sawyer passed on your details. I'm very keen to meet, I'm back home this evening. How would 7pm be, in your hotel bar?

What's this in connection with, by the way?

Regards,

Peter Bailey

I used Peter. I thought it sounded more impressive.

It was a waiting game now, we needed some replies. Our plan was to finish off our breakfast, buy a couple of cheap T-shirts from the seaside shop along the road, and get changed in the hotel before checking out. Alex still had knickers to spare from her previous day's purchase, I'd need some new boxers.

As I'd anticipated, I could only eat about half of my giant fry-up. Alex ate even less. We sat at our window table checking our phones for news, updates from friends, emails and social media feeds. My phone vibrated again, it interrupted me as I watched the waves crashing out beyond the promenade.

'Damn, it's Becky!'

Alex looked up from her phone, waiting for me to tell her more. There was a video attached to the text. I clicked on it instinctively before reading the message. The hotel had dodgy Wi-Fi, it was taking a while to download. I read the message.

Screw you Pete and damn that bitch! You don't just ditch me like that. I want to see you again. Tell me where you are now. I want to meet you there. Look what I've got btw. Wouldn't want anyone seeing that would we? Becky xxxxxxxxx

I got a bad feeling about this. She'd taken my rejection badly. The progress bar on the video showed that the download was complete and I opened it up. The other guests turned towards me as the sounds of a couple having sex came from my phone. I couldn't find the volume control, I was too stunned by what I was seeing.

It was me and Becky in my caravan. On the bed. She was wearing the masquerade mask, her tattoo clearly visible on her neck, her long red hair falling over her face. She was moving gently up and down, all you could hear was the sound of our groans as we slowly moved to climax.

'Take off your mask,' she said in the video, and there it was, clear as day: my face right on the screen, completely naked, having sex with a masked Becky.

She had to have set that up. I'd been lured into a trap and now she was going to blackmail me.

Chapter Thirteen

There was no hiding it. Everybody in the dining area had heard the sounds of my encounter with Becky. I finally managed to turn down the volume on my phone. I felt as if everybody was staring at me. After a few seconds, the hubbub returned to the room.

'I daren't even ask you what that was.'

Alex looked at me, waiting for my answer. I steeled myself to tell her. I knew she wouldn't give me a hard time over it, but I was shocked.

'It was Becky. Looks like I got my reply. She doesn't want to cool things off. She's threatening to share it online. She wants to see me again.'

'Can I look? Not at the video – I got the idea – at the text.'

'Sure, please don't play that video again.'

I handed Alex the phone. My face was burning red with embarrassment.

'That's certainly you on the video. I can see from the thumbnail image. Wonder if Diane would like to use that shot for your new publicity photograph: Peter Bailey, newsreader, relaxes at home. Not quite a Hello! photo shoot, is it?'

I didn't know whether to laugh or cry. Where had

Becky put that phone? Actually, it didn't take much figuring out, I just hadn't seen it. I hadn't even been looking for it. She must have set it up when she moved through to the bedroom. I think my trousers were tangled around my legs at the time.

'I think you're going to have to see her, Pete. Who knows how many copies there are? You could be backed up into the cloud already, it's so difficult to destroy these things nowadays. What do you think she wants?'

'It can't be a replay. Even I don't flatter myself that I'm that good in bed. Maybe she's annoyed that I haven't got back to her. Surely she'd have known the score. It was a one-night stand, a casual thing. There's no reason for her to expect an engagement ring, is there?'

'What is it with you and one-night stands, Pete? I hope the irony hasn't been lost on you. First Ellie, now Becky. This is God telling you to zip up and keep your boxers on. Maybe you should give monogamy a try sometime?'

I felt a momentary sting of judgment. That was unusual for Alex. I'd been faithful to her when we were together. I hadn't even thought about looking elsewhere, it never even occurred to me at the time. It was the same with Meg. When we were first married, I was happy. It was only when our IVF problems came along and things started to get difficult that I slept with Ellie in a moment of weakness.

Was Becky the same? I didn't think so. I was lonely, I missed Meg's company, although I was furious with her and not at all sure if we even had a marriage left. I'd slept with Becky because I was desperate for company. It didn't hurt that she was hot for me and had made no attempt to disguise it.

I was beginning to doubt myself and my judgment. Alex was right, it was in my lapses that I messed things up. Ellie was nice, she was no psycho, we were still friends. It was her stalker friend who'd caused all the problems in that scenario. Becky had seemed fine too. She didn't appear to be crazy, even if her sexual tastes were a bit exotic. But here she was, making a thinly veiled threat to release a sex tape. I had my own sex tape! Maybe I should be proud, I was finally a Z-list celebrity with my own porno.

'What do you think I should do? Will it make things worse if I see her again? I don't mean sleep with her. We can't do that again, not now. But I wonder if it will calm things down if I meet her?'

'She hasn't actually leaked the thing yet, Pete, it's only a threat. This text isn't quite at the blackmail stage. She doesn't want money. I could send it to the digital forensics woman that we use on the TV show, see if she can trace the user account and get it blocked … '

'Don't send it with the video, Alex. That's all I need doing the rounds. There's no way she'd keep that to herself, I know what the cops are like. Besides, I don't want anyone else seeing that. These HD phones … we might as well have had a film crew in there, the image is so clear.'

'I can forward it without the video. Maybe she can trace the source of the text, get a proper home address for Becky or something like that?'

'We know who sent it, though, that's no mystery. She wants to meet me again. I think she's angry that I gave her the brush-off. Filming us making love without my consent, that's got to be illegal, isn't it? Sharing it online is revenge porn, we did some reports on the radio about it, I know that much.'

'The thing is, Pete. If she shares it, you're closing the stable door after the horse has bolted. If everybody's seen it, it's kind of too late, isn't it? I think you've got to see this woman. Record the conversation with her on your phone. Make sure that she drops herself in it when she's talking to you. That should frighten her off.'

I considered the prospect for a moment. I didn't really have a choice. Had Becky not made the threat and got all heavy on me, I'd have been quite happy to meet up again after Alex had departed, have a rerun of our sexual encounter, then see her off on the Saturday at the end of her holiday. Why had she gone all wacko on me? I'd told her that we could meet again after Alex had left. Although Alex was right. With her stay extended, I had given Becky the brush-off.

'I'm going to have to meet her, I don't see that I have any choice. I'm really annoyed at this video, she has me over a barrel with that. Why did she have to film it? It makes the whole thing complicated.'

I took the phone back from Alex and started to key in my response. I didn't want to inflame the situation any more. I decided to hold up my hands and let her know where my new caravan was located. I needed to put an end to this thing.

I tapped in my reply, going back to delete a couple of times while I chose the right words.

Hi Becky, so sorry, I've been distracted. Happy to meet with you again. I'm away at the moment, but how about I see you in the bar tonight? 9pm?

Should I say anything about the video? I decided against it, it might inflame things even more. I'd give her what she wanted. I agreed to the meeting. Surely that would calm her down? I handed the message to Alex for approval.

'Yes, that's fine, Pete. Sign it off, maybe add in another apology. Don't type in any kisses. What will you do if she wants a rerun?'

The thought of more sex with Becky wasn't the worst prospect in the world, but her recent text messages had put a bit of a dampener on things. Would I go through with it, if it helped to defuse the situation? I'd be checking for a phone next time, that's for sure. It would make things worse. If she was like that after a first encounter, I'd be asking for trouble if I did it again.

'I've got to put her off. I need to get her to delete the video. I may have to lead her on a bit to make sure it's gone. Problem is, she could have a hundred copies of the thing by now. Once it's in the cloud, it's backed up in all sorts of ways. She might delete it on her phone, but that won't mean it's gone.'

I signed off the text.

Sorry again for being so distracted, I have a lot going on. Didn't mean to be distant or rude. Looking forward to seeing you again, Pete

Who knew what she'd read into it? It seemed vanilla enough, Alex was happy with it. I clicked on Send. I'd gone off my breakfast now.

'Have you finished your meal?' the waitress asked. She was trying to wipe a smirk off her face, she could see that we'd been discussing the video, the one that everybody in the dining room had heard.

'We're done, thank you,' Alex informed her. 'Shall we get packed up and checked out now, Pete?'

I nodded. I was almost reluctant to stand up. I knew that when I did the day would start properly. With two new bodies, JD, Becky going psycho on me and this Hannah woman doing the rounds, I felt as if I was right back where I'd been six months previously. I couldn't put my finger on it at the time, but I could feel things coming to a head. I'd have stayed there and asked for more toast if I'd known how that day was going to end.

———

The train out of Blackpool was very different to the one we'd taken on our earlier journey. We'd missed the morning rush, there weren't many people on board, and we had a table seat to ourselves. Alex kept her cap on and her hair tied back, it seemed to make her more invisible to the crowds.

I was becoming paranoid. I kept looking for JD, I checked the train twice. I had a go at some poor teenager in a hoodie and an *I Love Blackpool* T-shirt. Poor kid, he was with his girlfriend. I think he thought I was going to punch him. I apologised immediately when I saw his face. That was no JD, he'd nearly shat himself when I sounded off. I gave them twenty quid, which I couldn't really afford, to spend on getting lunch together, and I returned to my seat embarrassed and angry with myself.

'I don't even know what he looks like,' I cursed. 'I'm beginning to think that I'm a complete and utter prick!'

'Just a complete prick, Pete. No need to worry right now. I told you, he's not on the train. Calm down. Whoever he is, at least he's not violent. He's probably some socially inadequate, shy guy. He'll be easily frightened off once we work out who he is.'

I shuffled in my seat and took a swig of the coffee that I'd bought on the station platform. I'd even resorted to black coffee, that's how bad things were. My phone vibrated in my pocket. It was a message from

Hannah. At last, some progress.

'It's Hannah,' I said to Alex, moving my phone into the middle of the table so that we could read it together.

Hi Peter,

Thank you for getting back to me so quickly.

Happy to meet this evening. I'm staying at the Pine Trees Guest Lodge on the edge of town, they have a small lounge there. I'll meet you in the lobby at 7pm.

Regards,

Hannah Young

'She completely ignored my question about why she wants to meet up,' I remarked.

'Do you still think that she's Meg's sister? She could be married, it could be Hannah Yates. You've got to meet her, Pete, see what she wants.'

'I'm going to email her back and ask her what it's in connection with. I can't wait until 8 o' clock. She might be a journalist or another nutter for all I know.'

'Good point, I hadn't thought about her being a journalist. If she's after a scoop, you'd best stay wary. Fair enough, email her back, see what she wants.'

'Anything about Blackpool yet from that contact of yours?' I asked as I replied to Hannah's email. She was using a Hotmail address, there was no indication of her being connected with a newspaper or magazine. Although if Hannah were a journalist, she wouldn't make a rookie mistake like that.

'My signal is really bad out here,' Alex replied, trying her phone again. 'I'll keep an eye on it, but it's only work stuff at the moment.'

'Oh yes, anything interesting?'

'Only fallout from my leaving the show. A couple of magazines wanting interviews, the usual crap. My agent has a few offers in, nobody is supposed to know, but the word is out already in agent circles.'

'Will you take something, or will you carry on with your sabbatical plans?'

'I want a break, Pete. At least I'm getting offers, I won't be out of work for too long. I'll take a few months off, and then line up something new for the end of the year. What about you, any more thoughts about that job?'

'I'd like to go and see Martin Travis when we get back, before we return to the caravan. He's the only one who knows where Meg is, they've been in contact since we split up. I'm going to put pressure on him. I have to talk to Meg. She must have seen what's going on in the papers. She can't ignore it.'

'DCI Summers must have been in touch with her too, but she won't tell you where Meg is, not if you're estranged. Is that what you are? Estranged ... separated ... how would you describe it?'

'You'd have to ask Meg. But you're right, Kate Summers is too by-the-book to divulge Meg's whereabouts – if she's been able to track her down, that is.'

The journey passed quickly. I was absorbed in my own thoughts for much of the time. I was nervous about Becky getting back in touch, anxious to see what Hannah wanted, and worried about JD. If it wasn't for JD, things would be more straightforward. We could make a couple of visits before retrieving the car; the police station and Martin's office were fairly central, it was easier to walk.

I asked for DCI Summers when we arrived at the police station. I felt that she'd take the JD situation seriously. She was in, that was lucky. Probably bogged down with murder investigation meetings. She looked serious when she came to meet us in reception and escorted us to an interview room.

'Do you have any idea where your wife is, Mr Bailey? We've been unable to locate her. Are you still in touch?'

'I don't know where she is. Have you tried the probation service? She was getting a transfer as far as I knew.'

'We've tried them already. She resigned her post, she didn't transfer. I shouldn't really be telling you that. We can't find a record of her anywhere: no address, no job, no bank account. She's disappeared into thin air.'

I didn't know what to say. I hadn't expected that. She was pregnant last time we spoke. How had she managed to survive without her job?

'Have you spoken to Martin Travis yet? I'm on my way to see him myself. He's in contact with her still. He should be able to tell you where she is.'

'Yes, Mr Travis is coming in later. We only need to speak to your wife to corroborate some of our information, but we would like to find her. May I ask why you separated, Mr Bailey? We can speak alone, if you prefer. This is just an informal question.'

I hadn't expected that. She must have seen it in my face.

'Things were a bit tense after the murders,' I replied. 'Meg needed some space. I figured I'd let her have it, but we haven't spoken for some time now. I'm as keen to find her as you are.'

We exchanged updates. They had no leads on the break-in and murder at the house. Len's death in the caravan seemed to have reached the same dead end. The police were following up leads, but it was a holiday camp, everybody was a stranger there. Kate Summers believed that Len had disturbed somebody. It might have been a routine break-in gone bad. My gut told me that it was more than that. The storm seemed to have me at its centre, I could see that. I wondered for a moment if it was time to mention Becky. No, that was only a casual thing, there was no way she could be involved with what had happened to Len.

By the time we'd finished discussing our sighting of JD in Blackpool, I'd convinced myself that we must have been wrong. DCI Summers asked us so many questions about the episode, I felt like some crank who was reporting the sighting of a flying saucer. We were probably being paranoid. It was unlikely that he could have followed us to Blackpool.

She advised us to be wary of social media. With Alex in tow, that might be difficult.

My phone vibrated. It was Becky. I had no intention of sharing details of my sex tape with DCI Summers. That had to stay between me, Alex and Becky for now. I wasn't involving the police. There was no way that was staying private if they got involved, they'd all be watching it in the office.

I opened up Becky's latest text, hoping that I would have appeased her and calmed the situation down a bit.

'Is everything alright, Mr Bailey? You look like you've had a shock.'

'It's fine, DCI Summers, it's a weird text from my mum. You know what these pensioners are like! We'll need to be on our way, if that's okay? I have a couple of errands to run in town.'

She could see that things were definitely not okay, but she had no reason to stop me.

'That's fine, Mr Bailey, we'll be in touch if we have any more information for you.'

Alex had taken my cue and we were standing up to

leave.

'Oh, by the way, Mr Bailey. I almost forgot. We found your photographs. They'd been dumped in one of the bins on the caravan site. No fingerprints that we could use, I'm afraid. Vicky Walters is holding them for you at the campsite. You can collect them from the office.'

'Thank you, DCI Summers, we'll do that as soon as we get home,' I said, and ushered Alex towards the door.

'What was all that about?' Alex asked, as we exited the police station. 'You left that room like you'd farted and you wanted to get out before she smelled it!'

'Something like that,' I said taking my phone out of my pocket.

'Look, Becky got back to me. See what she says.'

'Oh fuck!' Alex replied as she read the words on the screen. But it was the attached picture that was even more alarming.

At last Pete, but the bitch has to go. Recognise these? They're all yours. I want this to be me and you. Want to meet. Your house. Tonight. 7pm. No masks this time :-) Becky x

Below the text message was one of those animated images that people post everywhere on social media. It was Becky sitting on the windowsill in the bedroom that Meg and I had once shared. Her legs were parted, her top raised up to reveal her breasts. There was the shadow of somebody else in the image, they were about to move into the frame. It was a man, but I couldn't see who it was, he was not even fully in the shot.

So Becky's intentions were clear. I wasn't going to get away with fobbing her off. This was some weird game that she wanted me to play and she had me over a barrel.

––––––––––––––––––

At the time I didn't even think of telling DCI Kate Summers about Becky. It was a private matter, a one-night stand. The video hadn't been leaked, Becky was just angry with me – and a bit kinky too, by the look of it.

I was concerned about the posing in my bedroom window. That suggested that she knew who I was. Had she sought me out on the camp? Perhaps she was some sexual thrill-seeker.

Deploying my usual good judgment in these matters, I had to admit to being excited by the prospect. Sure, I was concerned about Becky being a bunny boiler, but she hadn't seemed like that to me. I like to think that I can spot a crazy person. She wasn't mad, she was highly sexed and not at all vanilla in her sexual preferences.

Alex could see my mind working.

'You're actually considering it, aren't you, Pete? Do you never learn?'

I felt ashamed for a moment and then annoyed, as if I'd been caught by my parents reading a dirty magazine.

'It might get rid of her. And she's very attractive, you know. You can't tell me that you've never slept with someone you knew was bad news, but come back for second helpings?'

For the first time, I picked up jealousy from Alex. I'd never seen it from her before. I'm not very good at interpreting these things, but I'm certain that it was jealousy.

'In actual fact, no, Pete. I haven't ever gone back for second helpings, as you call it. You were my second!'

Another surprise. I couldn't remember if I knew that

already. Had we discussed previous sexual partners when we were together? We must have done. Maybe it had seemed less important when we were younger.

'You must have had partners since. Those footballers aren't really keepers, are they? I mean, they're not renowned for their intellectual capacity.'

Was I still prickly about who Alex had slept with since we'd broken up? Why did I even care? It was ages ago. It was none of my business.

'I don't sleep with footballers, Pete. These days, if you must know, I tend to use a very discreet and far-too-expensive escort service. It was recommended to me by Gloria Boardman. It's quite hard to form a decent relationship when you're in the spotlight all the time. I don't even do it for the sex. It's the company I like, without the fear of everything ending up on the internet.'

'What, Gloria Boardman off Lunchtime Bites? She's far too respectable to use escorts … isn't she?'

'I think you're missing the point, Pete.'

Even Alex was mad with me now. I couldn't see what she was getting at. I wasn't going to judge her if she used male escorts, it wasn't as if I was the moral compass in our relationship.

'Look, I tell you what, Pete. You go and see your Martin Travis chap, I'm going to go into town, see if I can get a few bits of clothing to keep me going until I leave. Is it still okay if I stay a bit longer?'

'Yeah, of course … if you want to?'

I wasn't sure if I'd done something wrong. One minute it had all been about Becky, the next minute it seemed to be all about Alex. There was something hanging in the air, half an hour apart might not be such a bad idea.

'Okay, text me when you're done,' I said. 'And sorry. Sorry, if I said anything wrong. I didn't mean it.'

'It's okay, Pete. I've known you long enough. It's just me, forget it. I'll see you later, good luck with Martin!'

She gave me a peck on the cheek and headed off towards the city centre, still wearing that *I Love Blackpool* cap. When it comes to disguises, I'd never have thought that a bit of tourist tat could be so effective.

Alex was right, there was no way I could sleep with Becky again, however tempted I was. I'd have to end it there and then, tell her I'd report her to the police if she didn't stop threatening me. I had her text message as evidence. I'd give her one more chance, try and end things nicely, then talk to DCI Summers in confidence if she wouldn't play ball.

I sent a reply text to Becky.

Hi Becky, see you there at 7pm, Pete

I was sure that Alex would approve. No hint of promise in there, only a confirmation of our arrangement. No kisses at the end of the message. I couldn't be accused of leading her on. I'd end it, no messing around. I'd ask her to delete the video. I'd get assertive if I had to. But I couldn't risk it with Becky, it was all getting a bit too intense.

Bollocks! I'd fixed my meeting with Becky at the same time as I was due to meet with Hannah Young. Much as I wanted to meet with Hannah, Becky was the more pressing matter.

I hastily typed an email to Hannah.

Hi Hannah,

Sorry, got to rearrange our meeting this evening. Earlier or later, but not 7pm now. Before we fix a new time, can you confirm what this is in connection with? Thanks,

Peter Bailey

I'd maybe catch Hannah later, if I still wanted to meet with her. Perhaps I'd got a bit carried away with the whole Blackpool thing, maybe it was too big a leap for her to be the Hannah in those pictures. She was probably a journalist, trying to get the scoop on the recent deaths.

It took me about a quarter of an hour to reach Martin's office. I was hot and sweaty by the time I got there. It reminded me of that night when I'd had to climb up the drainpipe to enter the building. I'd thought I was coming to rescue Meg, but it had been one episode in a very sad and violent evening. I'd have to remember how honourably Martin had acted that night, he'd even been shot with that air pistol that Sally was carrying. Poor guy, there was not a lot of warmth between us, but he had at least been a friend to Meg.

I passed by reception with no challenge. They were used to me being in and out of the building. First Meg and I came to marriage counselling with Martin, now it was one-to-one counselling with Blake Crawford. I hoped I wouldn't run into Blake in the corridors. We didn't have an appointment, he'd know I was there for Martin.

Their offices were on the upper floor. I popped into the gents, it's always best to have a confrontation on an empty bladder. I couldn't believe my luck. Martin came in for a pee and stood right next to me.

'Martin,' I said, keeping a firm fix on his face, while shaking and zipping up.

'What brings you here? Have you got an appointment with Blake?' he asked.

'No, actually, I was hoping to catch you … Have the police been in touch yet?'

'I've seen what's been going on, Pete. It's all over the

news. I even had your radio station chasing me for an interview about what happened last time. Can't you tell them to back off? I want to put it all behind me.'

'Me too. Me too, Martin. I'll have a word with the news team, I know how you feel. Have you heard from the police?'

'Yeah, I'm popping over to the station during my lunch break, some woman called Kate Sumners, something like that.'

'Summers,' I corrected him. 'She's going to ask you about Meg. They need to speak to her about the murder at the house. She's still a joint owner and all that. Did you know she'd left the probation service, Martin? When were you going to tell me that?'

His face changed. He finished drying his hands on a paper towel, then threw it into the bin.

'I beg your pardon?' he said, staring intently at me.

'You must know that Meg left the probation service? Kate Summers told me. They can't trace her.'

'Shit!' came Martin's reply.

'If there's something you're not telling me, Martin, I need to know. Come on, I have to talk to Meg. We have to get this all sorted out once and for all. You can be the mediator if you want to – if she prefers it that way. But we've got to get the house sorted out, I need to know what happened with the baby.'

Martin looked at me as if he was trying to work out if I was trying to catch him out.

'To be honest with you, that makes sense, Pete. I know I'm supposed to respect client confidentiality and all that, but … '

He stalled. This was testing him. Martin was a stickler for the rules.

'Come on, Martin. What is it? If there's something I

need to know, tell me. I'm her husband.'

'Look, you mustn't let Blake know that I told you this. I could lose my job. The truth is, I was in contact with Meg. By email. She told me the same thing as you, I thought she was transferring jobs.'

'Did she tell you, Martin? Did you find out if it was Jem's baby? Come on, man. I need to know this stuff. I could be the father!'

He looked down at his feet, then met my gaze.

'The truth is, Pete, I haven't heard from Meg in four months. It all went quiet. I tried to get her to talk to you, but she was having none of it.'

I believed him. I didn't particularly like Martin Travis, but I thought that he was a trustworthy man.

'Do you have any idea where she is, Martin? The police are going to ask you exactly the same thing. Where is she?'

'I don't know. I didn't have an address or anything like that. We rarely texted, we usually communicated via email. But she did mention somewhere once. She gave it away by accident. She mentioned a hospital and I looked it up. It was easy enough to find.'

'Where was it, Martin? I need to get an idea where she is.'

'It was called Queen Elizabeth Hospital. There are lots of those, I couldn't tell where she was from that information, but she let it slip in another email – I could tell where she was.'

He paused and I looked at him, urging him to spit it out.

'So where was it? Come on, where was she?'

'It was a place called Bispham. I'd never heard of it before, I had to look it up online. But there it was:

Queen Elizabeth Hospital in Bispham. It's in Blackpool,
Pete. Meg's in Blackpool.'

Chapter Fourteen

So I'd been in the same town as Meg that very day. It would still be like looking for a needle in haystack, but Blackpool wasn't so bad. She'd returned to her home town, the town that she'd never bothered to mention to me, other than in passing.

That place must have held so many horrible memories for her, I wondered what had made her go back. In truth, I was no further forward – I still didn't have an address for her. But I did have the name of a hospital, that was a start, only I'd hit the same old nonsense about privacy. There was no way they'd let me near Meg's personal records. I'd tell DCI Summers and let her work it out. At least now I had a geographical location to shoot for.

'Why did you stop emailing, Martin? Did something go wrong?'

'We fell out over you, actually. I told her that you'd been putting pressure on me to find her and that she should arrange a meeting, if only to put you out of your misery. She was having none of it, said she had some important things to sort out first. She had a real go at me when I pushed her about the baby. That's when she stopped speaking to me.'

I sighed. What was Meg up to? Why had she cut herself off like that? I wasn't the enemy.

'Okay, Martin. Thanks, look I appreciate you telling me that. Is she still using the same email address? I keep getting bounces from her old one.'

'Yes, Pete. She's got an new email address, but you know I can't tell you what it is.'

There was a shuffle in one of the toilet cubicles and the sound of toilet paper being torn. Damn, someone had been in the toilets with us. I hadn't even thought to check the traps. There was a flush and the sound of the lock being drawn back. Blake Crawford stepped out.

Bollocks, that's all we needed. Blake Crawford was the worst person who could have been listening in on that conversation. I didn't handle the embarrassment particularly well.

'Good shit, Blake?'

'Martin, wait in my office please, we need to talk. Pete, I have asked you repeatedly not to push Martin about Meg's whereabouts. Now I've heard it all. You and I will need to cancel our future appointments pending a review of what Martin has discussed with you here. I'd like you to leave the building now please.'

Martin slunk off, no doubt for a bollocking in the headmaster's office. He had that look about him, the pupil about to be hauled over the coals.

'If you would leave now, please?'

'Okay, don't be hard on Martin, Blake. He's a good guy. I put him under a lot of pressure. And remember to wash your hands, please. It prevents germs spreading, you know.'

I left the toilets and Blake watched me head down the stairs. It was a long time since I'd been asked to leave anywhere. In fact, I was a teenager when it last happened. A friend had recently passed his driving test and I was messing about in the back of the car. He was a bit nervous, I wouldn't quieten down, so he asked me to get out. I had to walk five miles home.

That's how Blake had made me feel: embarrassed, caught in the act with no way out of it and still save face. Poor Martin, I hoped he wasn't in too much trouble.

I stepped out of the building and pulled out my phone. Nothing from Alex. Had I really annoyed her? It wasn't turning out to be one of my most diplomatic days. Where was she?

There was an email from Hannah. I opened it up eagerly.

Hi Pete,

Sorry you can't make our meeting at 7. Could do it earlier, say 6.15pm? I'm not press btw, this is about a personal matter. I promise you, not press. Would prefer to talk face to face,

Hannah

Excellent! Yes, I could do it earlier, but I'd need to head back home first. I needed a shave, I hadn't bothered taking a razor to Blackpool. I wanted to freshen up too, and get the photos from Vicky. I'd take those for Hannah to look at. She'd described it as a personal matter. That was encouraging. But where was Alex? I needed to get back home.

I texted her, then went old fashioned and dialled her directly. Nothing. Alex was good with her phone, not one of these people who carries it around then completely ignores it when it actually rings. I left her a voice message.

Hi Alex, I hope you're not fed up with me? It didn't go brilliantly with Martin, I think I got him into trouble. Look, if I said something, please let me know. I'm sorry if I put my foot in

*it. I have to go back to the caravan now, I've rearranged my
meeting with Hannah. I'll speak to her, then finish things with
Becky. Can you get a taxi back? Unless you pick up this message
before I get back to the car. Sorry to dump you like this, but I
need to get home now. Hope you catch this before I leave, see you
later!*

I rang off. Alex wasn't the moody type, unless she'd
changed in the years that we'd been apart. People don't
change that much. I couldn't recall her ever going off in
a huff. She was nice and straightforward, there were no
mind games or any of that nonsense.

I replied to Hannah, told her I'd have to be there
earlier, at 6 o'clock, and that I'd have to make it brief. I
was intrigued. What might a personal matter be? I still
suspected that she was from the papers, they're devils
like that. They lure you onto the hook with a bit of
bread then jerk the fishing rod so the hook gets lodged
in your mouth and you can't get away. I'd be wary, but I
was definitely turning up for that meeting.

I kept my phone in my hand as I walked through the
city, making my way to the station car park. I was
hoping I'd hear from Alex, but there was nothing. She
wasn't waiting by the car either. I tried her phone again.
Another text, then a final voice message. I felt awful
leaving her to take a taxi, but I was keen to get back to
the caravan. She hadn't really left me with a choice, she
should have answered her phone.

Reluctantly, I got in the car and drove away, looking
out for her in the distance. I felt unsettled all the way
back to the site. My phone didn't vibrate or ring, there
was no word from Alex. Half an hour we'd said, but it
had been almost two hours since we'd gone our separate
ways.

I replayed the conversation in my head. At worst, I'd

been a bit insensitive. She'd confided in me that she was using male escorts from time to time. She'd been trying to tell me that she was lonely. Why would a woman as good-looking as she was use escorts? Because she felt isolated, Pete, that's why, you idiot! She was reaching out to you, confiding in you. She's unhappy, you dickhead.

Alex had been trying to connect with me for the entire visit. The penny dropped. Way too late as usual. I'd assumed everything was cool with her, she seemed to have it all: the TV career, the glamorous events, the articles in magazines. But she was feeling isolated by everything, that's what she'd been saying to me. It's why she'd wanted to sleep in the same bed as me. She wanted a companion, one she didn't have to pay for his company and discretion.

I felt the weight of guilt in my stomach. It was the realisation that I'd completely missed the point. How bad must it have got for Alex to leave her job and admit her loneliness to me? I had a sudden thought, but I dismissed it immediately. Surely she wouldn't have done something stupid, would she? No, not Alex, there was no way she'd do that.

I called her again.

Alex, it's me again. Though you knew that already. I'm guessing you recognised the voice? You'd make such a great detective …

Stop stalling, Pete. Apologise. Just spit it out.

Look, I realised what a prat I've been. I'm so sorry, Alex. I'm really sorry. Come back to the campsite, I'll get Hannah and Becky sorted out, then let's go out and eat. Let's talk. I'll be listening this time, honestly. I get it now. I'm sorry, Alex. I'm such a dickhead sometimes. Please text me or phone when you get this. Let me know you're okay. Love you.

I did love Alex. Not like that. We'd spent years of our lives together, we'd always loved each other. It started with us being friends and that's how it was now. We'd been lovers in between. That was over now, but we still cared deeply about each other. I hoped she'd call back. Soon.

Unusually, Vicky wasn't in her office. At that time of day, with the bars closed and the punters off on day-trips, she'd normally have been seen at her office window, wading through paperwork.

I peered through the glass. There was no sign of her. The office was a mess. Something wasn't right. I walked through the main entrance and took a left towards Vicky's office. It was all quiet. Late afternoons were the dead zone for the Golden Beaches Holiday Park.

'Vicky? Are you in here?' I asked, opening the door slowly. 'It's me, Pete.'

There were papers all over the floor. The place looked as if it had been ransacked, either that or Vicky had been reading a feng shui book upside down. My eyes picked out the photos that I'd found in the lock-up. They were strewn all over the floor, like all the other paperwork. Vicky's phone was flashing where several messages had been left unanswered. She'd been gone for some time. Had there been a break-in?

My hand hovered over the phone, wondering whether to call the police. As I moved towards Vicky's desk, I saw what they'd come for. Customer contact cards were thrown all over the place, but it was my own which was lying on top of the untidy pile. Whoever had been here had been looking for me. They wanted to know which caravan I was in.

Was this Becky's work? We'd agreed to meet at the house, so why would she do something like this? I'm no great judge of character, but she seemed sane enough to me. A touch Fatal Attraction perhaps, but I was certain that she was no nutter, not in the knocking-people-over-the-head-and-killing-them way.

I needed to find Vicky. I had to check my caravan. I gathered up my photos and rushed back to the car. It would be quicker walking rather than sticking to the 10mph limit and having to drive over the humps. I hurried back to the caravan as fast as I could. The door was open and a key was in the lock. It was one from the office, it had the blue key fob attached to it. Whoever had been in Vicky's office had helped themselves.

I was almost scared to walk in. Last time this had happened, we'd found Len's body. This had to be connected with me now, I couldn't kid myself that these were random events.

The lounge looked fine, exactly as we'd left it. I walked along the hallway that ran down the length of the caravan, glancing in at the bedrooms, until I reached my own.

'Oh Jesus!'

It was Vicky, lying on the bed with her throat cut. The white quilt cover was stained with blood. There was so much of it, how could there be so much blood? I began to sob.

She was wearing a Venetian mask, one that I'd seen once before. It was the same one that I'd been wearing in Becky's video. This had to be Becky's work. How had I missed that? She seemed okay, perfectly normal, why would she kill Vicky? Why had she gone totally psycho on me?

Stupidly, I ran through all the things that you see people doing on the TV. I felt for a pulse, but there was no way that Vicky was alive.

I removed the mask from Vicky's face, at least I'd give her that dignity. I felt the crushing weight of guilt. Why did I bring so much pain into people's lives?

I reached for my phone. I'd need to call the police. For the second time, the cops and the medics would be surrounding one of the caravans on the park. The press would have a field day.

I sat on the bed next to Vicky, avoiding the bloodstain that was covering much of the quilt. I'd seen this scenario before. I felt sick, faint and exhausted, but my mind was steady. I knew what had to be done. I felt strangely calm and still.

I checked my messages first. Hannah had confirmed receipt of my short email, saying that she'd see me at about six o'clock in the bar. I read it quickly and then saw that I'd got a text from Alex. It almost got deleted in my rush to read it. It had a photo attached.

If you want to see ur bitch alive again, tell no one what you've seen. Go to the police and your bitch dies. You see Becky tonight and you wait for me to tell you where to take her. I've got your bitch you fucker!

This time, I did throw up my guts. All over Vicky's bloodied body. I couldn't even give her that in death – I had to mess up the evidence too.

The photo was Alex. She looked petrified, her right eye was blackened. She'd been hit, hard by the look of it. She was still wearing that Blackpool cap. Her mouth was taped and she was in some dimly lit area.

Was this from Becky? No, it couldn't be – the text message told me to meet her as we'd planned. It had to be JD. He was the only other nutter in circulation. Like Ellie's stalker, he'd waited in the shadows and then turned out to be a killer. This had to be JD's work. It was me he was after. But why? What had I ever done to this madman? I didn't even know what he looked like. I couldn't give the police a description.

I hadn't got a clue what to do. I had to move from the bedroom. The smell of my vomit was disgusting, and dead bodies do horrible things that nobody ever speaks about.

I realised that I'd fouled up the crime scene nicely. DCI Summers wouldn't be offering me a job, that was for sure. Well, I knew who it was, it was JD. There was no sleuthing to be done, it would be an open-and-shut case.

I had to help Alex. JD must have snatched her on the street, that's why she hadn't got back to me. It was that weekend in Newcastle all over again: the deception, the lies, the violence. It was happening again. This time it was Alex who I'd placed in peril, rather than Meg. All because I couldn't keep my dick in my pants.

I considered phoning the police again. Would it have changed anything if I'd called them the last time? Vicky was dead, I couldn't help her. Alex was alive, and it was me that JD wanted. He'd warned me not to tell the police. He was a nutter, he'd proved that already. He'd killed Vicky, Len … had he killed Glenn too?

I had to help Alex. She was my priority. JD had hurt her already, and he might do worse if I called the police. It was me he wanted. It was time we brought the situation to a head. I'd meet with Becky and see what she was after. Then I'd tell DCI Summers and we'd catch that little shit JD together.

———

When I look back on those events, I can't believe that I did this. DCI Summers actually shouted at me afterwards, she was so frustrated with me. But she only had to mop up the fallout, I was right in the middle of it, acting on the spur of the moment. I did what I thought was best at the time. I was thinking of Alex.

I took a shower in the caravan. I actually cleaned myself up while Vicky's dead body lay on the bed. I covered her with a sheet and opened the window slightly to try to reduce the smell of shit and puke. I also closed the curtains. I didn't want some mischievous kids playing peek-a-boo at the window and discovering the bloody corpse of the campsite owner.

I showered and shaved as if nothing had happened. I had no clothes in the new caravan, so put my old stuff back on. I was serene. I knew what I had to do and I knew the order in which it had to be done. I would meet with Hannah as planned, and next I would go to the house and meet Becky. I'd see what JD wanted, then I'd tell the police. I'd make an anonymous tip-off as soon as I left the campsite, so they could recover Vicky's body. But I wasn't putting Alex's life at risk, I'd wait until I could figure out where JD was holding her. I didn't want to spook him.

I thought back to when Meg had been held by Tony Miller. They'd spent a lot of time together. I didn't know all the details. Meg had never made herself available to talk about it. I knew he'd fluctuated between befriending her and threatening to sexually assault her. That's when she'd killed him, she said, when he'd been trying to put his hand down her pants.

I burned with rage and frustration, thinking about Alex. Meg had worked at the probation service, she was used to dealing with thugs, rapists, thieves and burglars. She knew how to talk to them, she was accustomed to their nonsense. Alex was a different beast. She was on the TV too, there was little chance that she would go unrecognised by JD.

I wondered where he was on the psycho scale. If I was lucky, he'd be some lonely obsessive, thrilled by my involvement in such a high profile murder case, but if I'd drawn the short straw, he'd be a weirdo sexual predator. I began to sweat. I was anxious about Alex. I wished we'd parted on better terms.

If JD had been tailing us, I could have beaten the crap out of him myself. I'm not aggressive by nature, but my rage was turning to violence. If I met JD, I knew that I'd go for him. I wanted to hurt him.

Was this how Meg had felt? Had she experienced this rage? Is that why she'd stabbed Tony Miller so many times, to make sure the pervert was really dead? All I could think about was smashing JD's face to a bloody pulp. Is that what fear and anger makes people do? I'd be doing it for Vicky as much as for Alex. I'd never even met him, but I hated the man already.

I made sure that my phone was charged, and then sat on the sofa at the far end of the caravan to look through the photographs. I spotted the Yates's house. It had altered so much since being rebuilt that it was difficult to recognise, but the neighbouring houses were unchanged.

I looked into the young Meg's face, searching for traces of the woman I had known. She was in there. Even as a child, I could still see my Meg. I looked at the child called Hannah and wondered if this was the same person I'd be meeting shortly at the Pine Trees Guest Lodge.

My phone vibrated. It was another text from Alex's phone. It had a photo attached. Alex again. No more bruises. Not much light in the room. Reddened eyes, she'd been crying.

Don't tell police. Meet Becky. Don't say anything. You get clever I cut her throat like that other bitch

I thought about texting back. Would it be worth it? I decided to do it anyway.

I'll do what you say. Don't hurt my friend. I won't tell the police. Pete

I deleted the bit about breaking his neck if he hurt Alex. The hostage negotiator in me told me that one might not play out so well.

I placed the photographs in a plastic bag, grabbed my phone and headed for the caravan door. I considered taking a kitchen knife. Would I use it if I had to? It might offer some form of protection or leverage. I took a smaller knife, rather than one of the more sinister ones. It would tuck into my back pocket. It might come in handy. I dropped it into the bag, along with the photos.

I walked through the campsite towards the buildings at the entrance where I'd left my car. There were some call boxes near the small arcade – that's where I'd call the police. I didn't care about them knowing it was me, I had nothing to hide, but I didn't want the cops following me, or messing up my meeting with Becky.

I dialed 999 and got through to the police. I didn't chat with the operator, I said what I had to say. I told him that Vicky was dead and which caravan they'd find her in. I said that DCI Kate Summers should be notified. I told them that JD was responsible, that DCI Summers would know all about him. I finished by saying that I would be giving them a call later that evening. They should be ready for it, they might need to move fast. Then I did something weird. I apologised. To the operator. I said I was sorry for making such a mess again.

I hung up the phone, checked my mobile for messages, and then made my way back to the car. In the next two hours, I'd meet with Hannah and then see Becky, as we'd arranged. The minute I got any information about JD, I'd be onto the police. This thing had to end. I'd had enough, I had to finish it. That night.

Chapter Fifteen

The Pine Trees Guest Lodge wasn't the most inviting of tourist destinations in the city, but it was easy to get to and had parking. It was the sort of place that would attribute more value to a friendly welcome than to a decent Wi-Fi connection. It wouldn't be my choice for somewhere to stay. Who shares bathrooms with strangers these days?

The lodge was double-fronted, with two large windows facing the road. There were potholes in the car park and the sign needed a lick of paint. It should have read: *Welcome to The Pine Trees Guest Lodge, here's a knackered suspension to greet you!*

I locked up the car and checked my phone. No new messages. I was a bit early for Hannah. I left the small knife under my car seat.

There was a reception area inside the main entrance, filled with colourful leaflets for local attractions. After five minutes, a woman came through a door from the dining room where she'd been serving meals to the guests. I glimpsed a worn and drab carpet, grubby table settings and plates of stodgy unadventurous food.

'Can I help you? Are you checking in?'

The woman seemed nice enough, if distracted by her

dining room duties. She'd splashed gravy onto her white blouse.

'I'm not checking in. I have an appointment with a lady called Hannah Young. Would you ring up to her room, let her know I'm here?'

'Yes, of course, no problem. Would you like to take a seat while you're waiting? Or you can use the bar if you want to.'

'I'll go through for a drink, thank you.'

The bar was empty, except for a middle-aged couple making stilted and bored conversation with each other. They looked up at me expectantly as I walked into the room. They were probably hoping that I'd help to revive their tired conversation, but I was having none of it. I didn't make eye contact, and I kept my back to them at the bar.

A lanky youth, wearing a black bow tie which had seen better days, was busying himself wiping down the bottles in the bar. He had one of those half-formed moustaches across his top lip.

'Good evening, sir. What can I pour you?'

Very quaint.

'Just a soft drink please. Have you got a fresh orange juice? I'll have that with lemonade and ice, if that's okay?'

Eventually my drink arrived. I didn't dare to go anywhere near the middle-aged couple, they were like a Venus flytrap, waiting to gobble up the first person who landed near them. I moved into the corner, at the side of the huge window, it seemed safe there, they wouldn't catch me.

Then Hannah walked in. The couple looked up again, their tendrils alert to the newly arrived prey. She followed my lead, ignoring them completely, and waving to me from the door.

'I'll get myself a drink, one moment.'

She must have used the bar before. She ordered her drink, and then sat at a chair opposite me, asking the barman to bring it over to the table.

This had to be the girl who'd been pictured with Meg. She was the same age and same hair colour. She'd changed her look since she was younger, but I was certain that this was the girl that I'd seen in the Blackpool photographs. The resemblance wasn't as strong as with Meg, but then I'd known Meg for years, I could see her personality shining though in those pictures, even though she was so young when they were taken.

My heart raced. I'd been preoccupied with everything else that was going on before she'd arrived, but now this meeting seemed to hold the promise of some resolution at long last.

——————

I shook Hannah's hand, moving my drink off the table so that she couldn't knock it over as she sat down. The table was sticky, the beer mats stained. I wondered what had made her choose this place to stay. There was better in the city; an old-fashioned place like this couldn't last much longer in the face of competition from big chains like the OverNight Inn.

'Hi, Pete Bailey. Pleased to meet you!'

She had a firm handshake.

'Hannah Young. You'll probably be more interested in my maiden name, Hannah Yates.'

And there it was. Exactly the information that I wanted. No attempt to hide it. Straight to the point.

Hannah was the girl in the photos, the one who had been with Meg. However, they didn't look related. Even as an adult, Hannah didn't resemble Meg in any way. She'd changed a lot since those photographs were taken, she'd changed her appearance considerably in adulthood.

She was certainly an attractive woman, with strong features, a confident presence and a pleasant voice. There was no hint of an accent. You wouldn't have thought that she'd spent so many years living in Lancashire.

'I'm here to talk about Meg, but I'm sure you know that already.'

'I had guessed. I've got so many questions. Are you sisters?'

'Adoptive sisters,' she answered. 'We were adopted by Tom and Mavis Yates. I was sixteen and Meg was fifteen. You didn't know that?'

'Meg hasn't been entirely honest with me. For some reason, she decided not to share any information about her past. I've only known that you exist for a few days. I stumbled upon some photographs. Here, you might be interested in these.'

I picked up the bag, which was sitting by my feet. There was a sliced carrot on the floor – I'd crushed it with my foot. I'd have to keep my eye on the clock, I didn't want to be late for Becky.

She looked through the photographs, taking her time, studying each one.

'I don't know how she got hold of these. So much was destroyed in the fire. You know about that, I assume?'

I nodded.

'But only just. It's all recent news to me.'

'We lived in a children's home in Blackpool. It's been shut down now. We became good friends straight away – you couldn't separate us. We couldn't believe our luck when we were adopted together. We thought we'd hit the jackpot when Tom and Mavis took on both of us. As it turned out, it was the short straw.'

'What do you mean?' I asked, intrigued.

She looked up from the photos, met my gaze momentarily, then looked away again.

'Let's just say things didn't stay happy for very long. Did you know that I live in Spain now, Mr Bailey? Or can I call you Pete? I guess we're family, aren't we?'

I hadn't thought about that one. Did that make her my sister-in-law?

'I didn't know that. I thought that you were all dead. In a road accident, according to Meg. In fact, according to what Meg told me, you don't even exist.'

'Really? It's interesting that she should choose that as a way of killing us off. I moved to Spain to get away. I couldn't face the stigma of the past, I wanted to leave this sodding country behind forever. Sorry, I don't usually use bad language. It's being back in England that's done it. There's no love lost between me and this place.'

'How long have you been over there? Does Meg know?'

'Meg and I went our separate ways a long time ago. We had a difficult relationship.'

'Why don't you use Yates as your surname?' I interjected.

'I wanted to bury Hannah Yates forever, after the fire and all the press coverage at the time. Young is my birth surname. As Hannah Young I got my identity back.'

'Why do you think that Meg lied about her past?'

'I think we both did. We were anxious to put it all behind us. It wasn't only the fire. All sorts of bad things happened around that time. I went to hide in Spain. It's worked reasonably well for me. Until now. Until those murders. It felt as if it had all come back to torment me again. I thought I was away from it.'

'What do you mean? Surely everything was all over and done with, once the investigation into the fire was completed.'

'I wish! The journalists used to call us "the fire sisters", did you know that, Pete? You wouldn't have seen it in the papers at the time, but they were convinced there was something suspicious about the fire. Something our neighbour said, I think. One journalist in particular, who knew Tom Yates, wouldn't leave it alone. Kept chasing us for years afterwards. I hope he's dead now. He was a complete bastard. Sorry, that's the second time I've sworn now.'

'You know I'm a journalist too, don't you? A radio journalist, not the sort of investigative stuff the papers do. I'm surprised Meg even looked twice at me if you'd had a run-in with the papers. They give us all a bad name.'

'I can see why she fell for you, you've got kind eyes. When we were kids she always used to say that you need to look in the eyes, they're the gateway to a person's soul. If you look hard enough, you can see the evil in a person before it comes out. That's what Meg used to say. She used to yearn to meet people with kind eyes … like David had.'

'David?' I asked.

'A lad that we knew in the home. A long time ago. Someone Meg knew when we were younger.'

'So why are you here?' I asked.

There was so much more I wanted to ask Hannah. I'd have to keep on topic, I didn't have long. At long last her drink arrived. The youth from the bar shuffled the beer mat and the glass to make sure that it was right in the middle of the table.

'You don't want to join us for a game of Cluedo do you?' asked the boring chap. Fortunately, Hannah declined the invitation more gracefully than I would have done, and he went back to his table and began his game with his wife. They'd condemned themselves to an evening of traditional board games. It was like the seventies all over again.

I pushed my question one more time. She hadn't answered it yet.

'What brought you back to the UK, if you hate the place so much? Have you come to see Meg?'

'I'm not sure that she'd want to see me. We didn't part in very happy circumstances; I haven't heard from her in years. I'm not even sure if she knew that I was still living in Spain. I only found out that she'd married you when I read about the murders in a magazine. It was as if it was all happening again.'

Your entire life story has been plastered all over the press. I was buying fish and chips in our local expat café and happened to read a UK magazine. I don't know what made me pick it up. And there you were, you and Meg. I almost missed it at first, she was Meg Bailey in the article. But in the photograph it was still the Meg that I knew. She looked good, you must have made her happy. I'm pleased that you made her happy again.'

'Is that what brought you here then? To find Meg?'

'Yes, I want to find Meg. It's been too long, we need to speak. But it was important that I found you, Pete.

You know what I said about Meg looking at the eyes to see into the soul of a person? Have you ever looked really closely into Meg's eyes?'

'Of course I have. We've been married for years. What are you trying to say?'

'Meg is troubled, Pete. She's been like it since we were kids. Why do you think they called us the fire sisters? That was Meg's doing. Sometimes something would make her snap. If you looked into her eyes when that happened, you'd see a very different Meg from the one you know.'

I looked at her. What was she trying to tell me about my wife?

'I knew it as soon as I saw the magazine article. You look like a nice guy, Pete. I can see why she chose you. But you need to be careful. You need to know about Meg. When things turn ugly, you'll usually find Meg at the centre of things. She has a knack for screwing up people's lives.'

———

'Oh shit!'

I'd got distracted by our conversation. I was going to be late for my meeting with Becky.

'I'm so sorry. I have to go. This is really frustrating … '

'Oh, I thought we'd have more time to chat.'

'Yes, I'm sorry, something came up. I have to … er, I have somebody else that I need to meet this evening. It took so long to get served by Lurch over there, and that clock is wrong.

'Can we meet up again? I'm not in the country for long, but I had to come over. I needed to find you and tell you about Meg. I have to find Meg if I can. It looks like it's all happening again. Everything is turning to shit. And Meg is always at the heart of it.'

I wanted desperately to stay and talk but I had to leave. I should have consulted my mobile phone rather than the clock on the wall of the bar. I hadn't wanted to appear rude by leaving it out on the table. I was going to be late, I still had to drive over to the house. They were digging up the roads in the city centre, laying water pipes or something like that. I'd get stuck at the traffic lights, no doubt.

'Can we meet again? When are you going back to Spain?'

I have to fly out in two days. I have an early start, so that day will be a write-off. I've got your email address – can we meet again tomorrow sometime? I'm here all day. Maybe we can meet in town next time? This place depresses me, it reminds me of everything I hate about this country.

'Yes, let's do that. How about Fran's Coffee House in the shopping centre? You'll find it. Head for the town hall, the shopping centre is opposite.'

Hannah nodded.

'Do you mind if I hang onto the photos?' she asked. 'I haven't seen these faces for some time, I'd like to look at them again. I'll let you have them tomorrow. Okay if I make copies in town?'

'Yes, of course. How about 3 o'clock tomorrow afternoon? I'll send you an email.'

I shook Hannah's hand again, and then made my way out of the bar.

I was running late for Becky, but I'd been completely absorbed by what Hannah had been telling me. She was painting a picture of a Meg that I didn't know. Or did I?

Had I seen a glimpse of it in our final meeting in the cemetery, when she'd revealed to me that it was she who'd killed Tony and not poor old Sally who'd taken the blame for everything.

I checked my phone. I'd have to risk speeding through town if I was going to catch Becky. She'd texted me while I'd been in the bar. I'd half expected to see more naked pictures, so I got a surprise when I saw what she'd written.

Don't meet at the house, Pete. He might be watching. I'll be waiting by the corner shop at the end of your road. 7pm. Make sure he's not following you. I'll be there. Becky x

Who was she talking about? I was pleased that she didn't want to meet at the house, but why the secrecy? Had she run into JD too?

I texted her back.

Running late. Sorry. Will see you at shop soon, Pete

The roadworks at the traffic lights seemed to take forever. If watching paint dry is supposed to be slow, then this was even slower. I was getting agitated. I only wanted to get to the end of the road, but it was taking so long. I tried to stay calm, I needed to get to Alex, I had to locate her and then get the police involved. If I messed this up, it could all go badly wrong.

I reached my neighbourhood, driving past my house to get to the corner shop. It was quiet. The police had gone, and there was a bit of blue tape left on the drive.

I parked my car on a double yellow line, putting the hazard lights on in case the traffic wardens were about.

Becky was waiting a short distance from the shop entrance. She was smoking. I hadn't smelled that on her breath the night we hooked up – it would have been a complete turn-off.

'Becky, I'm so sorry I'm late. I got caught up in--'

'Is he here? Has he followed you? He's a nutter, Pete!'

She looked terrified. Her eyes were darting all over, scanning the street for something or somebody.

'Calm down, Becky. What's going on?'

'It's all turned bad, that's what, Pete. He's gone mental on me. He knew the deal.'

'Becky, take a breath. What's going on? You know he's got my friend, don't you?'

'Oh Jesus, no I didn't know that. I thought it was you and me he was after. He's really jealous of us, Pete. But he knew the deal. I told him what's what. Now he's gone psycho on me!'

'Is this JD, Becky? Was it JD who sent me those text messages?'

She looked at me.

'Who is JD? I'm talking about Lee. Lee Taylor. I don't know any JD. Why?'

'Who is Lee Taylor, Becky? Is he the one who's taken Alex? What is going on here?'

'Lee Taylor is a very violent man, Pete. I'm surprised you haven't heard of him. He was on that Crime Beaters programme that your friend presents – they're looking for him, you know. I'm out of my depth, Pete. I hooked up with him through a website. Fetish dating. I get off on crime scenes. I like to screw where people have died. It's my thing. It excites me.

'When I found out your house was for sale, I had to go there. I hooked up with Lee on the web. He was supposed to be you. It was a fantasy thing. I got him to have sex with me in your house. And at the cathedral. And then I had sex with you in your caravan. But when I found out that you really fancied me, I had to try it. I wanted to sleep with you again, in your house. It's the closest I've ever got, Pete: to screw someone who was actually there in the house where the murders took place. But Lee messed it up. He's a nutter, Pete. He's obsessed with me. He went off on one after you and I slept together. He was furious, but I told him he was only there for the sex. It was exciting, him being wanted by the police and all. But he got violent when I told him what we'd done. He made me tell him every detail. When he saw the video, he hit me. He's a nutter, Pete. Look at my arm.'

She pulled down her jacket, her right arm was heavily bruised. I was shocked, he must have really hit her hard.

'Damn it, Becky, are you okay? Has somebody looked at that?'

'It's fine, it hurt like mad when he did it. I had to sneak out on him after sex. It was all I could do to calm him down. I found somewhere else to stay. He's gone mad, Pete. He wants to kill you. I told him it was only ever about the fantasy, there was never any relationship in it, but he's got all possessive, like he owns me. I'm scared, Pete. I'm really scared.'

She looked frightened for her life. I was angry with her for bringing all this violence back to torment me again and for sending me those crazy texts. Those texts were screwed up. They were unnecessary and over the top. I was furious about her filming what we'd done together in my caravan. But as her stifled tears began to make their way out onto her cheeks, I could feel nothing but pity for Becky. She'd swum into the deep end without a float. Now she was scrambling around, desperately trying to reach safety at the edge of the pool. Only, it wasn't over for either of us yet. Lee Taylor had Alex. And the only way I was going to be able to locate him was by using Becky as bait.

Chapter Sixteen

'Was it you who threatened to send out the video, Becky? That was a crappy thing to do.'

'Look, I filmed it. Yes, that was my idea. But it was for me to watch, I wouldn't have shared it. Not with the masks off. I usually put them on porn sites, but only with the masks. I tore yours off at the last moment. I wanted to see your face. That video was only for my use. And yes, look, I'm sorry. When I thought you were blanking me, I said I'd send out the video. I wouldn't have done it. Honest, I wouldn't.'

This was opening up a new world to me. I'd never put anything on a porn site before. I was feeling a bit old fashioned. I'd never filmed myself in the bedroom either. I'd watched porn, and I'd look at stuff that I'd never done myself, sometimes, but it's like reading a book: you use it to inspire your imagination, to take you to places you've never been before.

'How well do you know this guy? Will he hurt Alex?'

'You saw what he did to me. He was really angry when I sneaked out of the hotel room. He's trying to find me. I daren't tell the police I've been with a wanted criminal. I can't get caught with him – I'll go to jail … won't I?'

'Who has a copy of that video, Becky? Does Lee have one?'

'He texted it to himself, but it's not backed up or anything like that. Lee uses disposable phones. They don't have anything fancy on them, like that cloud stuff. When I met him it seemed exciting using those throwaway phones, but it's so he can't get found.'

'Are you sure, Becky? I can't have that video leaking onto the internet. What happened was between you and me. It was private. That video has to go. Those texts you sent … well, they made you look like a crazy woman. A bunny boiler.'

She looked ashamed. I hadn't wanted to embarrass her. I don't mind people's sexual preferences, whatever turns you on, but it has to be legal and it has to be consensual. That video was not filmed with my permission. Becky's crime scene fetish was a bit niche for my tastes, but the masks and porn thing? I might have gone for that, with the right person. It's all a matter of taste. I wasn't going to judge her for it, but she had made a bad error of judgment getting mixed up with a wanted criminal. And she'd been out of order trying to force a reaction from me with those texts. She knew it too. I didn't need to hassle her over it.

'Has Lee been messaging you? Did he send you any pictures of Alex? We need to find out where he's taken her, Becky, and then we have to get the police involved.'

'I'll get into trouble, won't I, Pete? Lee's wanted, I knew that. It was part of the thrill. You have to help me to keep out of this.'

'Did you use your proper names anywhere? Have you only used those phones? It all depends on how careless you've been.'

'We called ourselves Alan and Ruth Simpson at the

hotel – and when we looked around your house. And we've used the same phones all the time too.'

'Look, Becky. I don't know if you can stay out of all this. I want those phones as much as you do. I don't want the police getting that video – the bloody thing will leak out somehow if they do. Even if it only does the rounds of the local police station, somebody will see it.

'You'll have to plead ignorance, tell the police you didn't know who he was. If we can get to Alex, she'll have some legal friend who can advise you and tell you what not to say. I'm sure we can sort it. You haven't done anything wrong, have you? You weren't involved with Glenn Elliot's murder or Len's at the caravan? Please tell me you didn't kill Vicky? I'll hand you in myself if you did.'

'What's he done? He hasn't hurt anybody, has he? That wasn't me, Pete. You have to believe me. I know you don't have many reasons to trust me at the moment. Jesus, Pete, I didn't mean it to get like this. Who has he hurt?'

'I don't know. There have been three deaths, haven't you seen that in the papers? They're all connected with me or the house in some way. It would make sense if it was Lee--'

Becky's phone buzzed. She looked at it anxiously.

'It's Lee again,' she said. 'He won't stop messaging me.'

'It's another threat, Pete. And more photos of Alex.'

Bring that fucker to me, then me and you will be okay. Have you got him? Bring him to me. Lee x

I took the phone from her to read the message for myself. There were three files attached. He'd moved to a new location. I opened up the images. More pictures of Alex, her bruised eye looked worse than before. It was swelling.

Two of the photos were dark, but in one the flash had gone off. I could see the background clearly. It took me a moment to figure it out, but then I got it. In the background was a box marked 'Meg's Stuff', exactly where I'd left it the other day.

Lee was holding Alex at my storage unit. He must have taken the key from the caravan, it had to have been Lee who broke in. I knew where he was and he didn't know I was coming for him. I was going to get Alex. And I was not about to sound the alert by telling the police where I was heading.

———

'You need to come with me, Becky. I know he's dangerous, but he has Alex at the storage units. We have to get her. If we play this thing right, we can distance you from this too. Is that okay?'

Looking at the expression on her face, it didn't look like it was okay, but she nodded anyway and put her phone in her pocket.

'My car is just up the road. Do you have a car of your own?'

'No, I've been using Lee's. I walked here from town, it was easier.'

We walked back to my car. It was getting darker, the hazard lights illuminated everything in the vicinity. We drove off. I was sweating, nervous about what we were about to do. Lee was angry with me and Becky. I had to get Alex out of there. I needed to alert the police, but not before I'd rescued Alex. The minute Lee heard sirens, he'd panic. If he thought his time was up, it could turn into a real hostage situation.

We were silent on the drive over to the storage units. I was thinking through the safest course of action. It would be quiet at that time of night. We had 24/7 access, but there would only be the night security guard on at that time. I don't know how Lee had got into the unit, but it was a great place to hold a captive. There was one way into my unit and one way out. He'd see me coming, I'd have to let him know I was there.

I had an idea. I had DCI Summers' mobile number. I could type in an emergency text message and leave it ready to send. As soon as Alex was clear, I'd send the message. She'd have the cops over there in minutes, and I'd have to keep Lee talking until they got there. I'd leave the car running for Alex, tell her to get away from there.

Would it work? It was Becky and me that Lee wanted. Presumably he wanted to kick the shit out of me. Would he go for a kill? Surely not. Becky had warned me about his violence. Perhaps I could take a few punches while I stalled and waited for the cops. But what about Glenn, Len and Vicky? They would have told a different story. I had a better idea. I'd call DCI Summers on my phone and let her hear my entire conversation. It would take the police a few minutes to get there, I'd have that time to rescue Alex. I could talk DCI Summers through what I was doing, using my phone like a walkie-talkie. That way the police wouldn't screw it all up. And I'd send her my location by text the minute Alex was safe. As a back-up.

We arrived at the road leading to the storage units. I turned off my sidelights and we swung into the parking area, pulling up as close to the door as I could. I left the engine running and my door open. There were two other cars parked at the far side, possibly people working late at the industrial units.

'Close it quietly,' I said to Becky, who had finally put her phone away. She clicked the door shut.

'How crazy is he?' I whispered. 'Will he launch straight at me, or will we be able to talk?'

'Who knows?' she replied. 'I'd describe him as unpredictable.'

'Have a look in that skip over there, would you? See if you can find a bit of wood or something that I can use as a weapon.'

Becky moved away, and I typed out my emergency text to DCI Summers.

I've got your killer. He's called Lee Taylor. He has Alex Kennedy, she's in danger. If you get this text, I'm in trouble. Send officers to Boxed In on Waterloo Street ASAP. Try to do it quietly, this guy is dangerous! Pete Bailey

I saved the message into my drafts, and then opened up DCI Summers' contact, ready to dial her directly. Becky walked back from the skip. She was carrying a metal pole about a metre long. It looked as if it had been part of a towel rail or a shower unit, something like that. Not the most useful weapon she could have found.

'Okay, thanks, if that's the best we can do, I'll take it.'

I pressed dial on my mobile phone and slipped it into the top pocket of my shirt. I made sure the speaker volume was low, I didn't want DCI Summers' voice being heard. I remembered the small kitchen knife that I'd grabbed before leaving the caravan. Would I even use it? I doubted that, but it might come in handy as a threat. I had a tiny knife and a metal tube as protection – great strategy, Pete.

As the call connected, I was close enough to hear her voice.

'Hello, DCI Kate Summers speaking … hello?'

There was a pause. She probably thought it was a crank call. I urged her to check her caller ID. If she knew it was me, she'd hang on. I needed to give her the sound of my voice.

'Okay Becky, I'm going to give the door a try. We've got the right place, haven't we? This is Boxed In storage?'

Becky looked at me. It wasn't the subtlest attempt to let DCI Summers know where we were, but it would do. I didn't want to tip her off that I'd contacted the police. I still wasn't certain that I could trust her.

The door opened. It was on the snip. The office light was dimmed and I couldn't see anybody inside. I signalled to Becky to be quiet. We closed the door gently behind us, I didn't want to alert Lee to our presence. I needed to do a bit of reconnaissance first.

There was a sliding glass screen between the reception area and the main office. Fresh blood was spattered up the glass from the inside. My stomach tightened, ready to vomit, but it didn't come. I knew what was in there, I'd seen these scenes before. Did I want check to see if he was still alive? I chose instead to announce it to DCI Summers via my mobile phone commentary.

'Becky, he's killed the security guard. We need to be really careful. He won't have a gun, will he?'

Becky didn't seem too shocked by the news of what Lee had done to the security guy.

'No gun, Pete. Not that I know of.'

I wanted everything to end. I felt numb, back in a terrifying nightmare. The sense of fear and the adrenalin took me right back to the events of six months ago.

The vomit came. Poor DCI Summers, I was the worst phone conversationalist ever. I hoped that she hadn't hung up, dismissing it as a crank call. If she had, I'd have to rely on my text message back-up. It was a long way off MI5 standards.

I quickly recovered and checked out the map on the wall showing the layout of the units. I'd looked at this when I came to my storage unit, but it made no sense to me whatsoever. I ripped the map off the wall so I could carry it with me.

'Stay together, Becky,' I whispered, looking over to the spot where Becky had been standing. But she was gone.

———

I was furious with Becky for going on ahead.

'Becky!' I whispered. 'Becky!'

Everything was silent among the units, and I had only the dim lighting of the night lights to help me to see. I tensed up, wondering if Lee had heard us already. Had he come to find us?

I took the phone out of my pocket and spoke to DCI Summers.

'Are you on the line?'

'Pete Bailey? Yes, I'm listening. What's going on? Wait for us to get here, don't go in on your own.'

'He's got Alex. He told me to come alone. Promise me you won't turn up with your sirens on. Becky's disappeared and there's a body – the security guard. There's a lot of blood. You mustn't spook him. And Vicky, did you get to Vicky at the campsite?'

'Yes, yes we did. There's a team down there now. Listen, Pete, we're on our way. Do not go in there alone. This guy is really dangerous. Repeat, do not go in there … .'

I slipped the phone back in my pocket, leaving it live.

I held up the metal pole and checked that the small knife was tucked safely into my back pocket. I looked at the map, took a right turn, and began to move deeper into the vast industrial unit. Every now and then I'd hear a noise and I'd look for Becky, expecting to see her waiting for me. As I cursed her for getting separated, I had a rare moment of clarity. I was an idiot.

Becky had claimed that she and Lee had split up; she reckoned they'd gone their separate ways. If that was the case, how come I'd got all those text messages from her phone? Had she been sent to deliver me to him? Was she some kind of decoy? It would explain why she had disappeared. Maybe she'd been warning Lee all along. They were probably waiting for me, ready to pounce. But what did they want? What was the point of all this? She'd done a good job of fooling me that she was scared of Lee, although it wasn't the first time that she'd played me for a sucker.

I was no better off with the map. I couldn't get the orientation right, and after a few minutes I didn't have a clue where I was. I dropped it on the floor and began to work by the unit numbers. They were all shapes and sizes. There were tiny units, presumably for students, people starting out who hadn't yet amassed a great number of possessions, and then much larger ones, for people like me whose lives were on hold.

I heard a loud crash in the distance. It had come from the main entrance. Was it Becky? Had I been wrong about her? Maybe she was looking for me and cursing me for losing her?

I moved along the lines of units, listening carefully. No voices, no footsteps. In the far distance, I heard a police siren. Was that for me? I hoped not.

I turned a corner along a long row of units and finally recognised where I was. This was my row. And to confirm it, I could see that the door was open and light was pouring out.

They were in there: Lee and Alex. I listened, I couldn't hear any voices. I hesitated. Should I announce myself? Or would it make more sense to get a feel for things first, maybe hatch a plan? I was desperate to rush in there to see Alex.

I moved silently towards the unit, listening, willing Alex to say something so that I could hear her voice and be sure that she was okay. There was more movement in the distance, an echo. Was it the police? Had DCI Summers got someone here already? I was too close to speak into the phone – all she'd hear would be my nervous breathing, if anything at all. My heart was thudding in my chest.

I made it to the side of the unit. The back of my shirt was wet with sweat. I had to peer through the door, it was the only way that I could see. I risked a quick glance, why wasn't anybody talking?

I saw her. Alex. She was sitting on a chair. That chair used to be in our kitchen, and now it was being used for a hostage. Her head was bowed, she was still. Her hands were tied too, she'd been restrained. I couldn't see her face. I wanted her to move, I had to be certain she was still alive.

I reconsidered my strategy. If I could confirm she was okay, I'd be better off backing away and letting the police deal with it. But Lee wanted me, and had threatened that I should not alert the police. Maybe I shouldn't have contacted DCI Summers in the first place. The cops might mess it all up.

The decision was made for me.

'He's here, Lee.'

It was Becky's voice. She'd been tailing me, making sure that I didn't get to surprise Lee. Alex immediately looked up towards me, her eyes full of terror. They'd taped her mouth with brown parcel tape – there was enough of it, left by the removal men when they'd dumped my boxes.

Lee was dark and muscular. He had tattoos up his neck, along his arms and on his hands. He was carrying a knife, which had smears of blood along the blade where it had been partially wiped clean. The knife was one of those horrible things you see on the internet. It had a long blade with five serrations at the end and a bright red handle. It was shaped like a scimitar. It actually had the words Zombie Apocalypse along the blade.

Are they really allowed to sell these things online? It got worse. There was a similarly branded crossbow sitting on the cushion of my one remaining armchair. I don't know why I hadn't had it taken to the tip. It was the only item of lounge furniture that hadn't been spattered with blood from Jason Davies' death in the house.

This guy had to be a nutter. Who carries gear like that around?

'Step into the light, Pete,' Lee commanded. 'Drop that feather duster or whatever it is you're carrying.'

I let go of the metal pole. It clanged on the floor, the echo ringing out across the industrial unit. Alex tried to say something, but I couldn't understand a word. Lee stepped up to her and struck her hard with his free hand.

'Jesus!' I cried out, lurching towards him by instinct to try to protect Alex. As I neared him, I felt him pull his head back and he struck my nose with his head. I heard the crunch. There was a sudden searing pain across my face and I could feel the blood flowing into my nostrils, and then running down my mouth.

I dropped to the floor, I'm not sure why, maybe it was a defensive action. I don't think I've ever felt a pain like it. My eyes were watering. I was half-crying at the shock of it.

'Shut up, arsehole!' Lee hissed.

There was another noise in the distance. I began to pray that the police were making their way through the units already, there was no way that I was going to be able to deal with this man. What had I been thinking of?

It took me some time to recover. Lee and Becky were kissing. He thrust his tongue deep into her mouth, pressing his hips firmly into hers and grabbing her buttocks with his free hand. He wasn't the slightest bit concerned about me. I clearly posed no threat to him. He carried on with Becky as if I wasn't even there.

Finally, I was able to speak. My nose was blocked with the flow of blood, my voice nasal and pained.

'What's this all about?' I asked. 'Let Alex go. You know she's got nothing to do with this.'

'Wads dis all abowd?' Lee mocked. He was a bully, through and through. I knew the type. Big, macho, good-looking, strong, with the cockiness of a violent man who knows exactly how to handle himself. A wimp like me was a joke to him.

'Keep your mouth shut!' He moved away from Becky and raised his hand as if he was about to strike Alex once again. She flinched. He'd trained her already. Alex knew what this man could do, I could see that she'd been struck several times. Her eyes looked empty, I'd never seen Alex like that. She was resigning herself to her fate. I'd seen that look before, when Sally jumped off the roof of the cathedral, at the moment when she decided to end her life.

There was a loud, metallic clunking sound deep within the warehouse. The lights went off. Complete darkness. Moments later, the emergency lighting came on, throwing out barely enough illumination to make out what was going on. Then all hell broke out.

Chapter Seventeen

I had been so preoccupied with my bleeding nose that I hadn't noticed the sound of sirens in the distance. When you live in a city, sirens punctuate your life, you think nothing of them.

When the lights went out, I was hopelessly slow to react. I looked around, trying to figure out what was going on. I was useless. But Lee knew exactly what to do. He was one of life's cockroaches, a survivor. He was ready to crawl under a new rock at a moment's notice, making himself scarce until it was time to crawl back out again.

I assumed the police must have arrived – I was praying that help had come. I was aware of a fast and sudden movement.

Lee grabbed the crossbow and handed the knife to Becky.

'Take her!' he said, motioning towards Alex.

I sensed him moving the crossbow in his hands. Oh please, no, Jesus, not the crossbow. He struck me on the head with its heavy iron handle. I felt myself fade momentarily, then my senses came back.

'Come with me. Don't make a sound. You utter a word, this bolt goes straight through your head. Got it?'

I nodded. I was cowed. This man had beaten me completely. There was nothing I could do against his strength and his casual violence.

He rushed me along the units. The fire exits were brightly lit, like beacons in the semi-darkness. He had this worked out already. He knew exactly how we were exiting that building, and it wasn't through the front door. He and Becky didn't say a word as they moved us silently and professionally towards one of the exits at the far side of the warehouse.

I listened for signs of the police. They had to be in the unit, surely? Who had cut the power? That had to be DCI Summers' doing.

My earlier cack-handed attempts at navigating my way through the maze of storage units were put to shame by the confident manner in which Lee guided us towards the exit. Every now and then he would push me to speed me up. I felt like a whining child out on a long walk.

Lee kicked open the fire door. It flew open and we burst out into the darkness. An alarm sounded on the door, announcing that it had been opened. We were at the far side of the warehouse, nowhere near the car park where I'd started out. I could hear a commotion at the front of the building – it had to be the police arriving. They were too late; we were well away from them.

I was dazed and confused, my head felt as if it had had a concrete block dropped on it. They had a van waiting at the back. It was unlocked. Becky opened the doors and pushed Alex inside. She offered no resistance, she'd given herself up for dead. Lee raised his fist and struck me hard on the side of my head.

Blood flew out of my nose and mouth onto the pavement. Barely conscious, I was aware of being thrown into the back of the van. I landed heavily on top of Alex, I felt her flinch, and then for a moment everything went black.

Lee was driving recklessly, throwing the van round corners and leaving me and Alex lunging from right to left, our limbs striking the metal sides of the vehicle.

He and Becky were silent. They knew what they were doing. This had been planned. She'd reeled me right in and made sure that I was delivered directly into the hands of Lee.

I was aware of Lee looking into his rear-view mirror. I recall thinking that he was checking to make sure that we weren't being followed. I couldn't hear sirens in the back of the van, neither could I see the flashes of blue lights.

My memories of that journey are vague. I must have been drifting in and out of consciousness. All I could think of was Alex, I didn't care about myself. She felt so small as our limp bodies rolled about in the back of the van, colliding then moving apart.

She'd come to visit me, as a friend, to support me. I'd been grateful for that, delighted to have her company. But I'd put her directly in the path of danger, exactly as I had with Meg when I'd slept with Ellie in the hotel. This was my fault. I'd brought Becky into our lives. I could have finished my shift the night before Alex arrived. I could have thanked Becky, told her I was flattered, but politely turned down her proposition.

Instead, I jumped into bed with her, urged on by my desire to sleep with her, not knowing who she was or what she wanted. I could have waited – I should have waited. And now Alex was paying the price. She'd got caught up in my crappy, screwed-up life and was picking up the tab for being my friend.

I felt a crushing sense of despair in that van, a feeling that I'd messed everything up so badly. I'd had two great relationships in my life, one with Alex many years ago and one with Meg. What was it about me that destroyed everything I had? I felt desolate, not even sorry for myself, just completely contemptuous of my actions.

Yet, in that darkness, in the midst of all that horror, Alex reached out to me again. She stretched out her hand, which was still bound, to hold mine in the darkness. It was a gentle action in among all that violence. In spite of all this, Alex could still reach out to me in friendship.

We'd arrived at wherever they were taking us. My head struck the back of the passenger seat as Lee braked hard. I let go of Alex's hand, fading out again.

I was aware of voices.

'Is it open still?'

'Yes, it's fine. Bring them through.'

The sound of the van doors being opened. Alex tensing as Lee reached in to pull her out. Then it was my turn.

'Walk, you dickhead. I'm not carrying you.'

I struggled to find strength in my legs. What were they doing to us? What had they got planned?

The cool night air helped to revive me. I became aware of my surroundings, slowly recognising where they'd brought us.

We were at the cathedral. I was standing opposite the spot where Sally had jumped to her death. This was weird and twisted. They were re-enacting what had happened to Meg and me six months earlier. And this is where it had all ended. This is the place where the final deaths had occurred.

I could hear the police sirens across the city. It sounded like a war zone. Lee pushed me towards the heavy wooden door of the cathedral. I was aware of dim lighting, mainly candlelight, I think.

'I'm sorry, you can't come in here now, we'll be locking up shortly--'

I was aware of Lee lifting the crossbow, swinging it towards whoever had just spoken to him, and firing off one of its bolts. I heard a thud as a body fell to the floor and sensed Alex go rigid with fear. Becky pushed her forward.

'Close the door, lock it if you can.'

Lee was completely in control and totally calm. Becky followed his commands as if he'd bewitched her. She pushed the door shut, I'm not certain that she locked it.

They were taking us to the bell tower. The climb up the stairs seemed to take forever, longer than I remembered. The blood was beginning to congeal in my nose, it was forcing me to breathe through my mouth. I was short of breath. The climb was exhausting.

Alex's eyes were red, she'd been crying. She'd sensed that it was coming to an end. I couldn't see how things could possibly play out in our favour. There was no sign of the police, I couldn't hear the helicopter hovering in the distance like the last time we were in this cursed place. I felt my pocket. My phone had gone. It must have dropped out somewhere, in the warehouse or the van. They'd never find us now. DCI Summers would find an empty storage unit. The police wouldn't have a clue how to track us down, they didn't know what vehicle Lee and Becky were using. If Becky had been telling me the truth, Lee was a wanted man, so at least they'd know who they were looking for.

We arrived in the bell tower. It was a funny thing to notice, but I could see that the bell rope had been replaced where it had been cut previously to tie Jem to the wheels of one of the bells.

'You're kidding me!' I shouted as Becky went to the ropes and cut a length off. It was a different rope, but she had the same intention.

'What time is it?' Lee asked. 'Are we near the hour?'

'Fourteen minutes,' Becky replied, checking her phone.

'This way!' Lee barked at me, signalling to the stairs.

They were taking us to the bell tower. I knew what they had planned before it even happened. Nobody tells you these things, but I pissed myself when I realised. I think I'd given up hope. Alex looked like she was walking towards her execution. We had accepted our fate. We knew we were beaten.

Lee didn't even have to show me what he wanted me to do. I placed my head and hands through the wheel, which was attached to the heavy iron bell. This is where Jem had been. This is where I'd left him, his head placed through the wooden spokes of the wheel, waiting for the bells to chime.

Lee tied me firmly. I couldn't move. I'd been struggling to stay conscious, but now I hoped that I'd pass out. I didn't want to experience the terror of waiting for the bells to chime the hour. It would begin with a click as the cathedral clock hands moved into the hour position. The wheels of the bells would begin to move, gaining momentum. As the sound of the bells marked a new hour, my head and arms would be torn off by the wooden spokes of the bell wheel. I'd die the same way that Jem had done six months earlier.

Lee, Becky and Alex moved away. They were going to the roof of the tower, the place where Sally had jumped, the part of the cathedral where Meg had almost fallen to her death.

How long until the bells rang? How long did I have left? I prayed that I would pass out again, but as I waited there in the silence, all I could hear was the sound of the minute hand making its way slowly towards the hour.

I didn't even know what the time was. It had to be nine or ten o'clock, it couldn't be any later. I wasn't getting out of this, those bells were ringing and they were taking my head with them.

What must have been going through Jem's mind when he was in this position? I don't think he'd realised what the bells would do. I didn't see it on his face when I left him tied there. But he must have got it when the clock struck. You could hear the progression of the minute hand as clear as anything. He had to have known what was going to happen in the end.

I examined the ropes that were tying me. They were tight, cutting into my skin, biting into me. I tried to work my hands free, but the rope burned, there was no room to manoeuvre. Lee knew how to tie a knot, but I had a go anyway, using my teeth to work at it.

What was happening on the roof? I thought that I understood, at last, what this was about. What a terrible way to die. This wasn't personal. Becky and Lee were thrill-seekers. It had to be that.

They'd spotted the story in the papers, got some kind of sexual thrill from it, and were seeking to recreate the events of that nightmare six months previously. This was some screwed-up replay. Becky had targeted me for sex, and Lee must have been in on it, in spite of the lies she'd told me earlier, luring me into her sick trap one more time. That's probably why it had been videoed, as a weird memento of what they'd done. God, there are some crazy people out there.

What would they do with Alex? What role was she playing in all of this? If Becky was Meg, and Lee was me, that made Alex Sally. Sally had jumped to her death that night. Oh shit, no, surely they wouldn't push her? Maybe they didn't intend to kill us, perhaps it was some role-play thing? Tell that to Vicky – and Glenn, Len and the guy at the storage units.

No, these two were nutters. This was some weird fantasy thing. I'd had a taste of it already. I carried on working at the knot with my teeth. The rope was too thick for it to make any impact, it was useless, but I carried on anyway.

There was movement. It was Becky, she was carrying her phone.

'You can't want this to happen?' I shouted at her. 'You're not really going to kill us are you?'

'It's the best snuff movie ever!' she smiled at me. 'They're going to love this one online.'

She was positioning her phone so that it would capture my final moments. I was aware of the minute hand moving once again. The bells must ring soon, surely?

'What time is that? How long until the bells ring?'

'Three minutes,' Becky replied. 'Three minutes until you both get it--'

'Don't you dare hurt Alex!' I screamed at her. 'Leave her out of this, she's nothing to do with it!'

'But she is, Pete. She helped you that night.'

'You're kidding me, she had nothing to do with any

of that. She was in a completely different place at the time. Let her go, you've got me.'

'Sorry, Pete. This is what gets me hot, it makes me want to fuck. Lee likes to hurt people. We make a great team. He gets to stick the knife in you, I get the best snuff movie ever, and we become online legends. See you, Pete! Lee's a better shagger than you, anyway. I look forward to watching the video when it comes out--'

'Becky! Becky!'

I screamed at her, but she ignored me, heading back to the roof. I could only imagine what was going on up there. The minute hand clicked again. Two minutes, two minutes to get out of this mess. It wasn't going to happen, the ropes were too tight. I hoped it would be quick. For both of us.

I can recall most of the detail of what happened next, but it was all so fast and unexpected, I might have missed some bits.

I'd stopped working at the knot. There was no way it was coming loose. I waited there, in the stillness, trying to hear what was happening out on the roof. I don't think that the hand had moved to the minute, but it must have been close.

Suddenly I heard someone burst into the bell tower. It was a man. I didn't know him. He rushed towards me. At first I assumed it was the police, but of course it couldn't have been. In the end, the reason Jem died was because the police had to do a risk assessment before they could rescue him. They didn't do it fast enough to beat the chimes of the cathedral clock. It was ridiculous, but that's what happened.

He went straight for the knot in the rope and began working at it.

'It's too tight,' I said. 'There's a knife in my pocket. Try that!'

His hand moved to my trousers. I remember hearing the minute hand move as he placed his hand in the wrong pocket.

'The other one, it's in the other one--'

'How long until the chimes?'

'That's the final minute before the hour, come on, cut it, cut it!'

He worked away at the knot, the knife was so blunt it seemed to take forever. It can't have been more than a minute, though, because I felt the rope loosen and was able to wriggle my hands out of the binding. I moved my body out from the large wooden bell wheel as the minute hand clicked into place.

There was the creak of old wood and iron as the bell wheels began to move. The force of them was massive, they'd have ripped my head and arms straight off. I moved backwards, well clear of the bell movements.

The noise was deafening, it was an assault on my ears. It took me a few moments to think about Alex. I hadn't a clue what was going on out on the roof, but I knew that I had to get out there as quickly as possible.

I didn't even think about my rescuer. He'd cut me loose, but I couldn't hear a word he said, because of the bells. Was he a cop, or someone from the cathedral? I didn't even give it a thought. I recovered myself, stood up and ran for the door to the roof.

'Alex!' I shouted.

They'd got Alex standing on the turrets, exactly as Meg had been. She was having trouble balancing. Her hands were still bound, she was struggling to stay upright.

'What the--?'

Lee turned around sharply. I was the last person he expected to see. He lifted his crossbow and shot it directly at me. A bolt came flying out. That thing was fast, I barely realised he'd fired it before I felt the pain. The bolt had stuck into the top of my right leg. It caved in on me and I fell to the ground.

Becky had Alex pinned to one of the turrets. She had the Zombie knife in one hand and Lee's phone filming in the other.

'You stay there, bitch!' she screamed, looking between Alex and Lee.

Lee was coming in for the kill. He was expertly loading up the next bolt, walking towards me so that he could fire it at point-blank range.

'What is this all about, Lee?' I shouted over the bells, which were still chiming.

'How did you get out of there? That rope was tied fast. Did she help you ... did that bitch let you go?'

Becky seemed unsure of herself suddenly.

'Did you let him go, Becky? Those ropes were tight. I knew you liked shagging him more than me. Was it you who did it?'

Becky looked frightened now. She didn't know what to do. She was trying to watch Alex as well as assess Lee's mood. My guess was that he probably wasn't the most even-tempered of boyfriends.

'I told you, Lee. You're my man. I did it for the video, you know there's no one like you.'

He'd got the second bolt loaded, and he was looking from me to Becky. The final chime rang out.

'That's it, Lee. Nine o'clock. It's time for her to go

over. That's what we planned, remember?'

'Only, it's not what we planned, is it Becky? You cut his ropes. He's free now. Is that so you can shag him again? Relive your slutty little fantasy.'

'I didn't let him go. He must have freed himself. He was tied when I left the camera there. Honest … look at the video on my phone if you don't believe me!'

She dropped to the floor as a bolt from the crossbow entered her left shoulder.

'Oh Jesus Christ!' she gasped and dropped the knife onto the rooftop floor. I watched Alex clock it. She'd spotted an opportunity. I staggered to my feet again, wary of Lee who was reloading. He was stronger than me and he was tooled up. I didn't stand a chance against him, but I'd have to do something. Becky was crying with the pain, screaming at Lee and swearing that she hadn't touched my ropes.

'You need to help yourself now, Becky. You're not like Lee, I know you're not. He's encouraged you to do this, Becky. You can still walk away … oh shit, shit, shit!'

Lee had fired a second bolt at me, centimetres away from the first one. The pain was excruciating. My trouser leg was soaked with blood. I had to buy time, give Alex a chance to run for the knife, or at least get down from the turret. I needed to sway Becky. The tide had turned now, Lee had tasted blood again and the dangerous killer was finally revealed.

Becky turned to face me. I could see she was looking to me for help. Lee was the killer; he was the one the police wanted. I assumed that bit was true, in spite of her other lies. He'd turned on her now, he was jealous. She was scared for her life.

How many of those bloody bolts did he have? Lee

had loaded another and was ready to fire. He seemed uncertain about who his next victim would be.

'How did he get away then, you bitch? I saw how you were enjoying yourself in that video. You don't moan like that when we screw. You never did. It's been about him all the time, hasn't it? You wanted to use me to get to him.'

'Look, Lee, we can all walk away from this. It doesn't have to be this way.'

I tried my luck by reasoning with him, but I didn't think it would be any use. I looked towards Alex. Her mouth was still taped, but she gestured with her eyes, drawing my attention to the knife. She wanted me to stall Lee.

'What if Becky did untie the ropes? She saved my life. She didn't want to be a murderer like you.'

I saw his rage flare up the moment I said those words. His eyes looked as if he'd flicked a switch. I'd never seen pure evil and hatred before, but I certainly saw it that day.

He turned to Becky.

'You stupid bitch … '

This was it, I had one chance.

With his back turned to me, I hauled myself off the floor and staggered towards him, pounding into him from behind. It was like trying to move a rock, but it caught him unawares and he stumbled, dropping the crossbow. Alex had been watching everything. She jumped down from the turret, ran towards the knife and kicked it towards me.

With her hands tied, she timed it wrong, kicking the knife away from everybody and falling hard onto the ground.

Lee and Becky looked at each other. They were an

equal distance from the crossbow. It was loaded, the bolt still securely in place. Both of them started to move towards it at the same time. Becky's shoulder must have been so painful, she cried out in agony as she thrust her hand forward.

Lee grabbed the crossbow, but instead of aiming and shooting, he threw it out of the way. I think he'd meant it to go over the side of the roof, but it hit a turret near the entrance to the roof area and fell to the ground.

He stood up slowly, clenching his fist, and then struck Becky across the face. She dropped down instantly. This was the Goliath we had to beat.

The knife and the crossbow were out of play. I needed to do something quickly. Alex was trying to turn over, but her tied hands were making it difficult for her to recover from her fall.

I got up and ran at Lee again, crashing into him from behind. He barely seemed to notice me, his strength was amazing. He pushed me away, then picked up Becky from the roof floor and threw her over the side.

I heard a thud as she hit the ground below. I was stunned, I've never seen violence like it. He just threw her over the edge. He didn't even pause before doing it. It must have been metres from where Sally met her death when she jumped. But there was no time to think about Becky, Lee was coming for me next. I was a bug that he was trying to swat away.

He saw the knife and began to run towards it. He was closer to it than I was, I didn't stand a chance. He beat me to it, picking it up and starting to wave it in my direction.

He was trying to back me into a corner, I was moving towards the far end of the rooftop area, towards the turrets and the furthermost end. The crossbow was too far away, Alex saw what was happening and began to try to move towards the only available weapon. Lee saw what she was doing and kicked her in the face. She dropped straight down to the floor.

I stumbled towards him, screaming now, ignoring the terrible pain in my leg. He struck at me with the knife, one of the serrations catching and slicing my cheek. Instinctively, I backed away again. He'd got me cornered, there was no way I could move. He raised the knife and held it to my throat. This was it. I was powerless to stop him, he was too strong for me, but at least I had given Alex a chance.

'You can go and join your buddy down there, and then I'm going beat your TV pal over here into a pulp. Great! I've been on her TV show and now I get to kick the shit out of her. Nice one.'

He moved his arm to slice my neck, but the pain didn't come. I was waiting for it. Nothing. Then I saw it. I'd heard it, but it took me a while to see what had happened. A crossbow bolt had come straight through his skull and out of his left eye. He fell against me, I almost lost my balance over the turret, but quickly steadied myself.

I looked towards Alex, who was moving once more, after Lee's violent kick. The man who'd saved me from the bells was there, he must have been waiting in the doorway, picking his moment to come to her rescue. But the look on Alex's face told me otherwise. I rushed over to her and tore the tape from her mouth. The man with the crossbow was reloading it, readying another bolt.

Alex was desperate to say something. The minute I ripped off the tape, the sentence flew out.

'That's him, Pete, keep away. It's him … it's JD!'

For an instant I thought we'd made it, only to have victory snatched away. So this was JD. Finally he'd decided to show his face.

'Stay where you are,' he said, pointing the crossbow directly at me. I'd had enough of that thing waving in my face.

'May I untie my friend?' I asked, anxious to help Alex. Her face was badly bruised and bloody. I hated to think what I looked like, covered in blood and reeking of urine.

He nodded. That was a good start, but the crossbow was still aimed at me. How long did we have until the police arrived? They had no way of tracking us from the storage warehouse, not unless somebody had spotted us driving out of the industrial estate.

'How have you been tailing us?' I asked. I wanted to know where this was all heading.

'It's surprisingly easy, especially with your friend here in tow. Social media provides a very useful map most of the time. You might want to think about removing location information from your social media posts, you daft buggers.'

I wasn't in the mood for a social media how-to session.

'Was that you in the warehouse, or the police?'

'That was me. But the police arrived about two minutes afterwards. That DCI Summers, she's a right tenacious cow.'

'Did you follow us here from the warehouse? Is that how you got here?'

'Got it in one. You're a great journalist, you are. I can

see why you're on the radio.'

'So what's this about? What do you want?'

'I'm pleased you asked,' he smiled. The crossbow didn't move one inch. It was aimed right between my eyes. I'd seen what he'd done to Lee, I wasn't going to risk anything. Besides, he'd saved my life twice already. I needed to know what this was all about. I helped Alex to her feet, although I could barely stand on my own.

'We need to move, fast. It won't be long until somebody spots our flying lady down there. I think she's still alive, you know, and she'll begin to scream shortly. Falls aren't nice. When she comes round and realises she's going to spend the rest of her life in a wheelchair, she'll get a bit loud. That and the spinal injury should do it.'

'Let Alex go. Lock her up here, leave her out of it. It's me you want.'

'Actually, it's both of you that I want. Our two crazy friends here did a fine job bringing you together. Now I'm going to finish it.'

He waved the crossbow and indicated that we should leave. I moved slowly, and JD picked up the knife before following behind us.

'You okay?' Alex asked. 'You've lost a lot of blood.'

'I think so,' I said. 'I'm beginning to feel a bit out of it--'

'Hey lovebirds, mouths shut!' JD said.

He wasn't like Lee. JD was calm and in control. There was no visible anger there. He was patient, he could wait for the right time to come.

JD was right about Becky. She wasn't dead. Her legs were both bent in ways that they shouldn't be able to reach; her hand was snapped back too. She'd narrowly missed the paving slabs, landing awkwardly on some small shrubs below. Because Lee had thrown her, she cleared the area that had instantly resulted in Sally's death. She was beginning to come round, shrieking wildly. It was the most horrible sound I'd ever heard.

'We've got to help her. At least call an ambulance,' I urged JD.

'They'll be here soon enough with all that noise going on. It won't be long until someone comes along to find out what's up. But now we're going to get in the car.'

———

Another vehicle. Another journey. Across the city, in darkness. Where were we heading now? And what was JD's intention? He made me sit on a plastic sheet in the car. It was the sort that you get from DIY stores, to cover the floor when you're painting.

'Don't want any blood on the seats, do we?' he'd chuckled. That didn't sound good. I'd seen the shows on TV. I knew how useful plastic sheets could be.

As we drove through the city, I began to get an idea of where he was taking us.

'Are we heading to the cemetery?' I asked.

He didn't answer, but I was right. He ushered us out of the car, and we began to walk along the path, past the graves. The cemetery was dimly lit and we could barely see where we were going. I couldn't feel my leg by that stage, and Alex had to support me so I could carry on walking.

'Where are we going?' Alex asked. 'What do you want?'

No answer. JD was worse than Lee, his silence was sinister.

We stopped at a gravestone. I'd lost my bearings, but I knew roughly where we were. I recognised Alex's flowers from our visit there a few days previously.

'What's this about, JD?' I asked. My voice was weak, I was slurring my words.

'I'm not JD. This is JD.' He pointed to the gravestone. 'While I'm touched by the flowers, I think we have something else to talk about.'

So JD were the initials of Jason Davies, our old contact from Special Forces. Alex had sent him over to help Meg when she was being held hostage in our house by that other nutter, Tony Miller. So how was this connected? I got my answer, but it was Alex who saw it first.

'You're his brother, aren't you?'

'Got it in one!' he replied. 'I'm Ian Davies, younger brother of Jason. I loved my brother, you know, I really looked up to him – I followed him into the Special Forces. So you can imagine how pissed I was to find out that he'd been murdered, seemingly by a housewife who'd never killed anyone in her life. Funny that, isn't it?'

'There's nobody who feels guiltier than me about that--' Alex began, but Ian spoke over her.

'I know how guilty you are. I checked out Jason's emails and phone messages. I know that you sent him over there. I know he was doing you a favour: Alex Kennedy, TV personality – that part of the story got buried, didn't it? But I know what you did. I know you sent my brother to his death.'

'Look, there's not a day goes by when I don't agonise over Jason's death. Don't you think I know that already? The police know, they checked his emails and phone records--'

'But your involvement was suppressed, wasn't it? Contacts in high-up places I assume? Who did you have to sleep with to get that matter quietened down?'

'I ... I ... '

'Alex?' I asked. 'That didn't happen, did it?'

She was silent. I could feel myself slipping away, I'd lost too much blood. I was tuning in and out of the conversation. I felt my leg giving way, so I slipped down to the floor on my knees. I could sense Ian waving the crossbow around.

'What are you intending to do about it?' Alex asked. 'Is that what all this has been about ... to get back at me in some way?'

'I want you to know that I loved my brother. I want you to understand that he survived all sorts of horrors in the forces: imprisonment, torture, weeks alone abandoned in the desert. My brother was a good man. There was no way he deserved to die like that.'

'I understand,' Alex answered. 'I know he was a good man. We heard his stories, we talked to him a lot on Crime Beaters. I'm sorry, I know how you must--'

'You do not know how I feel!' he snapped back. This was the first time he had shown any emotion. He was getting angry now. I wanted to tell Alex to tread carefully, but I was too weak. I desperately wanted to pass out, to let the pain end.

'I want to know who killed my brother!' he shouted.

'It was that woman who got the blame, there was no way she could have killed my brother. I want to know who did it!'

This was why he'd brought me to the graveyard. He thought that this was a secret that I held. I was in no state to tell him, and Alex didn't know the answer.

'Who was it, Pete? I know that the official version can't possibly be the truth. It was covered up, just like your friend here made sure that nobody knew she'd sent Jason to his death. You tell me what happened there. I have a right to know.'

I sensed Alex moving towards me. JD was getting angrier now, coming closer to us, waving the crossbow around. I was struggling to hold myself upright. It moved between us, he was getting closer.

The shouting continued. His body suddenly tensed, ready to hit one of us. I heard the release of the crossbow, then there was a scream from Alex whose hand had moved quickly towards my leg. She tore out one of the bolts that had sunk deep into my flesh and I was aware of her lunging with it before I passed out. The pain was more than I could take, I'd had enough. The last thing I remember was crashing onto the ground, to the sound of screams and shouting.

Chapter Eighteen

She might have seemed tough to her team, but DCI Summers was a pussycat when you met her over a cappuccino and carrot cake. If only the criminal fraternity had realised that she could be so easily bought.

It was two months almost to the day that I'd been recovered from the graveyard. In that time, I'd become an expert in the femoral artery, the large blood vessel that runs down the leg. When Alex had pulled that bolt out as a weapon to use against Ian Davies, she had selected the one that was lodged precariously close to that artery. I was bleeding profusely by the time the medics arrived, and I almost didn't make it.

I was given a blood transfusion, it was touch and go for a while. I battled on, as the doctors would have you believe, and I made it out the other end. What really happened was that I slept for several days in a hospital bed while medical professionals on very low wages worked hard to keep me alive and comfortable. I then woke up and took credit for the whole thing.

I was disorientated when I came round, I couldn't get the timescale right. How long had I been out of things? How can you be unconscious for a week? Did Diane know I wouldn't be coming into work?

My memories were all over the place, and it was some time until I remembered the important stuff. I think it was the hospital mashed potato which finally reminded me that horrific things had happened.

Of course, the doctors couldn't tell me anything, other than how my leg wound was healing and what a lucky fellow I was. I was too weak for visitors, other than my mum, so even that connection to the outside world had to wait. There was a bit of malingering on my part too. I'd discovered that near-death experiences really take it out of you.

It seemed to take ages for me to get back to a place where I could walk a reasonable distance, aided by a stick, of course. The first time I tried standing up, I got one of those frames that old people use. The shame of it, it felt like a taste of the life awaiting me in thirty or forty years' time.

That was one thing the experience had taught me. I desperately wanted to live. I was not ready to die at the hands of some crazy man like Lee Taylor, or from some potentially deadly leg wound. My life had got a bit shitty, but I was ready to move on and rebuild, it was time to put all of the bad stuff behind me. I was renewed, the experience had been cathartic. I wanted to get back to my life.

I was soon strong enough to walk around the hospital grounds and join the packs of long-term patients in their pyjamas smoking outside the front entrance. There were people who'd got cancer there, men and women who'd had heart attacks and strokes, yet still they gathered for their fags.

Every day I'd have doctors, nurses and the occasional consultant peering at my wound, examining my vital signs and making positive noises about my recovery. I'd received some head trauma too, plus a few other damaged bits and pieces. It was all very sore for a while, but like everything, I soon healed. I had a nice scar on my cheek too, that was the doing of the Zombie knife. I have to admit to quite liking that. It had needed three stitches, but I was out cold so wasn't even awake to whimper embarrassingly while they sewed it up. Instead I got this macho mysterious face scar like some dark hero in a Hollywood movie.

The problem of my release date was caused mainly by me having nowhere suitable to go for rehabilitation. With Vicky dead, the caravan park was going to close at the end of the season. With that wonderful woman no longer at the helm, things quickly turned bad and the site closed down and laid off the staff at the end of the summer.

I cried for Vicky. The shock of her death hadn't really hit me when everything was beginning to turn sour – I was too concerned about Alex and getting her away from her captor. But that woman had been good to me, she'd given me a home when I needed one, she'd given me extra work when I desperately needed the cash, and I'd got her killed by way of thanks.

I knew that I hadn't actually done the killing. Counsellors like Martin Jarvis and Blake Crawford would paint me as a victim in all of this, but I couldn't help feeling that I was poison in people's lives.

The caravan park was going to be turned into a seaside complex for elderly people; that's where the boom time was apparently, nobody wanted seaside holidays anymore. Particularly not Vicky's trustees.

I found my recovery frustrating. I wasn't given the go-ahead to drive for some time, there was some issue with healing and nerve damage. I worked hard to build up my walking strength. I was eager to spread my radius of travel, and I worked hard at my physio sessions. I was now getting still more benefit from the health insurance I'd been paying for with automatic monthly deductions from my salary.

Diane had negotiated a paid leave of absence for me, but reminded me that HR were on her back, using phrases like 'phased return to work' at every opportunity. One of the advantages of being an old boy was that I had a good package. I'd get up to six months before the HR guys could finally swoop and insist on my return to work. I didn't want the full six months, but I needed a decent break. I'd figure out what to do later.

My meeting with DCI Summers was my first expedition out on my own. I was still using a stick to help me walk and I had supplies of painkillers, just in case. I'd seen her already, of course. The police had been in and out of my room as soon as the medical staff would let them. But this was a social call, an opportunity to find out what had really gone on that night. The police had kindly assembled all of the missing pieces while I'd been in my hospital bed.

I took the bus into town. While I was sitting there, watching the world go by, I thought back to what Steven Terry had said. He'd been right again. The man had some gift, that was for sure, if it was only the ability to get lucky with his bullshit. It worked, he'd been absolutely correct in his predictions. He'd said that there was evil in our house. That was true, it had been the focus of much of the weird stuff that had gone on. Glenn Elliot had lost his life there.

Steven Terry had warned that the lies had to stop. I knew that. I had to change, I needed to get my life back on track. It had to begin with my poor choices in sexual partners. My encounter with Ellie had been my own fault; she was a wonderful woman, I was the party who was not free for a one-night stand. I brought that one on myself, but I'd also got unlucky with Ellie having a crazy stalker.

What about Becky? Maybe that was my fault. Poor judgment perhaps. I'd thought that Becky was okay, but she could have done the right thing when I was tied to that bell wheel. She was perfectly happy to leave me to a horrible death for her weirdo snuff movie or whatever it was. Even so, I still didn't feel as if she was made of the same evil stuff that Lee Taylor was forged from.

It was Steven Terry's final words that really stuck with me.

'The women you choose to be close to are what determines your path, Peter. There are some poisonous people coming into your life. You will need to decide who to trust. Your choices will determine the outcome, Peter.'

I had to make some serious life choices. I needed to get back on course. I had time off work, I'd put things back together again.

'You're looking better!' DCI Summers welcomed me as I joined her at the table.

'I couldn't have looked much worse,' I laughed. My face had been a bloody and bruised mess the first time that we'd spoken after those events.

'Can I call you Kate now?' I asked. 'DCI gets a bit wearing after a while. And call me Pete, please, we're a bit far removed from formalities now, aren't we? You've seen my groin area, after all!'

She laughed at that one, agreed to the informality, and kindly got me coffee and cake. My leg was hurting badly. I might have overstretched myself coming into town.

'So where are we up to?' I asked. 'Have you put it all to bed yet?'

'You know what it's like – paperwork, procedures and all that. But we'll get there.'

'What about Ian Davies? Will he be okay?'

'I think he'll be fine. It's a difficult one – self-defence and reasonable force are tricky bedfellows. But your witness statements are compelling, and if you're not going to file a complaint against him for the nasty emails that he sent to your office, he'll get off I think. The fact that he's recorded on Becky's phone releasing you in the bell tower doesn't hurt his case either. It kind of makes him a bit of a hero.'

'He was really frustrated about his brother. Angry. He had good cause to be. He saved us from Lee Taylor, I have no doubt about that. Lee was coming in for the kill, and I would be dead by now if it wasn't for Ian. He came to make a point, not to hurt us. He wanted us to understand what we'd done. I hope he gets released. I wouldn't be here now if it wasn't for him.'

I sipped my tea. It was good after the dishwater they served me at the hospital. It was made with real milk and decent tea bags. I had to get out of that hospital, private facility or not, I wanted my own place again.

'Have you got your timeline yet? I know you cops love a good timeline.'

'As much as we can, yes. It never helps when all your witnesses are dead. But yes, we think we know what happened now.'

'Was Becky involved in the deaths – Len, Glenn and Vicky? That's what I want to know. I still believe she was under Lee's influence. He was a scary man, you know. I don't believe that she's evil. Misguided, maybe.'

'No, there's nothing linking Becky to the deaths. They were certainly in cahoots – it was one of those Fred and Rosemary things. Lee had been a wanted man for some time. He was violent and terrifying, and there are a lot of people very glad that he's no longer on the loose.'

I thought back to the scene on the cathedral roof. My attempts to fight Lee had been pathetic. He was a formidable force, the kind of guy who only stops when he's dead.

'What about Glenn Elliot, what was that all about?'

'It was a case of wrong place, wrong time. Lee had been frantically jealous when Becky slept with you, and seeing that video seems to have pushed him over the edge. From what we can tell, he was besotted with Becky and went along with her plan, even though he'd fallen in love with her. She was just a bit kinky, as you keep saying. It's very weird seeking crime victims to sleep with, and even weirder keeping a video library of her sexual encounters. It's even more cranky to post them online. But, you know, each to his own. Nothing surprises me these days.'

'I'd liked Becky when we met, you know. I'm really doubting my judgment these days, but I was certain she was okay. Odd, yes, but I didn't have her down as a psycho.'

'She wasn't involved in the murders. Glenn Elliot had caught Lee in your house. We think he'd got some sexual encounter planned there for Becky, but we don't know. He'd stolen a key when they came to look around, posing as house viewers. They'd certainly worked it out between the two of them, but Lee was the killer.'

'How about Len ... and Vicky?'

It was still difficult to talk about Vicky in the past tense. I'd missed her funeral. I was upset about that.

'Lee was after you. He wanted to warn you off, or kill you, we'll never really know. He was waiting for you the day Len went to your caravan. Wrong time, wrong place again. Len walked in on him. We think he was jerking off to Becky's video. We found ... let's say, there was forensic evidence on your sofa. But that was Lee.'

'Why did he kill Vicky? Was it quick for her?'

'Yes, it was quick. She won't have known much about it, Pete. I know it's a horrible way to die, but he was a strong man, and that was a clean cut to the throat.'

I was relieved to hear that, but Vicky's was the death I was struggling with. What a terrible way to die. That poor woman. Whatever anybody said to reassure me, that one was my fault. I couldn't forgive myself for Vicky's death.

'He was looking for your new caravan, Pete. It's as simple as that. He wanted you out of Becky's life, but she was obsessed with you. She was desperate for that second encounter, she wanted to lure you back to your house for sex. It's her thing, you were a big catch for her fantasy. In the past, she's gone for robbery victims and victims of assault. You'd have been a hot prospect for her. Her father was a hit man, spent years in jail. Used to threaten people by crushing their hands with hammers. A really nice guy. It's some crazy psychological stuff, it's probably how she got it out of her system. Who knows with these things?'

'But she was complicit in what happened at the cathedral? She was going to watch us die there?'

'We're not sure about that. She says it was Lee's doing, that she was scared for her life. The aim was to re-enact the events that had taken place on the rooftop with Meg and Sally, but Lee had other things in mind. She's sticking to her story: they weren't going to kill anybody, or that was not what she had intended to do. She maintains it was all about fear, taking it right up to the end, as it would have been with the original deaths.'

'And how is she?' I asked. 'Will she walk again?'

'Unlikely,' Kate answered, 'but you never know. It was quite a fall, but she got lucky. The legs and arm have been put back in place, but the spinal injury is another thing entirely. She's in a lot of pain – your injuries look like a small scratch next to hers.'

'I know this makes me sound naive, but I don't think that Becky's evil. It feels like she's had her punishment already.'

'You might have lost your head in that bell tower, Pete. Remember that. I don't know what will happen to her. She's still in a right state, they'll need to put her back together properly first. But she's lucky. She got to live. There's no doubt that Lee wanted to kill her. It messes things up, sex, but you probably know that already.'

I nodded.

'I'm going to become a monk, I think. I've really screwed things up, I'm sorry, this must be a huge headache for you guys.'

'Don't blame yourself. You really should contact victim support, you know. You're a prime candidate for them, blaming yourself for everything. You can't help what these people did, Pete. They would do these things regardless of you. You're the same as Glenn and Len: wrong place, wrong time … only you got to live. These people do the things they do anyway.'

I knew all of that. But I still felt like shit.

My coffee with Kate Summers was in stark contrast to my drinks with Hannah Young. It was three weeks after my chat with Kate; my leg was far better than it had been, and my strength and resilience were returning fast. I was still using a stick, to boost my confidence mainly, but more and more I was leaving it behind.

I was sitting with Hannah at a street café in Alicante. The sun and blue sky nourished me, and my leg had begun to feel better the moment the heat began to work its magic on it.

This was the meeting we'd missed before Hannah had to return home. I was spending a few days out in Spain. I had other reasons to be there, but it made sense to catch up with Hannah after I'd landed at the airport.

I sipped my red wine and thanked her for her patience with me after standing her up. I was still using painkillers occasionally, so shouldn't have been drinking wine really. But I could see the light at the end of the recovery tunnel and I was ready to get back to normal life.

Hannah was full of questions.

'How are you feeling? I can't believe what happened after I left … Wasn't that B&B appalling? Did you make contact with Meg yet? You can see why I live out here, can't you?'

'Oh yes, I'm tempted to come out here myself. I love it in Spain. The warmth, the skies, the colour. It's wonderful.'

'I'm sorry that you had to go through all that again. I started buying the papers, I had to keep up with the story. Will they get off, do you think? Do you even want them to?'

'Yes, I do want Ian and Becky to stay out of prison. They're not killers, either of them. And Becky, well, she's in a right mess. I haven't seen her, mind you. I have contacts in the media, you know how it is. I'm interested, I want to know.'

She nodded and took a sip of her G&T. It really was lovely in the sun. Things always seemed so simple to me when I was abroad.

'We were talking about Meg last time we met. I'm sorry I rushed out on you like that. Have you heard from her?'

That's what I wanted to know. That's why I'd travelled all that way to see her.

'No, still not. I'm sorry, Pete. I wanted you to understand some things about Meg. We had ... it was a difficult childhood.'

I looked at her, not saying anything, a well-used interview technique. People become uncomfortable with the silence and continue talking. She took the bait.

'You know about the adoption and the fire already, but it was more complicated than that. There was a lot going on at the time. It was difficult. I want you to understand that things aren't always as simple as they seem with Meg. We're ... she's damaged. Things happened in her past which can make her unstable at times. I want to see her again. I'm desperate to make contact again ... if you find her.'

'I can't say that I ever saw it when we were together,' I said. 'For many years she was happy. We were happy.'

'Yes, I know that, Pete. But Meg isn't good when things go wrong. When her life gets unsettled, it can be difficult for her. She makes bad choices.'

Is that what I'd seen in my final meeting with Meg in

the graveyard? Was this her other side, the aspect of her personality that I'd never glimpsed? She had, after all, stabbed Tony Miller several times. Most people would have stabbed him only the once, to bring him down. It was a frenzied attack, perhaps more than just self-defence.

'Why are you telling me this, Hannah? Why is it so important to you that I know this?'

'I want you to understand that Meg can't help who she is. She's my adoptive sister – we had some wonderful times together and I'd love to be reunited with her. But we also went through some terrible things. You probably think it's you who's created all this bad luck, but it tends to follow Meg wherever she goes. It's not your fault, Pete. It's how life is with Meg.'

I was nervous about my next stop after Alicante. It had been a strange meeting with Hannah. I couldn't figure out what she was trying to tell me. It felt as if she was warning me of something, but what? She wouldn't spit it out. I'd seen none of it. I knew Meg, we'd been in love. Maybe we could still be in love.

I was sitting in the back of a taxi, heading for Alex's place. I wasn't ready to drive, and didn't think it would be a good idea to hire a car. I hadn't seen Alex since that night. I'd only heard the police account of what had happened.

I'd been away from my tech – it was a horrible experience not being able to text or email. I had no phone in the hospital and no laptop. It was almost a greater agony than my leg.

Alex had been short and sharp in her emails to me

when we finally reconnected. She didn't want to chat over Skype or video, but she did agree that I could come out and stay.

The taxi pulled up outside her house. She was renting on the outskirts of Torrevieja, it was a lovely detached place, I couldn't blame her for taking a break out there.

If I'd been in any doubt about how I would be received by Alex, I was wrong. She rushed out of the house when she saw that I'd arrived, and hugged me, really hard. I hadn't even had time to pay the taxi driver. Tears streamed from her eyes and she seemed distraught at how I was using a stick to walk. I paid the driver and we sat down in her garden chairs, the sun shining down on us.

'I'm so sorry, Pete. I thought I'd killed you. I've been out here hating myself for what I did to you. I thought I'd--'

'Alex, it's fine, honestly. I'm here, I'm fine, the stick will go soon. You did what you thought you had to do. You were scared.'

She hugged me again and kissed me on the cheek.

'I'm sorry. I can't say it enough, Pete. And I'm sorry I was too chicken to come and see you. I couldn't face the press. They haven't found me staying out here. It's off-season, it's really quiet at the moment.'

'It's okay, I get it, I get it. You don't have to apologise. We did what we had to do that night. It was terrible. But we lived. We're here now.'

'They wouldn't let me see you when I was still in the UK, Pete. I tried, but they wouldn't let me. I had this place arranged, so I ran away from everything. I know it was a horrible thing to do. I'm sorry.'

'Alex, enough of the apologies. It's fine. So what

happened after I keeled over? I want to hear it from you. I've heard the official version.'

'I thought Ian was going to fire that crossbow, I really did. He was so angry with us, and I didn't help things. He hadn't taken us there to hurt us, he wanted us to understand, I think … '

'Was he right about what he said? Did you call in a favour to make sure that you were kept out of the papers? Was he right?'

She looked down, and I knew that Ian had got his facts right.

'I didn't do anything wrong, Pete. I just know people. And I didn't sleep with anyone, it's not like he said. I called in a favour. It was definitely nothing illegal, honestly.'

'You know what, Alex? We've all done things we're not proud of. If the police don't need to follow anything up, then my view is, it's not that bad. I'm not bothered, honestly. I don't blame you. You did nothing wrong.'

I was all too ready to blame myself, but it was much easier to understand Alex's motives. She hadn't done anything illegal, but it was she who'd sent Jason over to help Meg. He'd got killed, yes, and that was nothing to do with her. She wanted to suppress that element in the press, she was in the public eye, I understood that. It wasn't illegal. It was only a refocusing of the truth.

'How did it end then? What's your version? I want to hear it from you.'

'Where do I start?' Alex said. 'I've been trying to forget it all. I thought Ian was going to get violent, and I had nothing to defend myself with. I saw those bolts in your leg and grabbed one. I don't know what made me do it. I thought it would come straight out. I didn't know what it would do, but I felt it tearing your flesh and I knew I'd cocked up the minute I did it. You let out a horrendous yell. I bet you don't remember that bit.'

I didn't. I was out cold the minute she pulled the bolt. I had no recollection of anything after that. I woke up magically in a hospital bed.

'It was that yell that saved you. Some old codger at the back of the cemetery was taking his dog into the garden for its night-time walkies. He heard your scream and called the police, thinking it was yobs at Jem's grave again. They've had quite a lot of trouble there. Two beat bobbies arrived and then, within minutes, the entire emergency services were there.'

'How did it play out with Ian?'

'He's okay. He hadn't got over his brother's death, he wanted to scare us, it was frustration. He was waiting for his moment. He was so angry with you when he sent you the letters. When I popped up on social media, he followed us for a bit, to get a sense of what we're like. He was frustrated that we were walking around and his brother was dead. I've been to see him since. They're holding him locally. He let me visit him before I left the country.'

'How did that go? Did you hurt him with that crossbow bolt?'

'No, I was waving it at him and then he put the crossbow down on the floor. "We'd better help that friend of yours," he said. "He's going to die if he doesn't get some help." He dialled the ambulance, but they were on their way already.'

'I'm pleased you made your peace with him. That was my impression; he's not a violent man, he needed to get it out of his system. And he saved us from Lee Taylor. I really thought we were goners there. Can you call in any more favours to help his case?'

'I'm not sleeping with anyone, if that's what you mean. I know it looks like I've been doing sod all out here, but I have actually been doing some useful work. Yes, I've done what I can for Ian. I think he'll be okay, we've both vouched for him, portrayed him as a hero. The crossbow was the only weapon that he had, he had no choice but to finish off Lee like that. And he saved your life, twice. He saved me too. I think he'll be fine.'

It was lovely there, chatting to Alex in that beautiful sunshine. It was good to put things behind us, to reassure myself that things had played out as I thought they had. We chatted about Becky and Vicky and thanked our lucky stars that JD had turned out to be harmless.

Alex shuffled in her seat, and I sensed the mood change. I didn't want to ruin the moment, I was enjoying myself again. I felt comfortable and relaxed for the first time in months.

'There's something else I need to tell you, Pete. I hope you don't mind.'

There it was. The gear change. The warning that something bad was on its way. Maybe I was judging too fast, I needed to hear her out.

'What is it, Alex? Please tell me it's good news?'

'I don't know, but I think that it's going to be helpful news, if nothing else.'

'What is it?'

'You know how we spoke about you getting your life sorted out now: the house, your job and all that? I've made some progress. I've been doing some digging on your behalf. I wanted to do something for you, to apologise for messing up your leg like that.'

'Okay, so what is it? Surely you haven't tracked down

the Bailey family fortune? You're not here to tell me that I'm rich, are you?'

'Not quite.' She laughed, but I could see that she was anxious to share her news.

'What is it then? Come on, this is killing me. What have you found?'

'It's *who* I've found, Pete. And where I've found her. I've located Meg. At last. It's taken me ages, but I finally managed to track her down. It was a devil of a job, but you can sort your life out at last. You can put things back together again.'

So there it was. The information that I'd waited more than nine months to learn. The best part of a year. As I sat in the sunshine talking with Alex, for a moment it had seemed that our troubles were behind us. But the knot had yet to be fully unpicked.

The Forgotten Children is available now. Start reading the third part of the Don't Tell Meg trilogy today!

Find out more about Paul J. Teague's thrillers at:
http://paulteague.co.uk

Made in the USA
Middletown, DE
03 December 2017